COFFEE, CARS, AND NECROMANCY

NEEN COHEN

EVIL KOALA PRESS

COFFEE, CARS, AND NECROMANCY

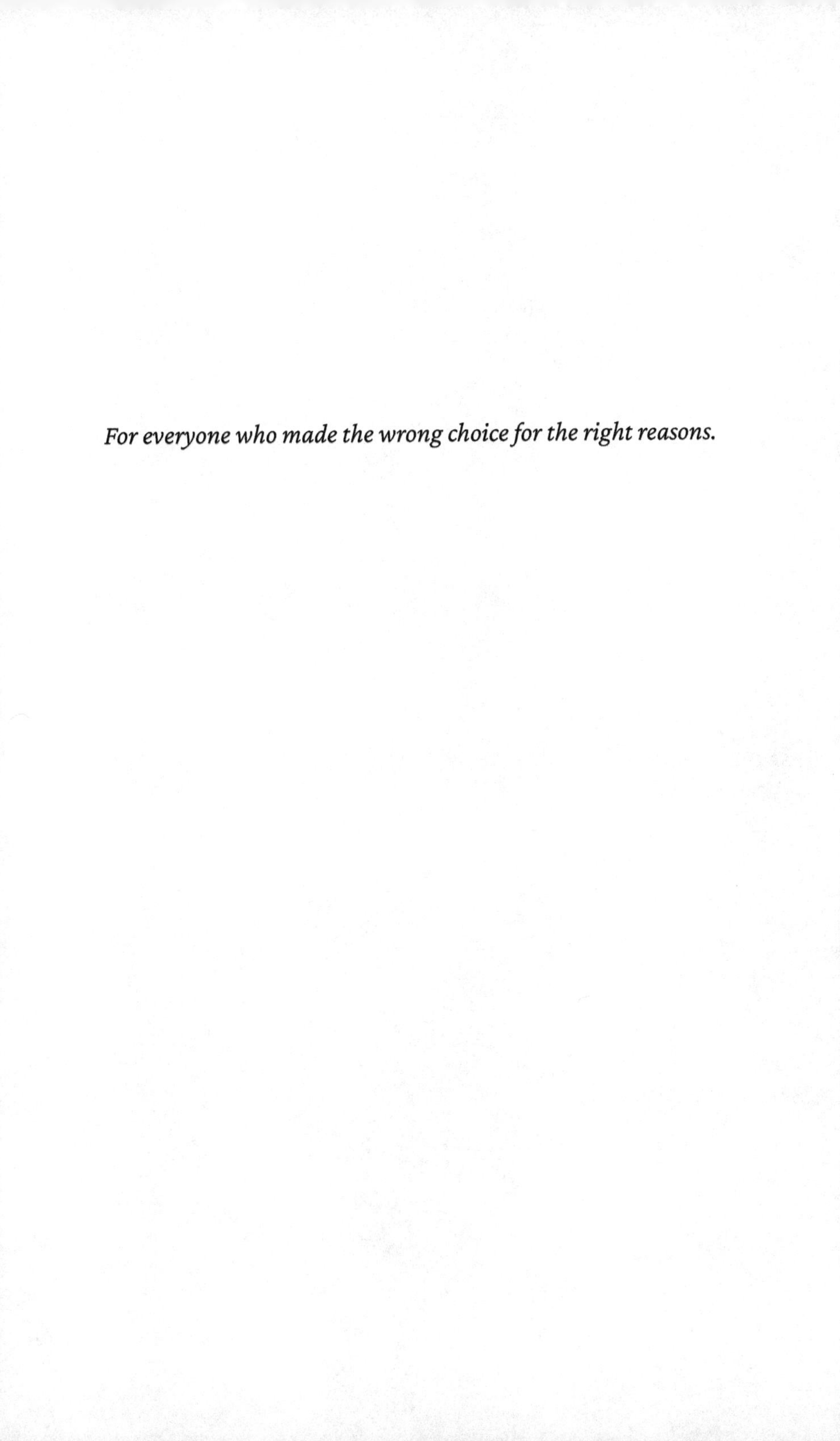

For everyone who made the wrong choice for the right reasons.

CHAPTER

ONE

"What did you do, Lilekai?" Theamin's fingers dug into the flesh of my upper arm. She glared down at me, her dark eyes boring into my own, right through to my very bones. Her words barely held back the anger that pulsed in the vein at her temple.

"Let me go!" I screamed as I yanked against her grip trying to move closer to the body. No, closer to Katy. My stomach churned. How easily I had shifted my thinking. It was a product of the profession, but this wasn't a job.

I couldn't pull my eyes away from the soul of my friend, as she screamed silently into a void that I couldn't reach. I didn't know what she saw, and she gave no indication that she heard me.

I had arrived at Katy's apartment early because her distance over the last week gnawed at my stomach. I sensed it in a way I had no way to explain, much like I couldn't explain the magic I used every single day.

Her home was on the third floor, in the middle of a building that sat in the middle of many others. Though it was a small studio, she had filled it with colour and contradiction, and it suited her. Depending on the day, Katy could be called a goth or a hippie, a femme or a butch. And that eclectic nature of hers had been just one of the things I loved about her. But now. Now she screamed silently and her body lay still, growing colder the longer Theamin held me, stopping me from helping. But I couldn't help. I had tried. Not only had I failed, I had also made it worse. So much worse.

I had arrived early. But it hadn't mattered. I had ignored that gnawing inside of me for far too long. Because I had still been too late.

She hadn't been able to fight the black dog of depression any longer, and I hadn't been there to stop her. Not this time. Why hadn't I come earlier, why hadn't she called me, like she had on previous nights when darkness all but consumed her.

She should have called me. But instead, she had taken the only way out that she could see. And when I had shown up, that gnawing in my stomach had turned to churning, and I now fought against the rise of bile.

I hadn't let her go, I couldn't.

I needed her. The Worlds, all of them needed her. There was so much she could offer.

The ritual had been more complicated than I anticipated. I had no right to perform it, I knew that, but I had always gotten through by asking for forgiveness instead of permission.

I had seen Death do the ritual. Once. I had only seen it done once in over fifty years of servitude. What the hell had I been thinking? I had to fix my mistake, and I had to do it now.

I pulled harder against Theamin's grip, fury mixing with my grief.

Only Death was allowed to touch one of their minions.

Theamin might rule Death's Necromancer minions, but not here. She did not have permission outside of the training rooms held within the Grey World.

"I need to help Katy. I need to save her," I said.

"You've done enough," Theamin spoke between clenched teeth, waving her free hand toward Katy's dead body. Katy's soul continued to scream soundlessly. Her essence remained pinned and trapped to her dead body. The bile scraped daggers up my throat as I fought it to stay put. My breath rasped in and out loud enough to make my skin crawl.

"Let me go, Theamin." A small sob escaped with my demand.

Theamin ignored me as her eyes shifted focus, and every muscle in her tensed and solidified as though she were made of stone. But I didn't need to see Theamin's physical shift, her eyes darkening further until they shone a glossy black. The energy crackled around us and danced over my skin.

"No." I yanked with all my might. I might as well have thrown myself against a brick wall instead of throwing it away from Theamin's iron grip, the good it did. Bones cracked in my wrist and still she didn't let me go. "I can't go back. Not yet. I need to save her."

The familiar sensation of bubbles fizzing over my skin intensified and washed its way up my arms.

Theamin Shimmered out of the Green World and took me with her.

Whether I liked it or not.

The cold hit my lungs the moment we arrived, and I gasped as shards of the air scraped down my throat. She hadn't even given me enough time to prepare for the transition. At least the bile now retreated.

With an animalistic growl, Theamin finally let me go and threw me to the ground.

I landed with a thud, knees and palms stinging as they hit the protective layer of hardened resin. Only one place in all the Grey World had this floor.

This was where everything had begun.

Grey World 101 did not have the complications of rocket science. Though, it did usually take new minions of Death a while to take in the reality of what they saw and what they felt.

One doesn't simply stand in the cavernous Central Chamber of Death for the first time and not feel overwhelmed by the sepia toned decor of bones. From full skeletons to disarticulated sections, the place was decorated in such a fashion that there was nowhere to look and not see a bone.

The spine candelabras always intrigued me, though my best friend, Jen, had always been drawn to the skulls with their jaws opened and their faces eyeless though seeming to look in all possible directions.

The Grey World had been created to stop the Green World and the After Worlds from colliding again. If that were to ever happen, hell on Earth would no longer be a poetic macabre ideal.

The original Death had stood in this spot and made the floor I had been thrown down upon. Beneath the clear resin lay the collected bones of the earliest dead, killed when the Worlds first collided together. The magic from the bones combined with Death's own skills created the Grey World, and since then every Death who had sat upon the throne had maintained that very balance.

But the Grey World was large and dense, and the first Death learned quickly their need for minions. From Collectors to Necromancers.

I pressed my palm hard against the floor, watching as the pale skin on the back of my hands turned almost transparent.

My tanned skin had faded, and my skin shone as bone white as ever.

I sensed Death's presence where they sat on their throne in front of us.

Death's Central Chamber wasn't the biggest space in Death's palace, but it was the most important for all who lived in the Grey World. The World had not only begun here, but all the important matters were decided in this room.

Death judged and punished those who would interrupt or threaten the balance between the Worlds.

They condemned and banished the Grims.

They centred the Worlds and carried on the legacy of Death.

They had the power over every single soul's final walk.

"I can fix this. I can save her." Tears wet my cheeks. I didn't know who I spoke to. All of us, none of us. "I can't leave her there, not like that."

Silence lingered in the chamber.

"Take me back, you cold-hearted bitch." I stared up at Theamin, my chest rising and falling fast, my throat raw. But Theamin stood at attention, her face and body turned away from me, and I knew exactly who she looked at.

"Theamin!" I screamed.

"Save her?" She turned her head only far enough to lock eyes with my own. "You should be far more worried about saving yourself, Lilekai."

"Myself?" I spat. "I don't care about myself. I need to save her. She can't be left that way."

"You stupid child." Theamin returned her attention ahead of her. "One day you will learn you are fallible, Lilekai. That rules exist for a reason. When will you grow up and start listening?"

"Why did you bring me back here? Why not just walk me

through to the end? You finally have your excuse to do it," I asked, looking up at her profile. I imagined her back in the days before she became a Necromancer. I could see her being sketched in the light and shadows of a drawing room. The curves of her face with its strong chin and prominent nose. From where I remained on the floor of Death's Central Chamber, I could almost admire the General of the Necromancers. Except, of course, I knew Theamin, and we had never gotten along, not once in my fifty years.

"I would also like to know the answer to that." Death didn't yell, though their voice filled the room.

I turned to watch as they rose from their throne. The dark heavy looking cloak swirled around their feet, and their cowl perched perfectly atop their head.

"Death, a soul has been pinned. Trapped to the mortal flesh." Theamin's words came out in a rush. "Because of her."

"Lilekai? Explain." Death looked down at me. The pressure of their gaze rested like a physical weight upon me.

"It's Katy, the one I told you about." I looked up from half closed lids, not wanting Death to see just how much fear and pain I knew swarmed in my eyes. Without words, I begged for them to understand, to see what had happened without making me retell it, without making me relive the nightmare.

"The one you wished to become a Necromancer?" Their voice revealed nothing, but their eyes flickered, fiery flames licking against black irises. Their beauty paralleled their power, but I saw the danger lurking in the depths of every slight movement.

I nodded, biting my tongue from words that would only make us linger longer. Painfully aware that every moment we remained here was another moment Katy's soul remained trapped.

"What of her?" Death's words held a tightness new to my ears.

"She killed herself," I said. The edges of a sob stopped any more words from coming out.

Death paused and got that look on their face. The look that told us they were checking the gates at the furthest end of the Grey World.

"She has not crossed at either gate, Light or Dark. Nor does she wait to cross." They stared at me, waiting for my response.

Fear, raw and ragged, rippled around my edges. For all that I adored and admired Death, there remained inside of me always a fear of their power. A fear of them. Despite what Theamin believed, and despite my actions, there was still fear.

But the fear had never been like this.

This fear gripped me, changed me, and I no longer knew a thing about this World or my place within it.

Silence pressed hard against the pressure in the cold air around us.

I forced myself to move and get to my feet. I would stand in front of my creator. The one who made me the Necromancer I was.

Screw fear and cowering.

I would admit to my flaws.

I looked over at Theamin.

She narrowed her eyes at me, lips pressed into thin lines. Her eyes were stones that could have literally killed if she were given even the smallest hint of more power over me.

"I tried to change her," I admitted through a throat thick with emotion.

"Oh, Lilekai." A stone gargoyle would have been able to call my name using a softer tone. "What are you, Lilekai?"

"I am a minion of Death." I said the words I knew by heart,

but they tasted like ash on my tongue. "I am a Necromancer. I am one of many in a vast sea."

"And your job?"

"I collect the souls of the dead. I place your mark on the bones left behind. I lead the souls on their final walk."

"And who am I?" Now Death's words were slower, harder around the edges.

"You are Death. You rule everything within the Grey World. You alone hold the power to change mortal to minion."

My heart beat with a thud against my ribs. And then another.

"Lilekai, with me now." Death walked between the gap of me and Theamin, not breaking their stride as they spoke. "Theamin, direct Sara and Kensley to watch the gates, permission for extra Keepers should they feel the need."

"Yes, Death." Theamin walked off without even a casual back glance at me as I turned to follow Death.

Not even getting a smirk from Theamin did not bode well for the depth of trouble I had placed myself in.

Death's grip on my arm made Theamin's own vice-like grip comparison to a lover's caress.

I scurried to match Death's stride, step for step. I had little choice. I had to either keep up or be dragged.

We walked out of their Central Chamber and down the corridor of the Necromancers' rooms. Each corridor that shot off from the main chamber, like spokes on a wheel, housed one of Death's ranked minions. Five in all—Necromancers, Resurrectionists, Collectors, Witches, and Keepers.

My own door whisked by without acknowledgement.

A few heads appeared from doorways and disappeared just as quickly.

I met Jen's eyes and her face paled more than her usual chalky complexion. Not sure what she was doing in the hall of the Necromancers, but I didn't care. I was simply grateful to see her. At least she knew something had happened. She knew I hadn't just disappeared without a word, without a care.

I mouthed a quick sorry, hoping she understood.

Her wide grey eyes, blue fire flickering within, filled with tears.

I struggled to keep my legs moving and my heart from bursting through my chest as we walked on and on. I focused on the full skeletons pressed into the walls of the corridor. At first glance they looked identical, a repeating pattern. But if you stood long enough, if you knew the truth you saw the subtle shift from skull to skull as the skeletons surveyed the hallway. Each head had been placed the merest fraction off from the ones either side of it.

Death had once told me that they didn't know any of the bodies the skeletons had once been, having all been interred long before they became Death. I had jumped on the topic, asking question after question about their own time as Death, about how many came before them. They avoided my curiosity with ease, redirecting my attention to something else every time.

"Breathe." Death's single command warranted no time for an answer before we stepped out of the building. Outside of Death's castle, the heavy thick fog of the Grey World loomed. Death walked with the confidence of unnumbered years.

They knew the way better than all others. Of course they did. This was their domain, and I knew for a moment–a moment that might just turn into my final walk–I had forgotten that simple fact.

We stopped at the barrier to the Green World. It shimmered like rain on an oil slick, one moment black and the next purple, then yellow, and finally green.

The fog of the Grey World dissolved behind us as we drew closer to the vertical oil slick.

Shimmering between Worlds took energy and permission. Stepping through the actual barriers was in Death's power alone.

Every human dies, and every soul finds themselves in the Grey World. Only those with Death by their side are granted permission to step through, body and soul intact, through the barrier gate.

I had stepped through it once. The memory of it lingered, never to be forgotten. An experience I had hoped never to know again.

I shuddered, memory and anticipation blending to create a new foreboding in my stomach.

Death released my arm. The long sleeve of their cloak rolled back to reveal their hand as they curled their fingers into a fist. Without speed, as though this were just another ordinary day, another ordinary moment in our Grey World lives, they reached up and gently bumped the barrier with their knuckles.

The barrier rippled, colours warping around us. The foreboding turned to roiling in my stomach. My body could not hold back the bile and upset much longer. I knew that. But I kept my mouth shut and watched in silence. Even with the fear, I stared, mesmerised and in awe of how Death's body shifted and changed. The gentle fist bumps against the rippling gate increased into hard thumps.

"I am sorry, Lilekai.," Death spoke between one punch and the next.

I took my eyes from the moving barrier and looked over at them. Their silhouette looked wrong in a way I couldn't place.

"I don't understand."

The barrier took longer to get to the mortal realm, and we didn't have time for this. But I didn't say the words.

"You will." They punched again and the movement of the barrier reminded me of a storm-tossed sea at night.

"Never forget I am sorry." Death took my arm once more. Their touch held a gentleness that frightened me far more than their grip of anger.

Before I could reply, they pulled their hand back once more and slammed their fist again into the doorway. The sound cracked around us like thunder on the horizon. The oil slick rippled and, for a heart stopping moment, I thought it would not open for us, would not allow us to step through.

I didn't want to step through, but Death not being able to access it scared me in ways that made my skin shiver in goose pimples.

My stomach lurched.

Without Death's grip on my arm, I would have collapsed to the ground.

Finally, the rippling oil spill barrier opened, and I sighed with relief.

But we weren't done. Through the opening sat another doorway.

This doorway was more green than black.

Without waiting, Death pulled their hand back a second time and punched their way through into the Green World. Heat washed over me.

I blinked a few times to acclimate to the Green World.

While time worked much the same in each World, I often found myself surprised by how quickly day and night changed here. There was never anything but the mists in the Grey World.

With relief, I took in the darkness of the sky and the false light of electricity that hummed around us. Shimmering from the Grey World into the Green World's daylight stung the backs of my eyes and throbbed at the tattoo at the base of my skull. And it was still night. We had not been gone so long.

But the World sat differently on my skin and through my eyes. My mortal body hadn't been in the Green World for over fifty years.

Worry gnawed at the back of my mind, but I left it there.

Nothing else mattered but Katy. Nothing else could matter. Theamin told me to worry about myself, but I would not. I would face whatever consequences Death deemed appropriate. I had prepared for my final walk long before I met Death, and I did not fear it now.

"Where is she?" Death's voice held none of the warmth I had come to know and love.

"At her home," I replied. We were not far, but time scratched against me like an insistent bug.

"Picture it."

Instantly I did. I obeyed though they did not place an order on my blood. They had every right to. They could do so to any minion at any time. But I had never seen them do it. Or heard of it happening. Not since they sat upon the throne.

The Shimmer washed through me, faster than what I could have conjured up myself and in a moment there we were, standing in the middle of Katy's small living room.

The view from the window normally took my breath away. The lights from buildings and cars dancing on the river and calling to the lovers and the creatives. It reflected on the surface of the water, warping and undulating with the gentle movement of the wind. But now all I saw were the mechanics and none of the magic or beauty.

Inside Katy's apartment, the only light came from outside, filtered through the glass windows.

"I had hoped Theamin had overreacted." Death's words were clipped.

I turned away from the view to see Death kneeling beside Katy's dead body.

Her eyes were closed, and her face looked soft and at peace. A look I had rarely seen on her during her far too short life. I had tried to understand the extent of the depression she suffered, but only now did I truly grasp how painful so many moments of her life must have truly been.

How much stronger she had been to have gotten through so many days. My heart ached.

I breathed slowly between barely pursed lips and saw the wavering soul, Katy's soul, buzzing and fighting to get away. It moved from her dead body, so close to escaping. She was so close but then the stitch I had not meant to make pulled her back. She collapsed back onto her body. On and over, but no longer within.

"Can you help her?" My voice, rough and raw as I forced it out of my mouth. "Please?"

"Of course I can help her." Death lifted their arms and shook their hands until the sleeves of their robe dropped back once more. The long slender fingers didn't curl into their palm but flicked out with a small movement of their wrist. Hands turned to bones, stripped of flesh as though they had merely taken off a set of gloves.

"Necromancer?" My voice squeaked as my confidence seeped out of me. I had once known, once believed in all that I did and all that I was. Now I stood stripped bare of it all.

"No!" Death snapped out. Their teeth clacked together as though stopping themselves from saying anymore.

I stepped back involuntarily and took a sharp intake of breath.

Death looked up, with a head tilt as sharp as my gasp. After a deep breath their eyes returned to their task at hand.

"I cannot save her and keep her soul intact." They spoke without looking at me. Their focus solely on where it needed to be.

"She will be gone?"Vines wrapped a grip around my heart.

"Yes. And the magic of her bones can only be used to balance her death once the soul is removed."

"I will never see her again." Memories of our times together flashed through my mind. I was her senior in all ways, and yet she had taught me so much about living. She convinced me to get my first tattoo, got me drunk, which is no mean feat for a Necromancer, and introduced me to coffee.

Tears slid from my eyes and over my cheeks.

"You are lucky Theamin dragged you to me as swiftly as she did." They shook their head and the softness of their voice cut into me sharper than the 'no' they had snapped out. I wished for their voice to rise and yell, to scream at me. I would have sold my own soul, if I could, to have them look at me with anything other than the disappointment I had seen.

"A soul once tethered will go crazy if left alone. You are old enough to know these things."

"I haven't forgotten." I shouldn't have said anything.

"Then you wilfully risked all of us for your own selfish purposes."

"She would have been yours."

"No, she would have not." They shook their head. "The longer she remains, torn between life and death, the more she puts all of us in danger. The magic Death creates shifts in the Green World. You know this. It is why I need all my Necromancers to respond to a death, to guide the souls through and ensure the Green World is not brought closer to the After Worlds. You have risked everything we hold dear. Her magic grows strong in its confusion and anger. If she is not walked through, and quickly, then we risk more than her soul."

"It's not just the bones that have the magic. The souls shift the Worlds as well." How had I never realised that? It seemed so obvious now they had stated it so clearly.

"Of course they do. These are just one of the many lessons you must know better than your own soul before trying to turn a mortal into a minion." Death's face looked at Katy's fighting soul, their eyebrows furrowed, and their lips curved down in sadness. "She is becoming desperate and soon the soul's magic will turn into power. Power this soul alone cannot use. She will be able to use the body, and the bones, but the power will turn dark."

"A Grim?" I had been scared before, now terror rushed through my veins. Grim's existed, I knew that, but no one had ever explained how they were created. ?This is how a Grim is made?"

Death nodded. "One of many ways, yes."

"I'm sorry," I mumbled. "Please help her."

"What were you thinking?" Death shook their head.

"I couldn't let her cross over until she had a chance to see what being a minion, maybe even a Necromancer, was like. Until she truly knew how special and unique she was." They were words Death had once said to me when they offered me this World and this life.

"And you thought so little of me." Death snapped finger bone against finger bone, lights burning transparent between. "You think so little of my powers, that I would not stop her from making that crossing? Do you think me unaware, so forgetful of what every single one of my minions asks of me? I do not sit upon that throne and become fat and oblivious to my duties. It has been many lifetimes since those mortal failings were my own."

While they spoke, they worked. The light grew and stretched, hovering around their flayed hands to the sound of bone clacking on bone. I watched, mesmerised, as Death gently worked their way inside the flesh that had once been Katy. I knew their work would leave no mark, just as they created no wound and spilled no blood.

I trembled beneath their rage and power, gasping for breath that mocked my lungs instead of filling them.

When Death finally stood, I no longer had any concept of time or how much had passed.

Katy's quivering and blurred soul now shivered in their arms, finally unpinned from the horrors I had put upon it. She looked like nothing more than a sleeping child in their parent's strong embrace.

"You are exiled from the Grey World." Death's words were quiet.

"What?" The word tumbled out. They cannot have said that. "It's my home."

"You are exiled from the Grey World. You will continue to do your job, I will not see you walked through to your end. Though I should, I cannot." The resignation in their voice broke me and silent tears spilled from my eyes and over my cheeks.

"Will I be mortal again?"

"You are my Necromancer." Their words were fierce. "I do not relieve you of your duty. Outside of walking the dead through, your physical body will return to the Grey World once every six months. I will walk you through the barrier myself. That will allow your powers to remain active. If you Shimmer without permission, if you step inside my chambers without my leave, I will take you through your final walk myself. Do you understand?"

"Yes, Death," I spoke on a whisper. I couldn't bring myself to speak any louder. "For how long?"

"For 30 years you will be a Green World Necromancer. Only then will I consider reinstating you as one of my Grey World minions. If you want the luxuries that you have come to rely on, you will earn them back one by one. Just as you did in the beginning. I hope you finally learn something from this, Lilekai."

"Please." I didn't know what words I could say. I didn't know what I even wanted, not really. But this had definitely not been it. I would be alone, completely and truly. Belonging to nowhere. I would not return to being a mortal, and I would lose the family of the Grey World.

I did deserve the final walk, they were right. But this punishment would serve a more painful lesson. And I had promised to accept whatever punishment Death chose.

I stared at Katy's insubstantial form in Death's arms. I deserved this.

Her presence acted like a barrier between the two of us and, for a moment, I found comfort in knowing I would only need to see Death once every six months. Though never seeing them again had its own charm I yearned for.

"If only you had had more faith in me, child." The look they gave me broke what little sense remained. "Learn while you are in your banishment."

"Please." I grabbed the bottom of their cloak, my resolve to accept the punishment fading me. "Do not leave me, please."

But leave me they did.

And with it my consciousness.

I woke with a start. A fist banged on a door nearby. The sound mixed and fought to be heard over the screaming of Katy's name, over and over.

FIVE YEARS LATER

"Hello?" She was young. Too young. Her voice, trembling and confused, echoed as though from the end of a long corridor. It was nothing like it had sounded in life. I knew that now, I knew so much more about the mortals I guided on their final walk through the Grey World.

She stood in the shadows between two red brick buildings. She had been drawn to me as I had been drawn to her.

It was all part of the job, all part of being Death's Necromancer. That hadn't changed, though it had been one of the few things that hadn't.

"Hi. What's your name?" I stepped toward her and smiled as softly as I could. She flinched at my presence. I didn't take it personally, they all flinched.

After blinking a few times, she replied, "Rose."

"Like the flower?" I bent my knees and crouched so we were face to face.

She nodded.

"My name's Lily. I'm a flower as well." I smiled and Rose met mine with a watery but confused version of her own attempt at smiling.

"Where am I?" She turned around, unable to see the scene that surrounded her. She did not remember, so she could not process the reality of her own death.

"You are where you died." I spoke soft but firm. If I hesitated, if I got clever with the wording in hopes of softening the blow, the soul would fight harder against the idea. It made it worse, for all of us.

"Died?" Her eyebrows knitted together, and bile burned at the back of my throat. Still so human and expressive. But it wouldn't last much longer. It never did. Once she accepted the truth, the soul would quiet. I would walk her soul in silence through the Grey World and to the gate it needed to step through.

"Yes, you died," I repeated, wanting both to let the truth remain evasive while also finding a way to hurry all of this up. The young ones were some of the hardest souls to collect. Their lives had so much potential, but all of that life and talent were stolen too soon by tragedy or disease.

Every soul I collected weighed on me. Not as it had when I lived in the Grey World. There had been so many things to adjust to when I had no choice but to live in the Green World again. So much had changed.

It had been only after I had returned to the Grey World after my first six-month recharge that I learned I was not the only Green World minion. Things had gone easier after that. But only thanks to Lita and Isla.

"I'm not dead." She pulled me from my thoughts and forced her smile to widen. Her bottom lip quivered anyway, and part of her already knew the truth. "I've got exams next week, and Ma is letting me help her on the holidays with the letter run so I can earn some pocket money."

"You crossed the road, and the person driving was distracted. They didn't see you until it was too late."

"They killed me?" Silver drops slipped from her eyes and shimmered against the misty form of her soul. There was never just one tear sliding down a face, I had never seen such a thing in any Worlds, or any forms, despite the number of movies I'd seen it in. Movies that professed to mimic life. Thankfully they never truly did.

I nodded and offered her my hand. "Look around."

She looked me over closely. The heavy black cloak covered my hands and my feet. The cowl, though pushed back a little to show my face, rested at the top of my forehead. The girl gasped and then turned away from me and moved in a slow circle.

I closed my eyes as the soul beside me sobbed out a word of denial, the reality of her stolen life hitting as hard as the car had hit her body.

"No, no, no, no. I can't be dead. I can't. I had more things I had to do."

I let her sob while the surrounding noises, like symbols struck at the wrong time during a performance, created chaos in my mind.

It hurt my ears. It was always too loud. Death should never be so loud, but mortals had a way of screaming when silence was required.

It reminded me of that sci-fi movie tagline. But it wasn't space. The truth was that in death no one can hear you scream. At least, no one who remains living can hear you scream.

"I don't want to die. I don't want to go to Hell." Her words snapped me out of my own head.

"Why would you think you are going to Hell?" I wanted to stroke her hair and kiss her forehead. At moments like this, I wanted to be mortal again. But no matter how or where I lived, I would never be one of them again.

"I'm not good."

"Oh, sweet child." Screw it, I could pay the price of a fractured heart later. I wrapped her soul up in my arms and she clung to me. The touch of souls had never been forbidden, but it tore away a little of myself when I had to let them go again.

Her tears wet my cloak, and her voice whispered in my ear the dark sins she thought had been her own.

"You're going to the Light World."

"What's it like there?" A smile, small and hesitant, sparked a joy in her eyes.

"I don't know." I smiled and shrugged. "It's not my time to go there. But I've heard it's beautiful, and there's no more pain."

Her eyes welled with hope. "Will you take me there?"

"I can take you to the door."

"Okay." She nodded and I mourned the loss of her strength for this World. The Green World would have been privileged to have her for so much longer than it had been given. "I'm ready."

"You are." I smiled and nodded in return.

Her breath changed and I knew, from years of experience, that the last truth sounded within her. She looked down at her feet. The silence slid over her like a shutter window being pulled. What made her human, what made her mortal, drifted away as simply as that. I always expected there to be more of a fanfare.

No, I didn't expect it, I wanted there to be a fanfare. There should be a celebration of each life, with confetti and balloons. Once, I asked Death about my concerns, about the disappearance of their noise but they reassured me it was temporary. I held on to that more now than before. But it never made enough of an impact when they had to walk such a young life through to the After Worlds .

I crouched beside the body and slipped my hands through the flesh, tagging the bones as soulless as now belonging to Death. The Collectors would be there soon.

The scene surrounding us carried more confusion and disbelief. There were young voices, high pitched with hysteria. Sobs from a man who leaned on the bonnet of his car. Cries from girls who could just have easily been the one to stand beside me, silent but ready.

A stern authoritative voice cut through the cacophony, demanding an ETA on the ambulance. A teacher held back school children, all wanting to know what had happened. Another teacher leant over the girl's body. They muttered a song without rhythm or emotion as they moved their hands, arms slightly bent, pressing against the girl's chest in time with the words.

Slipping the soft vibration of her soul into the armhole of my cloak, Rose found my fingers. It was time to leave.

We walked through the door I made with the Shimmer, and together we crossed into the Grey World. The final walk of the Grey World never took the same amount of time. For years it frustrated me that I had not learned the pull of the Light World well enough.

It hadn't occurred to me until my first year living as a Green World Necromancer that we were merely guides, and the time it took had nothing to do with me. We were really only needed to interfere if the soul wandered too far toward Death's home or turned themselves around.

Too soon, we reached the brightness of the barrier to the Light World. She had been ready, far more ready than she had realised.

Rose looked back at me, a small smile on her lips as she gave me a single nod. I returned the gesture.

She walked through the door of the Light World, and it closed silently and swiftly behind her.

I stood still, wondering if I would find my way here when I died again. Or if I would be punished, and pulled toward the door to the Dark World instead.

Soon, always too soon, the pressure built up inside of me, and I had to get out of the Grey World.

My job was done, and my next six-month recharge had not come around again.

Twice I had tried to ignore the pain, but Death knew their shit.

The Grey World had spat me out every single time. If I fought the pull back to the Green World, back to where my body remained in my banishment, then the headaches raged into migraines.

As soon as I stepped back through to the Green World the small ache behind my eyes pulsed. It would ease soon enough. I had not overstayed my welcome this time. I couldn't imagine doing that again. Twice had well and truly taught me a lesson.

My breath shuddered with relief. My body remained where I had left it. I stared at the shell of myself sitting at the small round table in my kitchen. It looked as though I were lost in thought.

There was always a danger in leaving the shell, always a small chance of damage while on a mission. One of the many things I had to adjust to during my banishment. As a Grey World Necromancer the body and soul could go with you on a job. They needn't be split. But that privilege had been removed, along with so many others.

"Urgh." I shook my head and focused on letting the two halves of myself snap back together.

What a fucking way to start the day. A child of all things.

Against the windows in the living room, light rain made a hush ing sound and mist of welcome. I smiled, relaxed the tense shoulders on my body and shed the metaphorical cloak of my job.

I changed from the loose sleeping singlet I wore into jean shorts and a sleeveless shirt. Even now, the hush of rain was slowing, and the heat built up again. The temperature would say something simply like "Bearable, quit your whinging". But after five years, my body still struggled to adapt to the mix of mugginess and the baking sun of another Queensland summer as it evaporated the rain. The ground would be dry once more before the sun reached its midday arc across the sky.

Picking up the specially designed phone Jen had made me, I slipped it into my back pocket. If Death knew about this connection I retained to the Grey World, to my best friend, they ignored it.

There were so many things that I hadn't known when Death had abandoned me, banished me back to the Green World.

How to live as a mortal in a World that had changed and progressed had taken time, but getting back into the groove of this new modern age hadn't been as hard as I had initially feared. Once I got used to my unique physical interference with the technology of the modern age. More specifically, electricity.

I didn't understand it, but since stepping through the barrier that second time, technology no longer worked correctly around me. The failure wasn't always instant, sometimes it would even work as long as five minutes. But in the end, it always screwed up. It was unpredictable at best, and dangerous at other times.

"Goddamn it, I need coffee," I muttered as I filled the pot, turned on the gas stove, and opened my pantry door.

"Fuck!" I slammed the door closed and flicked off the stove top with a little more force than needed.

I had run out of coffee. I had forgotten the plans to go and grab some before heading down to the cemetery. The last thing I needed after a final walk was social interaction with mortals.

My headache hadn't dissipated yet and after another minute the need for coffee overruled my need for solitude.

Resigned to the inevitable, I scooped up my house key and shoved it into the front pocket of my shorts.

I had only taken two steps out of the door when the phone rang, sending my butt cheek vibrating.

I smiled. Only Jen ever called me. Lita and Isla texted.

"Bitch, where the hell have you been?" I smiled as I spoke into the phone, now pressed to my ear. I knew where she had been, but it felt normal to talk to her as I would a mortal I got along with. There were few enough of them.

"Getting my rocks off, what else?" Jen replied with an accent she hadn't had last time.

"Which countries have you been to this month?" I smiled and stepped over a puddle in the middle of the footpath. Already the surrounding cement faded back from its former soaked state as the heat in the day built up again.

She laughed, and my shoulders relaxed as she told me tales of her latest adventures in the Green World.

I had hoped to see her in the Grey World during my walk. She often knew when I had been called on and found me in time for us to walk a little before the headaches began. But a call would suffice for now.

I took the well-worn trek down to my favourite coffee shop as I listened to Jen talk.

THREE

"I'm not going to your board game night, Jen," I snapped into the phone as she tried for the third time to assure me that I would have a great time. Jen's freedom often washed over me, and I didn't mind it, but today wasn't one of those days.

My foot slid a little as I tried stepping over yet another puddle that covered the cement footpath. How were there still so many damned puddles when the sun's rays on the back of my neck made sweat bead into my shirt, running down my spine and pooling at the waist of my shorts.

"Wow, not been a good morning, huh?" Jen asked. She stopped talking about the latest Green World party she had organised. I had no doubt it was yet another attempt to get me laid. I liked sex well enough, but I didn't need her running interference trying to find me someone to hook up with. I might never be able to have the kind of relationship mortals had, but one-night stands just weren't my thing.

But I missed Jen, and usually humoured her enough to attend. And I did often have fun.

"So why was today so much worse?" Her voice was gentle. I don't know how she did it, but she always knew when to push me and when I needed a little more understanding.

"A kid," I mumbled into the phone as I stepped over what was either a discarded plastic wrapper or a used condom. I didn't focus too long on the details for my own peace of mind.

"Ah shit." Jen could have passed for a Green World mortal any day of the week, but right now her casual tone made me ache in my isolation. There were other Green World minions and knowing them helped. Having Lita and Isla had made the difference between misery and life, but it wasn't the same. And none of them were my Jen.

"Yeah. Wasn't a good night either." I stopped walking long enough to close my eyes and take a deep breath. It wasn't Jen's fault. "Sorry, Jen."

"You should have come and found me." Jen and her ease with words, as though lingering in the Grey World would ever be a real option for me.

"You know I can't, Jen. Thirty years. No sooner than thirty years. I've got another twenty-five left." I laughed with all the bitterness of my situation.

I really needed my damn coffee.

"I know you and Theamin don't always see eye to eye."

"The bitch hates me," I replied instantly.

"She hates everyone. But..." Jen lingered on the word until I let out a sigh which seemed to be enough indication to her that I was listening. "You could ask her for leniency? For more training perhaps?" Jen's tone carried a begging she usually reserved for the need of a wingwoman in the Green World. "She's tough, but she is fair, Lily."

"Oh yeah, she's a peach." I smiled. "And why the hell would I want to inflict more of her training on myself. The bruises will be super fun to explain when I get back."

"You don't see anyone, Lily. So no explanation required." Jen, always with the logical argument.

"I see people." I felt smug in my honesty as I continued my walk toward the coffee shop.

My coffee shop.

It didn't have some fancy name and wasn't one of the shiny chain stores that charged three times as much for untrained baristas. Okay, so I had become a bit of a coffee snob since taking up the habit. But I stood by my opinion.

The coffee shop I frequented was nothing more than a small unremarkable building, sitting alone, surrounded by nothing but a carpark and some undeveloped land. On the top of the peaked roof was a sign that might have once been red with white letters. Now it simply spelled out "Coffee" in a faded blend somewhere between pink and grey. It hadn't always been a coffee shop. I had seen too many buildings with the same shape and design, with the banner at the top being a once arterial red. A fast-food chain restaurant maybe? I still couldn't remember the name of it.

"You've just got to learn how to handle Theamin." Jen's words pulled me back from my thoughts.

"No thanks. I don't want to think about anyone handling her, or her handling anyone else." I shuddered. "Besides, you can't even handle her, Jen. If Death's own daughter can't handle the General of the Necromancers, what hope do I really have?" I laughed, realising Jen had achieved precisely what she had intended. To get me out of my own head.

Jen's small chuckle came through the line. "Yeah, alright, but I wouldn't mind handling her, just the once."

"Oh my god, Jen. Ew, and no."

"She's hot, Lily. You can't deny that."

"Of course she is, but sooner or later the 'hot' diminishes in the light of her arrogance the moment she opens her mouth."

"I miss you, Lil. It's so depressing here without you."

"Of course it is, there's no hell-grown coffee there." As if on cue, that blessed building came into view, but my feet stumbled on the pavement as though they had forgotten entirely how to walk.

The carpark should have been busy with cars coming in and out. Movement should have been constant, while voices of those coming in and out of the front door should have carried over to me. Even this far away.

I stared, not entirely understanding what I saw. A few stationary cars were parked at angles incongruent with painted white lines, and a silence hung over the entire scene in front of me.

The sight made my heart speed up and my breath catch as I finally took in the finer details.

The cars, all of them were police cars, marked and unmarked. The unmarked vehicles were even more noticeable than their branded counterparts. There were big black bulky units on the dashboards and they sported more antennae than any insect would ever need.

"Sorry, Jen," I said, half distracted, cutting off words I hadn't been listening to. "Getting too close to civilisation. I'll catch you later."

"I'll send through the details for board game night."

"Ahuh," I replied, not truly taking in her words.

Tucking the phone into the back pocket of my shorts, I drew closer.

The noises cut in loud and sudden as though a bubble had popped around me, previously isolating me from the unnatural sounds that enveloped the coffee shop.

The World had come alive in my quiet little suburb. But beneath it, I felt the far too familiar pull of Death.

It wasn't unusual for me to walk to the coffee shop once a

day. I rarely missed a day. I even bought the ground coffee I used at home, the stuff I had now run out of, from here.

The routine and comfort of coffee was one of the first things I had truly embraced when I finally accepted my fate of being a Green World Necromancer.

Now it threatened to crumble around me and my mind stared at the incongruous site in front of me.

I forced myself to breathe a deep lungful of air. Slowly I breathed out before gulping in another breath. The World around me had never seemed so damn surreal.

But I could do this.

I imagined I could hear Lita and Isla cheering me on, just as they had many times over the years. Whatever had happened, maybe Daria needed a friend to help her get through it. Daria wasn't much younger than me, in terms of Green World living. She had invited me to her twenty-ninth birthday just a few months ago.

I had been thirty-three when Death gave me the opportunity to be one of their Necromancers. I didn't age. Even now, since my banishment, I remained the same. My body never changed despite what whirled and shifted inside of me. My insides took the brunt of my sins, turning them into a twisted blood-soaked portrait of my very own.

Daria seemed so much younger than what I remember twenty-nine having been. But the entire World had changed while I had walked souls through the Grey World.

I stepped around the cars, making sure I didn't brush too close to any of them. The police sometimes made it difficult to do my job, but overall, I had a healthy respect for their role in the Green World. They kept the chaos contained the best they could.

The sounds of muttering and shuffling grew louder as I pushed open the front door. The tug in my chest, a string pulled taught by Death, threatened to overtake all my other senses. Death lingered inside, any last strings of doubt snapping. A band gripped my ribs and squeezed. It couldn't be Daria.

The bell above my head tinkled and I blinked as a dozen heads swivelled and snapped around to see me.

Conspicuously, one head remained facing the opposite direction.

Electricity shot through my veins as I focused on the short black hair that cradled the back of the woman's skull. I couldn't remember the last time my body had reacted so intensely to another person's presence. It wasn't the same as the connection that I felt with other minions of Death. But there was something different about this mortal.

It couldn't be just hormones and physical attraction. The only other time I had felt this overwhelming zing had been...I forced my mind to trail off.

Death lingered in this space, and nothing as primal as lust could overtake that for me. My body chuckled as heat pooled within me, travelling down.

Focus, Lilekai, who cares if it is her.

The woman, I refused to acknowledge the possibility of who it might be until it was proven, blocked something on the floor in front of the counter. The curve of her neck made my fingers tingle with desire to touch it, to brush down the sides until I reached the broad shoulders and strong back. I let my eyes drift down to the curve of the woman's bum where black pants pulled in just the right ways. They were bunched at the side of her hips as though she had pulled the material a little before crouching down. As though she were more than used to having to do this task.

What the hell was wrong with me?

I was one of Death's Necromancers. Death lingered and yet

I was fantasising about this woman. I needed more than coffee. Maybe I would take Jen up on her board game night after all. I just needed to get through this moment first.

"For fuck's sake, Ben, I told you to get the barriers up." A voice I knew, despite the years since I last heard it, filled the space.

Shit! Of all the places to run into her again, it had to be where Death lingered.

She hadn't turned or looked up to see me. But I didn't need to see her face to know her. I hadn't even really needed to hear her voice. Having heard her, I couldn't deny it was her.

Detective Larissa Alanor. Detective Arsehole to anyone who spent longer than ten minutes with her on the job. And she was never not on the job.

She was also Katy's older sister.

Damn it all. Her bike wasn't in the carpark. I checked far more often than I cared to admit for that bloody machine. I'd walk to the Dark World myself if she no longer rode it as an extension of herself, so why wasn't it there?

I knew she remained in the city. And anyone in the area would have to be completely disconnected from all media not to know she had moved up in her career.

I knew too much about her, while neither of us knew the other at all.

I had taken great pains to avoid any more interactions with her.

"Thought the police cars were enough to stop any idiot from barging in," a uniformed police officer muttered. I assumed this was Ben. He scowled at me as it replaced the initial hang-dog expression that flashed over his features. I assumed that had been from the public dressing down by the Arsehole herself.

I watched him turn and pull open the door, the bell above jangled again, and he disappeared outside.

Larissa rose, her long dark pants unfolding, and my eyes mesmerised by the turn of her hip. Long, strong-looking fingers brushed down the front of the material. My eyes trailed up the rest of her body as it continued to unfold. I tried not to linger too much on the shirt that curved nicely around a good handful of breasts.

But I should have lingered longer. All that waited for me as I finished my slow upwards appraisal were those cold grey eyes. The colour was similar to Katy's but worlds apart in temperature and joy.

A myriad of expressions raced across her face. There was no way for me to catch them all, but I knew shock and disgust well enough to recognise them in the mix.

"You!" Her professional demeanour broke like a dam. It was easy enough to read the expression on her face then.

Hate and loathing.

The war raged in her eyes, professionalism versus personal fury. I followed her gaze and saw what she had previously been blocking. All thoughts of the past, and this strange electrical connection neither of us had ever copped to, fled as I focused on the torso of a dead man. Alanor's body blocked the bottom half while a uniformed police officer blocked the man's head.

In three long strides, Detective Arsehole blocked the rest of my view of the crime. She was too close, her face filling my entire sight.

"He's dead." The words tumbled out of my mouth before I could catch them.

She narrowed her eyes at me.

I knew the man had died. I had been pulled toward his death. But the words weren't meant for me. They weren't meant for anyone. They were simply words that fell out as I tried to recalibrate myself to the shock of Alanor's presence.

"Come back to check you've done the job right?" She hissed low enough that the techs and constables that moved and hummed around us couldn't hear the words, or the vitriol.

"What?" I stepped back and scolded myself for being caught off guard.

She unsettled me. Everything about her threw me off balance.

"I may not know exactly what you are, but I know you aren't right. I know all about you, Lily, and things do not add up. I will find out!" The words were the equivalent of ice-cold water splashed down my spine. A liquid pain that straightened my back and squared my shoulders. "Stay away from here and stay out of the investigation or I will bring you in for questioning as a suspect."

I had always known she could be dangerous. To me at least. The connection between us was a warning sign, and nothing else. She had always seen something about me, something that others couldn't.

I had suspected she shared more than similar features with her baby sister. But if she did, her sight had never been as powerful as Katy's. I supposed it contributed to why she made such a brilliant cop. And such a huge pain in my arse.

Her belief I had killed Katy would have been enough for me to actively avoid the woman for all these years. Her insistence that I had something to do with Katy's death never wavered. I couldn't blame her. Everyone else had so easily accepted Katy's suicide, and my unfortunate discovery. Alanor didn't let the inconsistencies go. She was good at her job. Unfortunately for me.

I needed to stay away from anything that brought me closer to this woman. But, I wanted to linger in her presence despite the threat she presented. To feel the electricity between us as it sparked and sizzled, continued to entice. The warning wasn't enough to stop me leaning into it.

But logic and self-preservation finally kicked in.

I was already paying for my crimes. I didn't need her adding any more shit to the list.

Death hadn't called me for this final walk which meant I could turn around and walk away.

So why were my feet still planted to the spot?

"Did you hear me, Lily?" She spat the name as though it burned the very flesh on her tongue. And even without coffee, my brain buzzed into overdrive. Maybe it buzzed louder because I hadn't had my coffee.

Damn the temperamental weather. It made me change my plans yesterday to come and collect the grounds. Riding a push bike kept me active, and fit. The serotonin boost helped as well. But riding in the rain wasn't all it was cracked up to be. Daria always kept the bag aside for me if I didn't show up. She knew it wouldn't be long before I made another appearance.

Daria. I blinked and focused on all the people around me.

"Where is Daria?" I scanned the ones doing their work and the ones pretending they were while being far too entertained by the conversation between me and Alanor.

No Daria. I knew why I hadn't noticed her absence right away. And anger boiled inside of me. The detective was a distraction, but she was nothing to me. I repeated it over and over in my head.

Daria was my friend. If she wasn't here, where the hell was she?

"Who?" Alanor blinked and I bit back a mocking laugh, more antagonism wouldn't get me to my answer any faster. Pissing off Alanor didn't matter. Daria did. But that didn't stop me mentally chalking up a point in my column. I managed to resist a smug look in her direction, but my thoughts rushed along that vein as I tried not to imagine Daria's own body laying lifeless nearby.

See bitch, I can be helpful, not just some punching bag for you to knock around when you have nothing but dead ends. I could also be incredibly petty. I would have liked to blame my years back in the Green World, but this same attitude and snark had raised its head too frequently in reaction to Theamin's arrogance. I couldn't even convince myself of that one.

"Daria," I said slowly, between clenched teeth. "She works here. She opens the shop every damn morning, and she rarely leaves before it's closed. She works harder than the damn manager." I baulked and looked around Alanor's body. Just a peek, just enough to see the face of the man before she shuffled to block my view again.

"He isn't normally here this early." I blinked, my mind racing with possibilities of what could have happened. I was a Necromancer, not a Witch. I didn't investigate crimes, I knew nothing of how to, except for an unhealthy amount of watching crime shows, with a strong focus on Olivia Benson.

"Daria is not the owner?" Alanor asked in full detective mode. At least she wasn't Katy's sister right now.

"No, she's not the goddamned owner. I don't know who owns the joint. But he," I pointed vaguely around Alanor's body, "he's the manager, and she is the main barista."

Alanor pulled a small notebook from her pocket, flipped it open, and started jotting in it.

I breathed in deep and focused. She was good at her job.

But I didn't care about the man or what happened to him. Not when I didn't know where Daria was.

Had she missed work? I couldn't remember if it had happened before. I wasn't there every day, so it could have. But

I was there often enough. Daria had been there every single time, sometimes with others, sometimes on her own, but she was always there.

Detective Arsehole glared at me. I hated how it set a flame in my core. "Daria is someone you know well. And no doubt she's younger than you."

"Seriously?" I didn't have time for her old wounds. I didn't have time to have the same old arguments. "This isn't about Katy. This is about a woman who is missing while her manager is dead."

"Don't say her name around me." The detective's mask slipped just enough for me to see the hint of anger flash in her eyes, but her words remained calm.

"Are there any signs of Daria?" My teeth clenched so hard they hurt as I forced the words to come out strong without yelling, but it was close. I wanted to give myself a pat on the back but thought better of it, at least for now.

At least until I knew where Daria was and that she was okay.

"There is someone locked in the storeroom."

"What?" I glared at her. "Who?"

"We are working on it." Alanor pinched the bridge of her nose. "They won't tell us their name or unlock the door."

"Can I..." I let my request trail off as Alanor's eyes narrowed at me.

"You need to leave my crime scene. Willingly, or I'll have you escorted out."

I rolled my eyes and turned back to the door.

The sun hurt. It was too bright and harsh. I had far more to worry about then my caffeine withdrawal, but a cup of the good stuff would definitely help me figure out what to do next.

No one followed me out of the building. The door closed and no further jangle of the bell to announce anyone else.

I stepped under the roof overhang and leaned against the red brick wall. The warmth soaked through the back of my shirt, and I relaxed a little against the bricks.

I needed to concentrate, and I needed to stay away from my past. The five-year itch had crept up on me, but being around Alanor made me stupid and snarky. Even against my own self-preservation.

I had to get the hell away from here. Lingering would do me no good. But I enjoyed Daria's friendship, and that was enough to stop me from leaving just yet.

Daria was kind and bubbly. There was a sense of purpose to her that radiated from within. Something I didn't often see in the humans I was forced to spend time around. If I were honest, I didn't often see it in the Grey World either. We had a purpose, but not our own. It would always be Death's.

I sighed into the heat and watched as Ben dragged out an orange plastic bollard from the boot of a marked police vehicle. Bright crime scene tape looped over his arms like giant bracelets. He placed the bollard a metre away from another one, making three in total that cut off the driveway entrance to the coffee shop. I chuckled. Did anyone really believe the faded white arrow pointing out of the driveway would truly be enough to stop people coming in?

I closed my eyes as Ben struggled to untangle his limbs from the tape.

"Lily," Alanor barked from the entrance of the coffee shop. She slid a pair of grey tinted sunglasses over her eyes and walked toward me.

FOUR

I leaned my head back against the wall and closed my eyes, counting her steps as Alanor drew closer.

"I'll leave in a second. It's bloody hot in the sun," I muttered, keeping my face tilted up toward the sky.

"I need you to come inside."

My eyes flew open. I turned my head so sharply to look at her I heard the pop of tense muscles releasing in my neck.

"What?" I laughed incredulously. It didn't matter how horrible a situation became, it seemed I would live my entire life laughing when I found nothing funny. The sound wrapped around us, the laugh that held no humour. One day I might be able to deal with emotions, with the overwhelming things I saw and confronted on a daily basis, but this was obviously not that day.

"It appears that you are correct."

"Really?" This time my lips spread wide across my face, filled with the best shit-eating grin I possessed.

"She confirmed her name is Daria, but she refuses to open the door and let us in."

"Oh," Pieces fit into place, there was no holding back the smugness now. Especially when my main concern–Daria's safety–had been lifted. "So you need my help?"

"She might respond better if you were to talk to her." Alanor trying to hide her fury behind a layer of politeness screamed all manner of fucked up to me. The politeness rankled me, as though that were more insulting than all the amount of things she had accused me of over the years.

Larissa looked at me, eyebrows raised above the dark grey tinted lenses.

"Please." It was forced out between clenched teeth, but I'd take it.

And once again, inappropriate laughter bubbled in my chest. I pushed it away, as I pushed myself off the building's wall.

I reminded myself this wasn't about me. This wasn't even about our own history or Katy. Once I got Daria out, I would be rid of this entire nightmare. I had twenty-five years left living and breathing each day as an outsider in this World. I needed to get my equilibrium back.

Alanor led the way. I couldn't imagine a time when she wouldn't. I followed with my chin up and my footsteps steady. I didn't turn my head to look at the body. I saw death too often, and I was intimately familiar with what it looked like.

At the door to the storeroom two plain-clothes officers stood on either side. They were silent and serious. The perfect little lackeys for Alanor.

Getting a sick little thrill, I pushed roughly past Alanor's shoulder. I didn't know what was wrong with me. Why this woman brought out the very worst of who I could be. I wanted to show I had grown, I had learned to be better, but I wasn't beyond getting my digs in while I could.

Officer number one shuffled in front of me. I stopped and turned back to look at Alanor.

"It's fine." She directed her words to the officer, and he shuffled back to his sentry position beside the door.

I stepped between the two of them and knocked.

"Daria?" I held my breath and knocked again. "It's Lily. Are you okay?"

"Lily?" Daria's voice strained in a way I had never heard. I knew her laughter and jokes, and had seen her bubbliness and her excitement. But fear strummed her voice like an instrument, and it rasped in ways that shook me.

"Yeah, it's me, Daria." I smiled and breathed out loudly, the last knot of tension in my shoulders dissolving. "It's good to hear your voice."

Footsteps shuffled behind me, getting closer.

"We need her to come out. We need her statement." At least Alanor had the decency to whisper the words.

"She is shaken up."

"I know."

I looked at Alanor and saw hints of kindness hiding within the grey of her eyes.

"Hey, Daria." I turned back, unable to process those eyes holding much more than contempt and anger.

"Yeah?"

"The police are here. They need to make sure you're okay. Can you come out for me?"

"Is Brian okay?" She asked, the door still closed and locked between us.

"I'm sorry, no. He's gone."

"It's my fault. I ran and hid. I should have helped him, but I hid instead," she scratched out between sobs.

"None of this is your fault." I pressed my palm against the wood grain of the door. "Please come out."

Silence filled the space. Moments ticked by and then the click of the door sounded like a gunshot in a small space.

The door swung inward, and Daria stood half hidden behind it.

"Hey." I smiled and apparently it had been all she needed. She stepped out and into my arms the moment I held them up to her.

"You did the right thing." I shushed out the words, rocking her gently in my arms. "If the monster had gotten you as well, where would I get my coffee from?"

She chuckled, pulling back out of my arms and meeting my eyes. The smile wobbled as she brushed her fingers along her cheeks. They swept the fresh tears away but did nothing for the streaks that ran over her face.

"It was so scary." She spoke as though no one could understand what it was truly like. And maybe no one ever could.

"You did the right thing coming back here," I repeated. She had to know that. I cared about her. I cared about so many of the mortals I saw struggling as they forced themselves to understand the world within them and the world around them. I cared more than a Necromancer should.

"Brian's really dead?" Daria's eyebrows pulled together as she asked.

"Yeah. He's dead." I nodded.

I moved to Daria's side and placed my hand firmly but not forceful on her back. I used the same techniques I had often used for souls who struggled with their deaths. Those who struggled far more than Rose had this morning. How was that only this morning?

I looked at Alanor, unable to see her eyes behind the sunglasses she still wore. I raised my eyebrows in question, and Alanor nodded at me, though her lips were a thin line and her eyes narrowed. Talk about your mixed messages. The woman was a conundrum wrapped up in an enigma. No wonder she intrigued me.

No, infuriated. That's what she did. She infuriated me.

Before I could ascertain if the nod took precedence over the expression, several officers shuffled to make a line blocking the crime scene and Brian's body from view as we passed.

Alanor stepped around us and took the lead. Naturally.

I had to admit I was impressed she didn't jostle me the way I had her. The lack of tit for tat made me feel a little chastised. Damn her. I had to be at least fifty years older than her. Not that I could admit that, and I definitely didn't feel as such right now.

She waved her arm for Daria to sit at one of the booths. The padded chairs wrapped around the table and faced the opposite direction of the murder scene.

Daria looked at me without moving.

"If you want me to stay as your friend, I can do that. But you've gotta tell the police what happened." I looked over at Alanor, eyes begging her to take my lead.

For a moment she stared at me, eyebrows furrowed, and head slightly tilted. I wanted to laugh and call her a puppy dog. I definitely needed to get out of here. Not only did she make me feel years below my age, she made me reckless and my thoughts fuzzy.

Now was not the right time, I knew that and yet it took everything in me to keep my words and thoughts locked away around her.

She had made my life a living hell all those years ago. A life that I had to adjust to, fresh and broken and without a single break from her.

But this wasn't about me. I gave myself the pep talk I had when she asked the same questions over and over again about Katy.

Soon I would be gone, and I hoped this time I would never see those grey eyes again.

"Lily?" Daria asked. "What's wrong?"

I looked down at her where she had slid into the seat of the booth, next to Alanor. She had shoved her sunglasses up onto her head and stared at me as intently as Daria did, but with suspicion replacing concern.

What had my face done to cause both worry and suspicion? I cursed myself and my lack of concentration. I cursed Alanor for all of it.

"I'm sorry." I gave Daria the best smile I could muster. "I'm okay. I'm just a little exhausted."

I forced my face to remain as neutral as possible as I turned to Alanor.

She met mine, and after receiving a second nod from the Detective I decided I would buy a lottery ticket when I left here. I stepped to take my place at the end of the seat but stopped before my bum hit the cushion.

Warning bells rang inside my mind. What I needed was to get the hell out of there. It was one thing to have to live among the mortals, but something else quite entirely to be wrapped up in the affairs of the individuals. The last thing I needed, the last thing I wanted was to be caught up in yet another investigation. I lived by their rules only as much as I had to, but they weren't the rules that mattered.

And caring about the living hadn't worked out for me the last time. I had ignored Death's unspoken yet ever-present opinion of spending time in the World enjoying the company of mortals. And they had been right, it had all turned to shit.

Daria was as close a friend I allowed myself to get, but I couldn't do this. My heart sped beneath my chest. Knowing she was safe and unharmed physically relieved that fear, but it also allowed the greater picture to take back over my thoughts.

I needed to get the hell out of there.

As soon as the thought entered my mind, my skin tingled as though I were about to Shimmer. But the sensation wasn't quite strong enough. Instead, a pulling like a hook behind my navel tugged me to turn around. It yanked and caught within me, demanding I pay attention to what lay behind me instead of those who sat in front of me. The two in front of me mattered more than Brian ever did. In my four years of frequenting the place, the number of words the two of us had exchanged could have been counted on the fingers of both hands.

Yet the tugging wouldn't stop.

"She can stay if you'd like her to, Daria." Misinterpreting my hesitation, Alanor's words came out clipped but not hard.

"Yes please." Daria's reply was instant.

"I'll stay," I said just as quickly. "I just need the bathroom first."

I had my hand on the door of the bathroom when I noticed the storeroom door remained open and unguarded. I don't think I had ever seen the door open before.

"Clever girl," I muttered. The door standing open looked far stranger than when it was closed. Perhaps the person who did this thought the same.

I had never learned to tame my curiosity, no matter where it ended. Not when I was mortal, not during my fifty years as a Necromancer living in the Grey World, and most certainly not during the past five years.

Inside the storeroom, shelves were stacked with containers, boxes, and bags. Some looked to weigh as much as a grown man. I turned, shaking my head but from the corner of my eye the shelf along the back wall grabbed my attention. Turning back around, I looked harder. Noticing the shelves weren't as loaded or as even as those on either side, I stepped and saw why.

Behind the shelves stretched out on the floor looked like a camping bed. At the end sat a half-closed suitcase. The more I focused on the makeshift room the more I found other evidence of habitation. My heart dropped to my stomach.

"Oh Daria," I whispered.

I had never questioned Daria's willingness to allow me to be my loose interpretation of a friend. She had appeared willing to remain in the dark about my past or my life, and it satiated my need to connect to others. We enjoyed chatting and laughing, and I obviously cared about her and her safety. Nothing else would have kept me here with Alanor's piercing gaze that drilled accusation at me every time she looked my way.

But It hadn't dawned on me that Daria might've had her own reasons to remain an association instead of allowing for a deepening connection toward friendship.

I wouldn't break that trust. Daria could keep her secrets, no matter how hard my heart ached for her. Curiosity had its merits, but it could also be dangerous. I would not let myself step over this line, not with her.

I took one step back into the dining room and for the first time I got a complete view of the murder scene. Brian's body had now been covered by a white sheet but that didn't stop me seeing exactly what stared back at me.

My heart thundered in my chest.

The next step echoed in my ears, too loud as my sneakers sounded more like tap shoes. The next shuddered inside me like a clap of thunder drawing ever closer. A throb behind my eyes raised its trembling hand for my attention. The headache that had dulled to ignorable now increased its presence.

In my ears, my breath roared as it came faster and harder. Beneath the skin at my wrist, my blood pumped harder against my veins, wanting desperately to escape. The hairs on the back of my neck and all up my arms rose to attention.

It couldn't be.

I knew what I saw but it couldn't be.

I didn't do this, I didn't make the same mistake twice, not with this.

But I would be blamed.

Hands grabbed at me, but I shook them off without much thought or effort.

Detective Arsehole's voice screamed at me, but the noise was more akin to the buzzing of a mosquito near my ear. Annoying but ineffective and unintelligible. Whatever small truce we had found in helping Daria had vanished. I didn't care what she said, I didn't care about anything else. My mind was focused on a single image. Nothing could tear me away from it or stop me from getting closer.

When I reached the covered body, I dropped to my knees and let the reality of what they couldn't see truly wash over me. If I had eaten recently the contents would have interfered with their precious crime scene. But the scene around them didn't matter. What I saw would be yet another thing to haunt my nightmares.

Brian's soul stood up through the thick white sheet that covered the physical body.

If I hadn't seen it before. If I didn't continue to see it every single time I closed my eyes, I might not have been able to tell. But as it was, there was no way for me to deny knowing that his soul remained firmly pinned to his dead body. His translucent eyes flew around the room wildly, not resting on any one thing or any one person.

His mouth moved, open and closed forming words, but no sound came out. A thick swirling darkness outlined his soul, leaving an afterburn behind it as Brian's soul moved.

"No." My fingers itched to reach out. My horror stilled my hands. "This can't be happening. I know who did this. I can't have done this, can I?"

The noise that had swirled around me disappeared as if they were all instructed into silence by a conductor.

"What do you mean, Lily?" Detective Arsehole's words were quiet. She wasn't in the seat anymore. Instead, she was crouched down beside me. For a moment I couldn't understand what she referred to. "Are you confessing to this man's murder?"

I blinked and forced the curtain of my horror back just far enough for me to focus on those around me. Everyone stared down at me, eyes filled with accusations. Daria remained at her seat but her eyes were filled with a combination of fear and confusion.

"No." I shook my head. I clung to the pain the movement caused. I needed it to ground me in the here and now.

"You said you knew who did this." Detective Arsehole's words slurred. No, they weren't slurred. They came out slow. Too slow. And were pushed out with a heavy breath. "Then you said, 'I can't have done this, can I?' What did you mean Lily?"

"I..." I blinked, my mouth opened and closed trying to catch words that would let me out of this coffee shop. It wasn't my coffee shop any longer. Whatever warmth and calm it had once offered no longer remained. It never would again, I knew it couldn't.

"I meant." I swallowed audibly as I stood up, Alanor mirrored my movements. "I know what kind of person did this. How could anyone do this, and sleep at night I have absolutely no idea?"

But I had done it once. It had never been with any intention to harm. My actions had been stupid, but not dark. I took the smallest bit of relief in knowing this wasn't the same. But that didn't change the fact I hadn't slept a full night through since I had been banished and named a Green World Necromancer.

There hadn't been any sign of a dark shadow lingering around the soul of Katy. Katy had been tired. She had said so on many occasions. I hadn't known that time had been so much worse than any other. She had willingly left behind the potential of life. The pain had been too much, and sometimes I forgave her. Sometimes I understood and knew I couldn't hold that against her. How long would I last if darkness surrounded me so entirely? Other days, I grieved that she had been so overwhelmed that she saw no other way out. And some days, not good days, I hated her for giving up.

But Brian's case gave me no emotional dilemma. Not only did I not care either way for the man, but this many police wouldn't show up for a suicide. If that weren't enough, what I saw confirmed it. Brian's eyes searched for life and for his future. The trauma and the fear that overwhelmed him created dark streaks across his face, and I would bet on my final walk that beneath that protected white sheet, his physical body was not at peace when he died.

The contents of my stomach, what little there were, flipped and began their journey upward.

"And what kind of person is that?" The Detective pursed her lips and stared at me.

"I didn't do this."

"You just as good as confessed." Detective Alanor stated, clear and forceful.

"Lily wasn't here. I wouldn't have come out of the storeroom if Lily had anything to do with it." Daria stood up at her seat and glared. But she was the only person in the room who wasn't glaring at me. "I'm not as young as I look, Detective, and I'm not stupid. Scared and traumatised, but not stupid."

"Did you see the person who attacked Brian?" Alanor asked, a slight edge remained in her voice.

"No, not the face, but they were tall and wide. It wasn't Lily." Daria insisted.

"Fine," Alanor huffed and let out a frustrated breath. "Who did this Lily?"

I saw the smirk on her lips and the scoff in her voice, but she couldn't touch me, not for this. Daria had been there during the attack, and she had just told everyone listening that I hadn't done this. I didn't for a second think Alanor was stupid enough to pursue me, not without something more.

"The person who did this is too clever to leave clues." Clues she wouldn't find no matter how much she looked. No matter how good at the job she might be. "You won't catch them."

"And you just happen to know this person?" Alanor's smirk turned into a full-blown sneer.

"No," I said. "I don't know the person. I don't know the one who did this."

But I did know the kind. Oh, it had been years since I had come across a Grim. I shuddered at the mere memory.

"Lily, you're a shit liar." Well, okay then. I couldn't really argue with that one.

But my head pounded, and I didn't have the time or patience for her shit.

"I don't know anything." I hid my worry behind a shrug and walked back to where Daria sat again. I slid into the booth beside her.

"Are you going to get an account from Daria about the events or not?" I asked.

"I already have," Alanor replied, staring at me with her hands on her hips.

"Ok then." I got back up. "I need to go."

I couldn't answer any questions. Not yet, and not here. The answers would make no sense, assuming I had any to give.

"Where are you going?"

"Home," I said.

The lie mingled easily enough with the truth for Alanor to narrow her eyes. I saw her struggling to know if she could believe me or not. Who the hell knew what home was. I had many, and I had none.

Good luck working that one out, Alanor.

My mind whirled with all the possibilities and none of them were any good. I had to contact Theamin. It was the last thing I wanted to do, but I knew my job, and no Necromancer had shown up yet to collect Brian's soul. Something was wrong here, besides the obvious.

I groaned inwardly as I thought about talking to Theamin again. I felt her fingers on my arm like phantom pain. We had never gotten along. She called me an upstart as often as I called her a self-inflated egotist.

Since the banishment, the dislike had hitched its way up to a visceral hate. We avoided each other, and when we couldn't, I was grateful she didn't have more power over me than what she already did.

We glared, we ignored, and we had not spoken a single word directly to each other since that night.

But surely she would look past our own personal issues with each other over this. She was a workaholic and a total suck up to Death.

The doubt gnawed at my stomach. Did I really have to contact her? The voice that asked the question in my head reminded me of a rich little brat who tried to whine her way out of death. I had been certain it had been the first time she did not end up getting her way.

I would step up. I had lived long enough to suck it up and do my job properly. I couldn't just turn away. Theamin needed to know so she could report the issue back to Death. And what I needed was time to think, and a goddamn coffee.

If Theamin heard about me knowing, and I hadn't gone to her immediately. If I had sat on this and done nothing. How much worse would it be?

I needed a plan.

I needed...I bit the insides of my cheeks holding back the smile as what I needed finally came to mind.

I needed Witches. Not just any Witches, I needed my Witches. Lita and Isla would know what to do. Witches were the investigators of the Grey World. And these two just happened to be Green World Witches.

I had to fight back the desire to smile while Alanor continued to glare at me, searching for a crack she could barge her way into.

"I need to know your number." Alanor spoke as I yanked open the coffee shop door. The bell jangled. I had been so close.

"Don't have one," I said, turning to face her while my hand kept the door from closing and jangling that bell again. I should have known better than to look back at her. Alanor really was the ultimate lie detector. She always had been. Somewhere along the line I had forgotten just how damn good she was at sniffing out the truth.

"Oh, hell no, you aren't going anywhere before giving me your number, Lily." Of course, the one time she didn't spit the name like venom was when she was pulling rank, thinking she could control what happened next.

Knowing she could, I conceded.

"Fine." I gave her my details and she scratched them down in that small flip book. She had never looked so much like Olivia Benson in all the times I had seen her. Memories washed over me and sadness crashed upon me like the tide coming in against the rocky cliffs. Katy had tried to convince me more than once that I would simply adore her older sister. We had so much in common, including our love for Law & Order: SVU.

"Make sure you answer it," Alanor said.

"Yes, ma'am," I snarled before turning to Daria.

"Thank you." Daria spoke before I could.

"It's okay. Let me know if you need anything, yeah?" I smiled and gave her a cheeky wink.

She smiled back and I finally made my escape from the coffee shop.

I could mourn it later.

As I stepped past the barrier of orange tape and bollards set a metre apart on the driveway, I pulled out my phone and dialled.

"Hey, I didn't expect to hear from you again so soon." I could hear the smile in Jen's voice and it almost broke what little control remained in me.

"I need your help."

"At your service," she answered instantly, though I heard the shuffling of papers through the phone line.

"I need a relocation."

"You can't Shimmer?" Jen's confusion had been expected, but I didn't have time to go into too much detail. The tick of a clock counted down in the back of my mind. I had no idea why or what it counted down to, but with each tick the pressure built within me.

"It's not for a job, Jen. Not one of mine. And, I need a full physical transfer." The silence on the other end did not bode well. "It's important. Please?" I begged. I let the urgency seep through my words.

"Yeah, yeah. Okay no worries," Jen answered. The shuffling of paper ceased. I had Jen's full attention.

"I need to get to Lita and Isla's." I spoke clearly with a fake confidence.

"Lily?" Jen's voice held the warning, but I still didn't have time.

"Jen, I wouldn't ask if it weren't important. You know that."

"Okay,"Jen answered, and I hated causing the worry that radiated in her voice.

"Thank you." I closed my eyes and took a deep breath. The relief washed through me. I would let my Witches know about it and then I could step away.

I didn't want anything more to do with this. And now, I could do my job without being involved. My shoulders relaxed as I put my life back into some semblance of order and normality.

"Stay where you are. Won't be long." Jen hung up before I could thank her again.

I tucked the phone in my back pocket as the door to the coffee shop opened.

"Lily!" Alanor's voice rang out, and cold washed through me.

"Fuck," I muttered under my breath, searching around for something that might help. This could not be happening. "No, no, no, no, no."

But nothing I did or said stopped Alanor's long-legged pace from drawing closer.

I couldn't move, I couldn't go anywhere. I couldn't let her get closer. She couldn't be allowed to see this.

"Shit." Nothing came to mind to stop any of the inevitable from happening.

"I have one more question," Alanor said, still a dozen paces away from me.

But I didn't hear the question. The wash of tingles raced over my skin and the Shimmer took me away from where Alanor looked.

I didn't even have time to say sorry.

I gasped as the air shifted from the humid heat of Australian summer to the bitter cold of the Grey World.

"What the hell?" I muttered, and stared around Death's Central Chamber.

"You of all people should know this is not hell." Death chuckled and the sound was incongruent to the swirl of emotions that had taken over me from the day.

I stared at them with narrowed eyes and confusion. My teeth clacked together from the cold and with the flick of Death's head, a minion stepped from the wall of the room and draped a cowled cloak around my shoulders.

"Thank you," I said as I snuggled into the warmth.

The minion had been here long enough to know not to answer, but I caught the hint of a smile as they met my eyes.

I remembered my time as a minion. Before being allocated to serve in one of Death's five ranks of service, all minions learn as they observe and serve Death and the Ranked. I had done my thirteen years, but Theamin pointed out every chance she got that it wasn't enough. I should have done seven more years. It was one of the many things that made her dislike for me palatable.

"Hey, Lil.," Jen said.

"Jen?" I forced the word out between clenched teeth as I

turned to where she stood beside Death's throne. I wanted to yell and scream, but all I could do was stare wide-eyed at her.

"I didn't have a choice, okay, Lilekai?" Jen's voice was filled with apology despite the harsh sounding words. Her usual voice, gravel and sand mixing together, held no hints of the sassy girl I had claimed as my best friend the moment she showed up in the Grey World. I had been five years into my servitude as minion, and I never once regretted my decision.

Now she called me Lilekai, always a bad sign. Things were only going to get worse from here on out.

Well shit.

"Some warning," I chattered between my still clacking teeth, "would have been nice."

"I know." Jen was at my side, helping me stand upright. I leaned into her, and she whispered, "I'm sorry."

"Lilekai." Death stood up from their throne, pulling our attention back to them. "I hear you have requested a special favour. A relocation unrelated to your job?"

"I need to consult with some Witches about an incident I have come across." There was never any point in lying to Death.

I had no intention of telling them everything though. Not unless they asked the right questions. If they poked and prodded and demanded it all from me, then I had no choice on the matter. They could enforce their thrall upon any of their minions at any time. But I didn't know whether they would do such a thing to me.

"And you approached a Resurrectionist for this instead of Theamin?" Death asked, eyebrows raised as they glided down the three obsidian steps from their throne to stand on the resin floor where Jen and I stood. They stopped in front of me. "Why?"

I debated how to answer this as diplomatically as possible.

"I needed to get there quickly, and seeing as Theamin and I don't exactly see eye to eye I believed I had a greater chance of getting the issue wrapped up faster and more effectively with Jen's help."

"Ah." Death moved their head to nod as they spoke.

They moved past me, their cloak brushing my own.

"And what is the situation that has you so concerned at this time?"

Damn them. They had once been a simple Necromancer. A minion to the previous Death. They had always been open and honest about the limitations of their own power. But that had only served in lulling me time and time again into believing them more limited than they truly were.

"I believe," I swallowed back the pain and guilt of the five-year-old memory, "that a soul has been trapped and bound to a dead body."

The silence was glacial. Even beneath the warmth of the cloak I shivered.

"Have you learned nothing?" Death's voice was a whisper, a waft of frosted air filled with anger and fury.

"I had nothing to do with this." I forced my words out, slow and steady though everything inside of me shook and trembled.

"You just so happened to have stumbled upon the scene? A scene reminiscent of your own banishment?" Death asked, their voice a little louder this time.

"Yes." I swallowed. I could have left it at that, but what was the point? "But I believe the death itself might also be unsanctioned."

A beat and another chill raced through me.

"Theamin?" Death's voice no longer whispered.

For fuck's sake. As though my day hadn't already been bad enough.

"Yes, Death?" Theamin pushed through the large double doors of Death's Central Chamber as though she were the most important person in all of the Worlds combined. And of course she was flanked, though one step behind her, by henchmen one and two, otherwise known as Sara and Kensley.

"Have you sanctioned any deaths this day, near Lilekai's home?"

Home?

I had been banished. But I didn't know where my home truly was, and I had never truly embraced the idea of it being the Green World. Apparently, Death had their own idea of where I belonged. The word hurt harder than I wanted it to.

Theamin took the time to glance a glare in my direction before returning her gaze to Death.

"No, Death. There has been no need to send a Resurrectionist to that area of the Green World."

"Then I believe it might be time to call in the Witches. Lilekai has stumbled upon an unsanctioned death."

"Are you sure?" Theamin asked, scorn and mocking in her tone.

One day she would have to take my word on something and eat her fill of crow.

"Yes, I'm sure. You trained me after all," I replied, my voice coming out guttural and reminding me of a feral dog being challenged over a kill.

But damn it all, I was a fucking Necromancer. I had been a bloody good one and I continued to be good at my job, no matter how much my heart was no longer in it. It hadn't been the dead's fault I was banished. I wouldn't take it out on them now or ever.

"It is an unsanctioned death."

Damn it, I wanted to get home, the word choked me even in my thoughts. I made one mistake, and now they thought I no longer even knew what a death performed by Grey World hands looked like.

"Theamin did not sanction a death. I believe her." Death spoke and I turned my head slowly back to them. Every word I had ever heard them utter had a purpose, and I wondered what the purpose of these words now were. "But how are you certain I did not sanction this expiration?" Death asked.

My mouth dropped open.

Fuck me, I hadn't considered that an option. I shook my head. No, I hadn't considered the option because that had never been the way. Death's way or any of the Grey World's way. It was the way of the Grim. To sanction a death would never be taken lightly.

"I know you have that right, Death." I bowed my head, staring at the hem of their cloak instead of looking into their deep dark eyes that beckoned me. "But I have never known you to leave a soul in such pain and agony. I know it's not my place, but it would surprise me had you sanctioned this for an individual. I cannot see what a soul would have to do to deserve this fate."

After a few seconds I dared to raise my head and look at Death. They nodded slightly and flicked their eyes over to Theamin once again.

"She is correct, Theamin. I have not sanctioned this death."

"And you believe her about the soul?"

"I know she tells the truth," Death answered and then turned their gaze to the nearest minion. The minion who stood ramrod straight against the wall of the room, stepped forward out of the shadow of a Skeleton. It had always been so easy to forget they were there. Even now, I had no idea how many stood in the shadows against the walls. "Please summon the Witch council to me so I might allocate an investigation."

The minion nodded and we waited for the doors to close with an echoing thud behind them as they left.

"Now, everyone out." Death's voice boomed around the Chamber. Their command crashed into me, their will pressing against my own.

Theamin turned on her heels, Sara and Kinsley following suit. I watched them leave before moving to follow.

"Lily." Death's voice was soft. "Do be careful. I know I have given you great leniency in the past, but do not push my kindness again."

"No, Death."

"Jen will escort you out."

We were not given a chance to respond or comment. Death's will to leave was enforced upon us with greater strength.

"Do you really think a Grim has gotten into the Green World?" Jen asked once we stepped out into the misty surroundings of the Grey World.

"What else could it be Jen?" I sighed and breathed in the damp air.

"A Necromancer turned bad?" She suggested, though she shrugged, scrunching up her nose and making me laugh. She didn't really believe her words, but she did have a tendency to voice her most ridiculous thoughts to me. And I loved her more for it.

"I miss you, Jen. You're the only thing in this place I still miss."

"Twenty-five more years." She sighed and leaned into me as she threaded her arm into my own.

"If I'm lucky." I looked ahead of us at the wall of grey I had once considered beautiful. "I'm sorry I dragged you into this."

"I'm not." I felt Jen chuckle against me. "I never would have known what the hell was going on if you hadn't."

"They would have told you." The lie stuck in my throat like dry bread.

"Oh, Lily." Jen chuckled again, her hand shaking back and forth in the periphery of my vision. "I'm a lowly Resurrection-ist. We get told nothing. And being Death's daughter has abso-lutely no effect on that."

"I'm sorry. I've always liked Death, but as your parent they really suck."

"They do." Jen didn't laugh this time, and the pain of our situations wrapped around us. "But this is Necromancer business."

As Death's daughter, Jen had surprised everyone by not arguing Death's placement of her as a Resurrectionist. She had excelled in the art of bones and life and had told me time and time again how much she enjoyed her position.

The barrier loomed up in front of us and my heart caught in my throat. I was in my body. Death had managed to summon me without stepping through the barrier. I had hoped for the same in kind.

"Jen, you can step through the barrier?" She had never told me so, and the shock mixed with hurt feelings and loss. Everyone lied, in some way or another. But this was the first time I had ever known Jen to lie to me.

"I can, but Death does not want others to know it."

"I guess that's their way of saying I love you?" Hope bloomed in my chest. They did wish to protect Jen. If others knew she could step through, if a Grim was to find out, Jen would become an easy target.

"Alright, looks like my welcome has well and truly worn out." I squeezed my eyes shut as pain behind my eyes thumped a techno version of every song I had ever heard, all jammed together.

"It's not just you," Jen panted out before her scream rent the misty air around us. Her grip tightened on my arm.

"Jen?" I called as though she were on the other side of the Grey World and not clinging to my side so fiercely that even her short nails cut into my skin.

"I'll get us to your place. I don't know what's happening. But this Shimmer is going to hurt."

Before I could argue, the bubbling sensation brushed over my body.

Darkness surrounded me as I landed with a thud against timber floors. I sighed with relief. I knew these floors well. They were mine, in my small house in the Green World.

"Jen?" I groaned, letting my eyes fall closed.

Jen laughed. "Well, that was unexpected."

I opened my eyes again and saw her standing over me, one hand offered to help pull me to my feet.

"I see you had no problem with your landing." I narrowed my eyes playfully at her and accepted her help getting up.

"Nope, but I'm not a lazy Necromancer who has their equilibrium automatically rebalanced for them."

"Ouch." I laughed and brushed myself down of fluff and dirt. I really needed to give the floors more attention.

"Are you okay?" Jen asked, but the smile on her face belied any true concern.

"Yeah, I'm fine. Except for the migraine." I rubbed at my neck as though it might grant me some magical relief from the pain.

"My pain is gone." Jen spoke with that curious tone that

would quickly lead to her forgetting all else, including my presence.

"That's because you aren't touching me in the Grey World anymore." I shrugged, but my words rushed out revealing my desire to keep her in the present instead of in her mind of curiosities. "You should've just let me go, Jen."

"It doesn't make sense."

"Maybe it's because my physical body had been pulled through by a Shimmer?"

"That's happened before." She waved her hand as though her words were common knowledge. They were definitely not. "But this, this has never happened."

"But you were able to Shimmer us here so it's no big deal, right?" Could she hear my desperate hope in need of her confirmation? I squirmed, uncomfortable in my thoughts. When did I become this person? The one who ran away from the unknown, the one who wanted the path to end, for me to pass the baton to someone else. I knew what had happened, but a sense of loss within me stilled my questions and forced me to push all the thoughts away.

"Oh, it's a big deal." Jen locked eyes on me and cocked her head. "Is that what happens to you every time?"

"Jen," I said slowly. I knew she could get wrapped up in her head, but this question didn't even make sense. "You know that doesn't happen every time. You're with me often enough when I Shimmer back."

"No, the pain." She shook her head as she spoke. "Does that pain take over with such force every time?"

"Did it feel like a marching band was stomping through your head?"

She nodded. Her face puckered as though she had sucked on something particularly vile.

"If I don't come back fast enough, then yeah." I winced as I made my way to my couch, hitting my shins on the coffee table, just for good measure. I really should turn some lights on. The sun was slipping below the horizon, and soon I wouldn't even be able to see Jen's face once it slipped past completely.

Instead, I collapsed onto the couch. It had been a long day. Far too long, and my body ached for rest, and for some damn caffeine. I doubted even that would be enough to ease the exhaustion that weighed upon me. "But it's not always this severe."

"Shit. No wonder you don't want to risk staying longer than you normally do."

"Yep. Death didn't fuck around with their punishment." I yawned and snuggled deeper into the couch.

"I fucking hate them sometimes," Jen muttered and flopped down on the couch beside me. She grabbed one of the cushions from the floor by the couch and held it to her chest.

"I know." I leaned closer towards her, and she met me half-way. The comfort of our shoulders pressed together, and the softness of the couch behind me made me wonder if home had to be a specific place at all. "But without them I wouldn't have you, so I kind of love them as well."

"Love you too, even though you are a Necromancer."

"Resurrectionist." I smiled at our irreverence to the tension that usually surrounded the different ranks of minions.

I woke up in a panic. I had dreamed of Katy again. Of that night. My heart raced in my chest, and my cheeks were cold and wet from shed tears.

The banging on my front door made me jerk enough to wake Jen. We had shifted enough in our sleep that Jen used my hip as a pillow, while I used the arm of the couch as my own.

"What the fuck?" She asked with a yawn and a crease in her forehead.

The banging came harder and more insistent this time.

"Come on Lily. Open the fuck up. I know you're in there," Detective Alanor's voice called through the heavy wooden door of my home.

"Who is that?" Jen whispered, as though afraid the person on the other side might hear her should she speak any louder.

"A detective."

"Detective?" Jen's eyebrows raised, and then a smile spread over her face. "As in the Detective Dick?"

"It's Detective Arsehole. And yes," I grumbled. Day two and still no coffee in sight.

"Excellent." The sleep had apparently improved Jen's mood. She jumped up from the couch and headed towards the front door. "I finally get to meet her."

"Like hell you do." I pushed myself up off the couch and blocked her from opening the door.

Alanor pounded again, making the glass in the windows either side of the door rattle in their frames.

What the fuck had I done now?

"Please?" Jen begged and gave me her best puppy dog eyes.

"Nope. She hates me and she's the one in charge of the investigation for the trapped soul."

"Oooh!" Jen's smile grew wider. "The plot thickens."

"Jen, I swear we can talk later, but please get the hell out of here." I returned her previous look with my own begging expression.

"Fine. But I'm calling you later." Jen smiled.

I waited for her to Shimmer. Nothing happened.

"Jen?" I asked.

Her eyes widened and I saw the fear in them. The grey of her eyes turned a stormy cloud colour.

"What?" I asked, my own heart rate speeding up once more.

"I can't Shimmer."

"Open up now Lily, or I'm breaking it down." Alanor's voice took on the traits of a wild animal.

"Okay, we'll figure it out. Let's just get rid of her first." I nodded, trying to convince myself as much as Jen.

Jen nodded and returned to the couch. Her previous enthusiasm and excitement about meeting Detective Arsehole now gone.

"Why hello, Detective, how kind of you to threaten to break down my door because I didn't come running instantly at your beck and call."

"Cut the shit." Alanor pushed past me, into my house. Without an invitation. "Where is she?"

"Who?" I asked, closing the door behind me as Alanor wheeled back on me. "And of course, why don't you come on in?"

"Lily, whatever you are up to I'm not playing your games. Not this time."

"I've never made you play games." I saw Jen sit up a little straighter on my couch, taking interest in the conversation. Had Alanor seen her or not?

"Then where is Daria?"

"What?" My body grew cold as the blood rushed from my head and torso. "What do you mean 'where is she?'"

"Did I speak another fucking language? Where. Is. Daria?"

"How the hell would I know?" I snapped back. "The last time I saw her she was with you."

"And the last time I saw you, you vanished into thin air. Why should I believe a fucking thing you say?"

"I'm wondering the same thing about you. People don't just vanish, or didn't they teach you that at the academy?" It was a low blow. I knew it even before it escaped my lips but while the sleep had helped, the headache at the back of my skull remained.

And my patience was still an absentee.

Alanor opened her mouth to speak but it wasn't her voice that filled the room.

"Who's Daria?" Jen piped up from the couch, and Alanor turned around slowly, eyes narrowing at me until they had to follow the turn of her body or disappear into the back of her skull. Which would certainly be an interesting party trick.

"Who are you?" Alanor snapped and that was the last straw.

"It's none of your business, Detective." I moved between Alanor and Jen who still sat on the couch, seemingly unphased by Alanor's question. "Now piss off and get out of my house."

"Where is she?"

"I don't know," I snapped.

"She's hiding something. And so are you. She lied about her address, and her phone is going directly to voicemail. Is she in on it with you? You suggested a way to get rid of Brian and she jumped at the chance?"

"Oh," Jen said. I closed my eyes feeling her shift behind me. "Now I get the Arsehole thing."

"Real mature," Alanor spat at me before turning around and walking to my still open front door. "I'm going to get to the bottom of this. You aren't going to get away with it again."

I waited until I heard her bike start up and the sound of its engine faded into the distance. Where the fuck had that monster been yesterday? It would have saved me this whole nightmare if it had just been in that carpark with all the other vehicles playing extensions to dicks.

"Fuck." The word didn't give me nearly as much enjoyment or relief as it normally did. Instead, the tension coiled tighter around my spine, as though testing just how much I could take before I simply snapped, physically and mentally.

"She's a serious piece of work." Jen shuffled around me and closed the door Alanor had left open.

"I need to find Daria." I nodded. I needed to do something. Sitting around had never been my strong point, especially without coffee to keep me company.

"You know where she is?" Jen asked. "You really were lying to the Detective?"

"No, I don't know for sure, but I have a pretty fair idea." It was a flimsy idea at best, but I didn't have any other place to start.

"Can I come?" Jen asked. I had never heard her sound or look so unsure in her life.

I looked at her face closely before wrapping my arms around her.

"Of course you can."

"Why can't I Shimmer home, Lil?" Her voice wavered, and for a second I froze with my arms still around her. I had never been certain Jen was capable of crying, but that waver hinted at the possibility.

"I dunno, Jen." I pulled back, unwrapped my arms from the embrace, but I gripped her hands in mine. "But we will figure it out. I promise."

She nodded and smiled. Her eyes were glassy, but no telltale signs of tears stained her cheeks.

I looked down at her bare feet and laughed.

"What?" She followed my gaze, wriggling her toes before she looked back up, her eyebrows furrowed. Her toes had apparently given her no answer to my amusement.

"We aren't in Kansas anymore."

"We weren't in Kansas," Jen replied.

I laughed harder and headed to my bedroom. She followed me in but took some convincing before conceding to my insistence that she needed shoes.

"Honestly, you need to come visit the Green World more often."

"There's not as much for any of us Resurrectionists to do in the Green World. At least not on a regular basis."

"I don't mean for work, Jen. I mean for fun."

"You like being here." Jen didn't ask, her mouth opening in surprise. "Is that why you never come and join in on the board games?"

"Jen." I looked her dead in the eyes, my lips pulled down. "Your game board nights are a cover for lots of sex."

"Well, yeah." She laughed. "See, I do come to the Green World and have fun."

"No." I rolled my eyes. "You come to the Green World to get laid."

"Aren't they the same thing?"

I shook my head and led us out the front door, ensuring I locked it behind me. Something I rarely bothered to do. But knowing Alanor was sniffing around, I wasn't going to take any unnecessary chances.

As we walked, Jen gazed around with a wide smile on her face. She didn't smile in the Grey World. I didn't blame her for it, the lot she had been given I didn't envy her for. I had known Jen her entire life, but I had never seen her in awe of anything, not like this. Her smile grew with each new discovery.

"Jen, do you remember anything from before Death brought you hom–" I cut myself off, the word cutting deep inside of me. "Brought you to the Grey World?"

"Not a thing." She shook her head, her lips pulling together in such a tight pinch.

"The Grey World had its benefits, more than just sex." I smiled and pulled Jen off the path for a woman who jogged past. She nodded her appreciation without missing a step in her long stride.

"Lil, why didn't you tell me you were surrounded by hotties? I would have understood why you hated coming back so much."

"No." I shook my head. "Definitely not."

"Not what?"

"You are not moving board game nights to my area of the Green World."

"Why not?" Jen whined and relief washed through me. I had genuinely enjoyed seeing her wonder of the World, as though she were a small child, but I understood the cocky Casanova far better.

"Because you will leave, and I will get stuck still being here, and they will come knocking on my door looking for the bitch who broke their hearts."

Jen scoffed.

"Don't pretend you aren't a player."

"Fine, I've been a player, but not for a while now."

"Define 'a while.'"

"Twenty-three months." She hadn't even needed to calculate the time.

"That's oddly specific," I said, trying to wrap my head around these changes in my best friend. "Hang on, you invited me to another board game night yesterday."

"Yeah well," Jen kicked at the path as we walked on. The tip of the sneakers she borrowed from me made contact with a small stone. The stone went flying and disappeared somewhere over the hill we had just begun to walk up. "I miss you, and wondered what might happen if there really was a regular board game night where I could just relax and hang with you again."

"Jen. Why didn't you just tell me?"

"You're busy, and it's depressing."

"What is?"

"Getting your heart broken."

"What?" I stopped, pulling at her arm to make her stop as well. "When did this happen, why didn't you tell me?"

"It's not like we get to catch up like we used to."

"I know, but Jen."

"It's fine. It did put some well needed perspective back into my life." She shrugged and got to walking again.

"Any other life-altering news you want to throw at me today? Not sure you can top yesterday's complete train wreck, but hey, what not give it a try."

Jen laughed and threaded her arm into mine. I let the topic go and we kept walking, but my throat felt thick, and a heaviness rested in my heart.

I had promised I wouldn't let anything get between us. Not even their parent's punishment for my stupid behaviour. But it had only been five years and already the wedge of distance had worked its way between us. What the hell would we look like after another twenty-five years?

"So, where are we going?"

"Back to the crime scene," I said.

"You can't be serious." Jen laughed. "Do you have some kind of screaming kink I'm not aware of?"

"What?" I scowled at her, and she laughed at whatever twisted look my features showed.

"Oh, come on. You and Alanor." Jen waggled her eyebrows up and down seductively.

"First, no," I said and shuddered. "Second, fuck no."

"Bullshit. She's smoking hot, and powerful, and did I mention hot?"

"And a total bitch and ice queen to boot. Ooh yeah, give it to me."

Jen laughed and for a few moments I remembered what it was like, before I fucked everything up for both of us.

"Okay, so if not to get into another screaming match with the mighty fine detective. Why are we going back there?"

"I'm pretty sure it's where Daria will be."

We were close to the coffee shop when Jen shocked me into stopping my stride.

"Why did Death and Theamin think you had killed the guy?" Jen asked.

"What?"

"Oh come on, Lily." Jen shook her head. "I know everyone thinks I'm stupid and not good enough to be Death's daughter because I much prefer my role as a Resurrectionist. But I'm really not that stupid. And I thought you of all people knew that."

"I do." Guilt washed through me.

"So, why did you think they would blame you, and why did they question you about it?"

"Katy."

"The human you got banished for?"

"Yes."

"Right." Jen's lips pursed together in thought before she rolled her eyes and shook her head. "And of course you can't tell me because it's Necromancy shit. And Worlds forbid us lowly, lesser minions be privy to the big boys club."

"Big boys club?" I laughed. "Where the hell did you even learn that expression?"

"Jesus, Lily. You really do think I'm some fucking moron, don't you?" Jen snapped and I knew this tone. The tone that meant she was ready to truly lose it.

"No, Jen. You are not a moron at all. But it's not like we get to see each other all the time and when we do it's the minutes between dropping off a soul and getting my arse back out of the Grey World. It's not like we've been able to keep up with the little details."

"I know," Jen hissed.

"So, you're finally admitting you are angry at me?" I'd been terrified of this moment for five years, but the relief that the waiting may finally be over was intoxicating.

"Of course I'm angry at you." Jen punched me in the arm. I wasn't certain if it were supposed to be playful or to hurt. It sat somewhere in the middle, and I forced my hand to stay by my side instead of rubbing at the spot.

"But?" I asked.

"You left me there with all the judgements and snickers. With Death acting like I am nothing to them, while Theamin struts up and down the corridors, all the corridors, with her lackeys on her heels acting as though she is Death already. And all I want is things to go back to the way they were."

"I'm sorry, Jen."

"I know." She shook her head and took a deep breath. "I miss you, bitch."

"I miss you too." I shoved her shoulder with my own and we started walking again.

"Good. Can you tell me that a little more often?"

"You betcha."

"Excellent." And just like that the spring was back in her step and the swagger back in her hips.

I was going to have to keep an eye on her.

Despite what she said about having had her heart broken, I knew a woman on the prowl when I saw one.

The sun had dried the dew from the grass, and the rush of traffic passing on the road beside us increased. The rhythm of wheels as they hit the road harmonised with the hum of the engines.

I had missed so much while I lived in the Grey World. The Green World had changed and shifted. The loss of exploring the new leaps in technology had hit me harder than I thought possible. How was it possible I could mourn something I had never experienced? Of course, I had seen the World change in the moments I looked around while retrieving a soul. But at some point, I had stopped looking around on jobs, and I hadn't even noticed when.

It was early, but the absence of people rushing in and out hurt a part inside of me. The crime scene tape and bollards still blocked off the driveway entrance and more tape had been added to the front door in an X marks the spot manner.

The sleep had helped. It cleared my mind enough for me to know without a doubt I had to stay away from all of this. That despite whether I liked it or not, I had changed and maybe it wasn't a bad thing.

No matter how much this situation pulled me towards it, I had to start learning my lessons somewhere. Besides having tornado Alanor heading toward me, getting tangled up any more was the last thing I needed.

I would just make sure Daria was alright. Then I could go back to working through the rest of my banishment in peace and isolation. I could stop thinking about how changed I was, how I no longer fit anywhere. I could forget about the loneliness my mind continued to unhelpfully remind me about.

I resigned myself to the task at hand. I stepped around the bollards and headed to the front of the building.

"Doesn't look like anyone is here." Jen stated the obvious.

"I know." My mind ticked over, working out the problem of Daria's situation. If I were right, and she had been living in the storeroom, where the hell would she go, and where would she go if she couldn't get back in?

I knew she had keys. Had she used them and snuck back in? Would she be brave enough after what she had experienced?

Shimmering was out of the question. Even for Jen. And that was a whole other problem we had to figure out at some point as well.

One thing at a time. I gnawed on my bottom lip while I pinched my top lip between thumb and forefinger.

"Can you hear that?" Jen asked, interrupting my thoughts.

"Hear what?"

"Listen." But Jen started moving around the building as she spoke.

"Shit," Jen spoke as she disappeared from view.

My heart leapt to my throat, and I raced after her. Skidding on the loose gravel at the back of the building I found Jen and Daria staring at each other.

"Oh, thank god."

"God?" Jen and Daria asked at the same time as they turned to stare at me. Synchronised as though they had planned it, they both turned back to face each other and laughed when their eyes met.

"I guess you must know Lily then huh?" Jen asked with a smile.

"Oh, yeah," Daria said as she moved her hands over her ear as though pushing back hair, even though none had escaped her low ponytail that sat at the nape of her neck.

"Jen, meet Daria," I introduced them as my heart returned to its rightful place behind my ribs. "And Daria, this is my best mate, Jen."

"Excellent" Jen held out her hand and Daria took it. She beamed as she continued, "I've heard absolutely nothing about you."

"Likewise," Daria chuckled as she replied.

"Yes, yes, it's all so amusing." I rolled my eyes as they bonded over my flaws. "Daria. Did you know the police are looking for you?"

"What?" Her face paled, and her hand dropped away from Jen's.

"You gave a false address, and you aren't answering your phone?"

"I didn't give a false address." Daria's voice was quiet. I didn't like that at all. "Just an old one, and my phone's battery died. I haven't been able to charge it."

"Ah." I squeezed my eyes shut. Should I ask her about where she had been sleeping? About where I assume her charger must be? I shook my head and focused.

"I guess I should go down to the station." She looked around her, as though searching for something.

"We can go with you," Jen piped up, and I had never

wanted to strangle my best friend before, but right now it seemed like a fantastic time to reevaluate that idea.

"Really?" Daria asked, a smile already returning some of the usual colour to her face.

I opened my mouth to say no but shut it before anything came out. I nodded, setting a mental reminder to yell at Jen when I next got her alone.

"It's not far. I don't have any money for the bus though." Daria wouldn't meet my eyes.

"We can walk." Jen pulled Daria's arm into the crook of her elbow and began walking, as if to prove her point. "It's safer this way."

"Safer?" Daria asked. The amusement in her voice was obvious and I grinned to hear the Daria I knew shining through.

"Oh yeah, Lily is a total nightmare around anything remotely electrical." Jen spilled my secrets as though discussing the weather we could all see and feel around us.

"Oh, I thought it was just early morning issues with the till." Daria looked over her shoulder and gave me a mock shocked expression. "And all this time it was you."

"Apparently." I shrugged and tried a sheepish expression. I'm pretty sure it didn't work, but I couldn't tell because Daria had already turned back and refocused her attention on Jen.

"Tell me all of Lily's dirty little secrets," Daria demanded in a mischievous false whisper I was pretty sure I was expected to hear.

"Oh, where to start," Jen replied.

I fell in line following the two as they chatted, heads bent toward each other. I caught words here and there but gave up trying to work out what they spoke about. I focused on how Daria gained animation in her arms as we crossed the road and headed toward the local station. Each sweep of her arms filled me with a calmness I didn't know I should be feeling. What I suspected she had experienced may be far more than she could deal with long term. Unease wrapped its cold arms around my shoulders.

But it didn't last long. How could it when in front of me the laughter floated back to me?

And the walk felt good, though coffee would have helped my mood. So might've my bicycle that sat behind my house.

By the time we got to the police station, my enjoyment of the walk and the day had turned. I was exhausted, sweaty, and having caffeine withdrawals for the first time since landing Green side.

When I was offered a coffee while we waited, I almost made out with the young police officer. Even after being warned that it was "just instant" my body vibrated in anticipation.

The first sip hit my tongue and it took all my strength not to spit the bitter rot out. By the third sip it was almost palatable and by the time I finished the drink I could have easily gone a second and third round. The caffeine buzzed through my system and my shoulders finally relaxed.

We sat in a small room filled with too much furniture. Two couches faced each other over a coffee table that was perfectly level with knocking shins. I found this out as I tried to skirt around the thing to take a seat in one of the individual chairs lined up against the back wall of the room. After some colourful words that sent both Jen and Daria into laughter, they sat side by side in one of the couches, while I took my seat and regretted my decision. The couches were low and would be annoying to get out of quickly no doubt, but if we had to wait very long, my bum would certainly be numb.

"Sorry for the wait folks." He was an older man with strong arms and a leanness that made me wonder if he'd ever been called "beanpole" while growing up. If so, I suspected it might have been one of the nicer nicknames.

"I was looking for Detective Alanor." Daria stood up and walked toward the policeman. Her confidence shouldn't have surprised me, but it did. Until yesterday, I wouldn't have even questioned her ability to handle herself. But she had just experienced something not many humans ever would. But I didn't need to know the details. I was staying away. I couldn't save her, that wasn't my job. I might not have learnt much, but that lesson had been seared into me. Yet despite that warning to myself, pride filled my chest. Daria was strong, and despite my desire to keep her at arm's length, I felt that pull of affection toward her. Danger screamed red and blaring in my head.

"Yes." The man smiled and nodded. He touched Daria's elbow and navigated her to the couch across from the one Jen still sat in. He sat and Daria perched on the edge beside him, not relaxing into the seat as she had when she sat next to Jen.

I moved from the torture chair, my bum well and truly beyond numb, and sat in Daria's vacated seat.

It didn't take long for us to realise that Alanor didn't work at this station and while they had left Alanor messages, she had yet to return any of them.

"We just need a way to get in contact with you. Something we can pass on to the detective."

Daria opened her mouth and closed it again.

"She can reach Daria on my number."

"You will be together the rest of the day?"

"Yes." I didn't look at Daria to confirm this was okay. I didn't want this to be the option, but I saw the setup in the storeroom where I knew without a doubt Daria had been living. I had no idea how long and that created knots in my stomach that made me want to jump up and start pacing the room. "She'll be staying with me for a while."

The police officer pulled out a notebook and I bit back a laugh. He even flicked it open the same way Alanor had. Maybe it was one of the classes at the academy. How to flip open the book with cool precision and command.

After he took down my details we headed back outside.

"Lily, I'm sorry." Daria's smile wavered. "You didn't have to do that. And you don't have to stay with me."

"Yes, she does," Jen interrupted and led the way back toward my house.

"The boss has spoken." I laughed and Daria's smile softened into something more genuine.

I had forgotten about the lack of coffee in my house until the moment we stepped through the front door.

"Bloody hell." I groaned.

"What's wrong?" Jen asked as she and Daria both turned to look at me. Their faces were a mix of worry and concern.

"I forgot I don't have any coffee left."

"Oh shit," Daria sucked her bottom lip into her mouth and flicked it back out with a pop, scraping her teeth on her lip as she did. I had seen her do this so many times. Seeing her do the same thing in the middle of my solitude and isolation shifted uncomfortably beneath my skin. "I was planning on doing up your grounds yesterday but then..." She trailed off.

"Why do you like that swill so much?" Jen asked as she slumped down on my couch and shook her head. "That stuff was garbage."

"Of course it was." I rolled my eyes. "It was instant. The good stuff rarely comes in a can or jar."

"There are different types?" Jen's eyes widened.

"Are you serious?" Daria's face screamed at how appalled she was by Jen's lack of knowledge about coffee.

"I've never had it before." Jen shrugged, not realising what the phrase might do to Daria.

"Lily, this is unacceptable." Daria rounded on me and put her hands on her hips. "How is she your best friend and you have not even bothered to offer her a real coffee. Not once?"

"Oh." I shook my head. I was determined not to get the blame for that one. "I have offered. Time and time again."

"Not with enough salesmanship obviously." Daria shook her head.

"Fine.," I said. "You two stay here and talk about how retched a human being I am, while I head down to the shops and get some grounds."

"Make sure you don't get the extra fine ones," Daria called out.

"Okay." I didn't even bother asking why. For years, Daria had been supplying me with the best coffee I had ever had, I was smart enough to take her word for it.

I pulled the front door closed behind me. Daria and Jen had already returned to chatting as if they had known each other for years but hadn't caught up in months.

The isolation was a soothing coat around my shoulders I hadn't realised I craved. It was the first time I had been alone since I led Rose through to her final walk.

Taking my time to walk to the shops would help shake the claustrophobia, but that tick, tick, ticking continued at the back of my mind. It should've gone the moment Death and Theamin knew about Brian's pinned soul.

I couldn't enjoy the walk no matter how much I wanted to. It had been a while since I bothered with the bicycle or the skateboard. There hadn't been a need. Pulling the bicycle from beneath the house, I jumped on and sped toward the shops which lay in the opposite direction of the coffee shop.

By the time I reached the shops I felt lighter than I had in days. My hair was a windblown mess and my cheeks were warm with the exertion.

The selection of ground coffee beans was overwhelming. Daria's instructions limited the selection to less than half otherwise I would have stood there even longer.

The ride there had been easy and mostly down hill. The return journey proved a little harder for my body that still had taken for granted the ability to Shimmer when I had to.

As I drew closer to the cemetery, I knew fitness hadn't been the only reason I walked beside the bicycle instead of riding past.

I t wasn't that I had forgotten about getting a call from the detective. I had however figured that if she did call, I wasn't too far away, and I could tell her exactly where Daria was. Besides, part of me hoped she might just show up again. What I would give to see her trying to intimidate Jen, while Jen gave Alanor a run for her money.

Still, I should have rushed back. But a familiar pull hooked me behind the belly button and dragged me forward.

I stood at the gates of the cemetery. They were open and inviting. They would be closed later but that meant little. Only one side of the cemetery had been gated. Some genius had thought the hill the cemetery resided against would be enough for people to avoid the ungated inclined sides.

I slowed my steps and took the familiar route, counting the 492 steps from the front gate to the headstone I knew as intimately as anything else in this or any one of the Worlds.

Her headstone.

It greeted me with its usual stoic silence. I smiled, knowing there would never be words or expressions or even tears enough to give voice to the storm that continued to rage within me, five years on. That knowledge had never stopped me from visiting, often. Perhaps it was too often, but I would keep coming until I finally stepped through a gate on the other side of the Grey World.

Kneeling in front of the granite block, I traced her name and let the tears fall silently. She saw me cry, at least her gravestone did. The only place I had cried since her death. It must have been over a year since I had shed tears for anything.

"I'm so sorry, Katy." My voice cracked, and I pulled in a ragged breath. It broke apart in my throat and I took every jab and scrape as part of a punishment that would never be enough. "I don't know if you know, I don't know what's beyond the Grey, but something happened. Something bad, and it's so much like what I did to you." I felt the bubble working its way forcefully up my oesophagus . I coughed the bastard back. "I never meant you harm or pain. Your sister is at me again. Not that I can blame her, I guess. I thought it would be hard to avoid her, but it's been five years." I let out a sigh. I didn't normally babble this much. "I don't think this one was an accident."

It wasn't the first time I had wondered at the ease of having avoided Alanor. At first, I dreaded her showing up unexpectedly, refusing to let the past go. After a while, relief replaced dread. In darker moments, moments when isolation overtook me, I convinced myself Death played a part in keeping me and the mortal apart.

Trees rustled around me. Hope surged behind my chest. I wanted to believe Katy had heard me, had breathed out on the wind. I knew better. I was so damned sick of knowing better.

I wanted to believe, just for a moment, that Katy rustled the leaves to let me know it was all okay. I yearned to know that somewhere beyond the Light World she had found the peace she desperately sought. And that she forgave me for the horror show I led her to.

More than once I had tasted Death's name on my tongue, the plan to ask for a mind wipe set in my thoughts. But I had never followed through, I was a coward after all of this. It was nothing but a hollow wish.

When Death came and showed me the truth of our Worlds and offered me more, I jumped at the chance. I hadn't been happy, I had barely managed content. Knowing I made the right choice didn't stop me wishing I could have been someone else.

The trees stopped their rustling and that precarious hope in my chest burst like a pin pressed to the skin of a balloon.

"I miss you. I know we didn't know each other for a long time, and I had promised you we would. I had told you I could make it all better. But I was too late, and then I was all levels of wrong."

Another rustling sound from the trees nearby was accompanied by a familiar voice. "Do you come here a lot?"

Always the wrong sister. When I craved one, it was always the other one that showed up.

I closed my eyes, swatting away the old thoughts like shooing away a mosquito buzzing too close to my ear. I counted to ten before I looked up and saw Detective Alanor standing in the shade of a tree. Her sunglasses protected her eyes, but she looked toward Katy's headstone.

What exactly did she see? What did she feel? And why the hell did I care?

"Whenever I can. Yes." Honesty had never been too hard for me. I enjoyed not having to think too much about lies and complications.

"That could be seen as a sign of guilt." Alanor plucked a

leaf from a tree, crushing its dry and brittle existence in her fist before stepping into the open.

"And how often do you visit?" I spoke between clenched teeth.

"Every damn day." She brushed the last of the decimated leaf from her palms and placed her hand over the top of the headstone, leaving behind several small stones. "Hey, baby sis."

The confession, the honesty, and the calmness in Alanor's voice froze me. I didn't want this air between us, this sadness.

I wanted to be able to tell Alanor to go fuck herself, but the wind had changed, and I felt it as surely as I felt death when it lurked around the corner.

"I need your help." Her tone returned to the more familiar snap, and I wondered what it meant that this put me more at ease. And then her words sunk in.

I burst into laughter. Maybe I wasn't doomed to be kind and sympathetic to her after all.

"I'm sorry." I waved my hand around, trying to stop the laughter, trying to breath and apologise. "But seriously? You want my help, again? Hell must have definitely frozen over this time."

"I know." Alanor almost smiled. Then the laughter on my lips died in an instant.

"Wait, you're actually serious?" I didn't laugh this time.

"I don't know what happened to that man, but I can't have another cold case in my life."

"What do you need? And why do you think I can help you with it?"

"We still can't find Daria Hart. I need to know about her, and you're the only person I can find that knows her."

"Daria?" My head spun with the whiplash of thoughts and emotions.

"Yes, you seemed..." Alanor paused, and I watched her throat work as she swallowed, "...friendly."

My hands balled into fists once more.

"Have you bothered to check your goddamn phone?"

"Why?" Alanor asked

"Because the station down the road has been trying to reach you for hours."

"Fucking cheap piece of tech." She pulled it from her pocket, held it up in the air and waved it around. "And now the bloody thing won't even turn on."

I bit the insides of my cheeks to stop from smiling. There had to be some benefits to fucking with electricity with my mere presence.

"Just so you know, Daria provides me with lifegiving sustenance. We're friends, only friends. Just like me and your sister were."

Alanor's chest rose and fell, speeding up with each breath. "This was stupid. Forget I asked. I'll find my information another way."

"She's at my place." I was just as surprised as Alanor looked when the words came unbidden from my mouth.

It shouldn't have bothered me to say it. As soon as she got back to the station, she'd have the messages telling her exactly what I just had. But why had I made it easier for her?

"What?" Alanor turned back, and relief flooded me that her eyes were protected by those dark lenses.

"Daria. She was behind the coffee shop."

"I told her to go home." Larissa shook her head back and forth. "Why were you back there? How did you disappear?"

"Do you want to talk to her or not?" I didn't want any more questions. Every time she asked one the answers burned up my throat like indigestion.

"I want my questions answered.," Alanor spat.

We stared, an impasse between us. My teeth clenched so tightly I worried I might snap a tooth if I didn't lighten up on the pressure soon.

"Ya know, all I wanted was to get my coffee. That was it. Nothing else. I had the day off work, and I was set to..." Oh Lilekai, she doesn't need to know what you do in your spare time! "...well, that doesn't matter. But I didn't get my coffee, I stumbled upon a bloody crime scene instead. I have a friend traumatised from witnessing it, and all you can do is hound me instead of looking for the actual bad guy. And here I was thinking you were a good detective."

"Are you done?" Alanor asked, no sympathy lacing the words.

"Not even a little bit."

"What were you planning on spending the day doing?"

"None of your business." Why did she have to actually be a good detective? Incompetence was highly underrated in my opinion, at least at the moment.

"Fine. You keep refusing to answer, I'll just keep asking on our way back to your place. Get up, I've got a spare helmet."

"That's not happening, Detective." I shook my head and turned back to the headstone.

Above her sunglasses, her eyebrows puckered and then she sighed.

"Fine, we'll walk."

"I'm not ready to leave yet." Though the itch beneath my skin wanted nothing more than to get me moving. "Besides, I've got my bike."

"You ride a bike?" The shock couldn't be hidden beneath the dark glasses this time, it curled her mouth, scrunched her nose and shuffled the stance of her shoulders.

"No, not that kind of bike, I'm not a moron." I rolled my eyes. "I ride a bicycle."

"I'm not letting you out of my sight again."

"Do you really think I'm responsible for this?" I meant to say Brian, I meant to say so many other things. I closed my eyes and wondered how she would interpret the words, how much snark I'd receive because of them.

"Take your time. But I'm not taking my eyes off you."

"Why, Detective? If I didn't know better, I'd say you might have a little crush on me. Or are you more the smitten type?" Playing with fire, great idea Lilekai. I would have rolled my eyes again, but those lenses remained fixed in my direction.

"Hurry up, or I'll just go knock on the door without you."

"Well, I've had longer hookups, but shit happens," I muttered, wondering why I couldn't just shut my mouth and my attitude around her.

Alanor shook her head. She stepped past me and up to Katy's headstone. With a touch gentler than before, she placed her hand on top of the headstone and covered the rocks once more. She muttered something too low for me to hear.

I kept my head down as she walked past again. I waited and I listened.

Her eyes bored into my back while I muttered words to Katy's memorial.

The weight of the morning had moved from the base of my skull, though a headache still lingered. I traced her name and the words her sister had etched on the stone in Katy's memory.

"See ya later, Kid. I'll be back when I can."

I didn't look at Alanor and she didn't look at me. I grabbed my bike, the bag of ground beans still hanging from the handlebars and started heading back up the hill toward home. The word still tasted like ash on my tongue, but it was the closest thing I had, and the last two days had reinforced that for me.

For a few steps we walked, my bike between us. But either

my pace or my smell, which I would take personally, pissed Alanor off and sent her back into Detective Arsehole mode. She stretched her long legs to full stride pulling away from my scurrying attempts to keep up.

"If you are in such a hurry, you really should ride yourself and just meet me there. Or you know, just call an ambulance now."

"What? Why?" That stopped her and I took a deep breath, unable to truly slow my attempts just yet.

"Slow the hell down you bloody lunatic."

To my surprise Detective Arsehole disappeared and Alanor returned, bursting out with laughter.

"Oh fuck, you sounded just like Katy." She smiled, and then her lips dipped down in sadness.

"I miss her as well," I said, knowing the moment the words left my lips that I had said the wrong thing.

"Fuck you." And just like that Detective Arsehole was back.

"Yep, knew trying to have an actual conversation with you was a futile effort, but I seem to be an eternal glutton for punishment. Why don't I just ask where your bike was the other day, how your weekend went, and ooh what's the latest gossip around the water cooler?" The words came fast. Always so fast whenever I spoke to her.

I hadn't considered it a long walk before, but I hadn't done the trek beside a woman who hated me either. The position of my house had not been an accident or even a happy coincidence. I needed to be able to get to the cemetery regularly and easily. Many didn't want to move on from their bodies until they had the closure of a funeral. Some transition Necromancers didn't care too much about that. But I lived in this World, I didn't just pop in and out for work—not anymore. And despite my attempts to remain distant from the World I lived in, I cared about the spirits that I walked through.

"Why is Daria at your place?"

"I told you." I forced the words out with as little inflection as possible. "She was sitting at the coffee shop, scared to go against your instructions."

"I told her to go home," Alanor repeated her earlier words, this time with an exasperated sigh.

"Well, she—" I puffed a breath upward from my lips, sending loose strands of my hair flying off of my forehead.

"What?"

"She's been living at the coffee shop." I would apologise and beg for forgiveness.

"What?" I half expected Alanor to rip off her sunnies like in some great reveal scene on a crime show.

"A makeshift room had been made behind the back shelf. Camping gear mostly, but a space that had been getting used."

"It makes more sense if she's been living there," Alanor muttered as she nodded.

"Than what?"

"Huh?" She blinked and focused on me again. Had she forgotten I walked beside her. I wondered if I should be offended or concerned.

"It makes more sense than what?"

"She gave us a false address. When I knocked, the woman screamed at me. Told me she didn't know anyone named Daria and not to go there again or she would report me to my superior," Alanor scoffed.

"Maybe." I forced my thoughts into words. "Maybe it wasn't a false address."

"She doesn't live there, what would you call it?" The arrogance dripped from the detective. Ah, Detective Arsehole and her spitting rage. Infamous in the right circles. We had avoided each other, but that hadn't stopped me finding out more about her over the years.

It had been what might pass as a nice minute of civilised conversation to a casual onlooker.

"I'd call it family." I had never met anyone else in my life who could get me to snap and lose my shit with a single sentence.

"Stop playing cryptic. I'm not playing your games again, Lily."

"Daria and I didn't talk much, and when we did, it was usually about coffee and my dire need for the elixir of life. But I know her folks weren't good people. And maybe..." I let the words trail off, already feeling like I had betrayed Daria for what I had already said. "Maybe she used to live there."

"Oh." Thankfully, Alanor closed her eyes for a moment.

"Yeah, see how easy it is to assume the wrong thing?" I should have kept my mouth shut, but really what would be the point. Larissa Alanor hated me as though the five years between then and now had never happened.

"If people told me the fucking truth, I wouldn't have to try to work out what the hell was going on."

"Isn't that the whole point of being a detective? To investigate? It's your job to figure shit out."

"Just tell me the tru—" her phone vibrated from her pocket, cutting her off.

I watched a little too closely as she slipped the phone from her pants again. I tried convincing myself I was impressed the thing worked, and not impressed by the curves of her body.

But of course, my mind mocked me, bringing to the forefront of my thoughts the memory of first seeing her bum walking across the barroom where Katy waited nervously to introduce me to her sister. Little did I know at the time.

"Alanor." Her eyes, now partially visible through her sunglasses thanks to the angle of the sun, widened, and then narrowed at me.

I listened as she spoke in short, sharp words. No specifics that told me what was going on. After a few snapped orders the call was over. Alanor slipped the phone back into her pocket. The silence lingered for a few beats, but I guess I valued my life more than I had realised.

"There's been another murder."

"The same..." Bile rose to the back of my throat, "...as Brian?"

"They think so. But I need to go see if there are any similarities."

"I told you I'm not connected."

"Maybe you didn't kill them yourself but that doesn't mean you don't have accomplices."

"Oh, for hell's sake. I'm not a murde—" I began.

"You're coming with me."

"To another crime scene?"

"Yep."

"You really think that's the best idea?" I forced the excitement from my voice. My skin fizzed in anticipation of finding out what was going on. My mind screamed at the rest of my body, demanding they chill the fuck out and remember this was not our job.

"Hope it's not far, because I'm not getting on that bike with you." I looked at my own handlebars as I gripped them between my hands. "Guess you could always try these handlebars."

"Not far at all," Detective Arsehole muttered, not rising to my bait.

Unfortunately, she was right.

Three cars were parked haphazardly in front of my house. I moved forward, a numb fear weighing down my limbs. Before I could move any closer, Detective Alanor's hand was on the middle of my chest, stopping me in my tracks.

"Let me go, Detective," I ordered.

She didn't move. Her hand remained pressed against my sternum. "I can't." Her voice was emotionless, flat, and professional.

"Fuck you. Who did they hurt? Tell me. Is it Jen or Daria?"

"Who is Jen?"

"Tell me, Alanor or I swear…" But the words died in my throat as images of Daria's trapped soul morphed into Katy's, and thoughts collided together in my brain—trains jumped off the track, metal squealed against metal.

Arms were around me before I realised I had lost my centre of gravity.

Alanor slowly lowered me to the ground.

"Who is Jen, Lily?" Her voice was soft and warm. I hated it and I hated her for dragging me back into any of this. For making my past shadow my present.

"Who is Jen?"

"My best friend." The words came out with a hitch and a sob.

What was going on and why did I feel like I was trapped in the middle of it all?

I watched as Alanor looked over my head, speaking words I couldn't concentrate on. Death shouldn't fill me with such dread. I was one of Death's minions, for fuck's sake. I was a fucking Necromancer.

"A man has been killed," Alanor muttered.

I blinked, the statement making entirely no sense to me. "What?"

"The body inside your home is a man's body."

The words made some kind of sense this time, but not enough.

What man?

I swayed as though I remained standing. I could feel the bumps and scratches of rocks and dirt beneath me, digging into my legs even through my shorts.

The softness in her eyes made me want to scream or fuck. Run or fight. I couldn't hold on to any emotion, any other thought.

Where were Daria and Jen?

I pushed out of her arms and stood back up. I swayed, but I would not fall again.

I took one step toward my home.

This was home. I knew it as home, the first real home I had ever known. The closest I had ever gotten to having one of my very own. And with pain, like a knife slicing between my ribs and into my heart, it was being trampled over and desecrated.

Alanor's eyes narrowed at me, and her long thin fingers wrapped around my wrist like a handcuff.

But the touch was soft. She had to stop being kind. I didn't want kind; I didn't want nice. I deserved neither, especially from her. I was Death's minion. I was not a murderer, but I had done something far worse than taking a life. Of all people, she thought the worst of me, but even she didn't go nearly far enough.

I held on to my anger and yanked my hand from her soft touch.

I didn't want her softness or her sympathy.

I needed Detective Arsehole. I needed someone to hate me as much as I hated myself.

"Who is the man, Lily?"

"There was no man in my house when I left. Where are Jen and Daria?"

"How long ago did you leave?" Detective Arsehole returned as Alanor's patience ran out. Good.

The problem with having known Katy so well, had been that I had also gotten to know about Alanor. Not a lot, but I knew how to hurt her. I knew her insecurities.

"Fuck you. Go find someone else to pin your incompetence to," I hissed.

"When did you leave your place?" She asked between gritted teeth.

I tilted my head back, face to the sky. I couldn't look at her, I couldn't calm my breathing, not enough for it to slow. The sun slipped further behind the horizon, bruising the sky in its wake. Everything came too fast, and I couldn't breathe. I needed space and time to breathe.

"Lily." Soft fingers brushed my forearm, and I pulled back as though burned.

"I don't remember."

"How long were you at the cemetery before I got there?"

"I don't know." I glared at her. My eyes pinned to hers.

I gasped. Where was the hate I had relied on, why wasn't there hate staring back at me?

"They aren't inside. My people have checked." The calmness of her voice made me want to scratch off my skin, or maybe hers.

"Right," I scoffed. "Just like they checked the café."

"Do you have any contact details for Jen and Daria?"

"I don't care who's dead. I don't care who's in there. My friends are missing and all you care about is holding a grudge from five years ago."

"A grudge?" Fury flickered over her face, but my own rage bubbled over within.

"I didn't kill your sister. She killed herself." I jabbed my finger toward her. "So, stop blaming everyone else because you don't want to believe the truth."

Ah, finally the hate flared back to life in her eyes.

A heartbeat, and then another. The rest of the world disappeared. No sound or movement intruded upon us. For a fleeting moment I fancied that even the birds in the sky froze mid-flight.

We stood, silent statues, eyes staring in a locked battle of wills, as though waiting for the other one to make the next move.

I didn't move a muscle.

Like a rubber band being snapped, the rest of the world intruded again, and Alanor moved faster than I would have thought possible for a mortal.

"You are under arrest for the suspicion of murder." She had me turned around, hands behind my back and wrists cuffed before I could even process the words she had strung together.

"Seriously?" I blinked at the darkening World around us.

More words tumbled from her mouth, presumably well strung together, but I couldn't be bothered to figure any of them out. Something to do with laws and rights.

I tuned back in when she mentioned something about a phone call.

I would get my phone call and she would be left without her answers. Again. The idea shouldn't have bothered me. It hadn't bothered me all those years ago.

Ok, that was a lie. It had bothered me. But not like this.

"I'll take this as well." Her hands were lightning fast as she grabbed the phone from my own back pocket.

"No." I struggled as she held it in her hands, just out of my reach. "You don't know what you are doing."

"I think I've finally figured you out, Lumbra." Detective Arsehole's face was a frozen mask, in an expression I didn't know and didn't like. She pulled me toward one of the police vehicles, while simultaneously looking at the phone.

"Whatever you think you have figured out, I guarantee you, you haven't got a motherfucking clue," I muttered, not caring if she heard or not.

She heard.

Her thumb slipped on to the side button. "Not as high and mighty or better than me anymore, huh?"

I closed my eyes, wishing the day away. "I have never been better than you, and I've never acted like I was."

She scoffed in response. She had a point, I'd acted like I was on more than one occasion, but I never believed it.

The fizz in the air rose goose pimples over my skin. I checked and, yep, sure enough, Alanor still held her thumb down on the pretty little call home button.

How had the day managed to go from bad to worse? And it wasn't even over yet.

"For what it's worth, I'm sorry." Something in my voice made her stop. Or maybe something in my face.

Whatever it had been, she stopped dragging me forward, tilted her head to look back at me, finally pulling her attention and her thumb away from the side of my phone. But it was too late. Her eyes bored into me, and I had the distinct impression she had never truly looked at me before.

Not once in all our confrontations.

The idea thrilled me to be seen, while it saddened me that all those little moments in the past were only ever in my head. Strange, the things that go through a person's mind when doom lingers in the air and wraps too tightly around them.

The thrumming through my body and the electrical pulse beneath my skin heated up. And the Grey World called. They had answered. I had never used the emergency button before. I had told Jen it was a stupid idea to have it there in the first place. I stood by that sentiment now more than ever.

I wanted to apologise again to Alanor.

I had never made the journey as a mortal. I didn't have a true frame of reference to begin preparing her for what she was about to encounter. But worry gnawed in the pit of my belly. Would she suffer? Would it hurt as much as the rumours and whispers told? Could it be as bad as walking through the barriers?

I didn't like her. Not Detective Arsehole who accused me of some wrongdoing, or the big sister Alanor who blamed me for her little sister Alanor's death.

But I did worry about Larissa.

Larissa? The name danced in my mind and an affection for the stranger I had locked eyes with rushed through me again. I never met that stranger. Instead, I had been introduced to Katy's big sister, who instantly took a dislike to me.

The sparks I thought had been mutual turned into little more than cooled and broken sparklers after writing the name of your true love in the night sky, hoping no one worked out the letters you spelled.

She stared at me now, the woman who hated me, with eyes wide and fear shining from within. I had never seen fear in her eyes before. Anger, pain, fury? Sure. But never fear. Cold fingers wrapped around my wrist, above the metal cuff.

"What's happening?" she demanded. Her voice didn't quiver and damn it all I had to begrudgingly give the woman credit for that.

I didn't answer. No answer would help, and we didn't have time anyway. The Shimmer happened and she gasped in a lungful of air. Oh damn, that's right, I should have told her to hold her breath. I had heard others talk about how that helped with the shift between Worlds for mortals.

Goose pimples rose over my skin as we landed in the Grey World. I stood still and waited. I knew what would happen next. And this wasn't solely limited to mortals either. I had seen plenty of minions lose the contents of their stomachs.

As if on cue, Alanor let go of my wrist and dropped to her knees. I heard the heavy thud as she landed on the thick clear resin floor. I looked down between my feet at the bones beneath the clear layer. I closed my eyes and listened, failing to convince myself that concern didn't eat at the corners of my mind. Alanor proceeded to throw up until all I could hear were the disturbing sounds of her dry retching.

I took a deep breath through my mouth. The cold air over-powered whatever stench might have been wafting my way from the bent over mortal. I steeled myself and placed the mask of the good little Necromancer securely over my features. When did the Necromancer in me become the mask? Urgh, was this some kind of midlife crisis? Had I been in the Green World so long that mortal ways were sneaking back into my psyche? That would suck, but the idea stuck because it sure would make sense of the last few days, at least.

Silence wrapped around me, and I became painfully aware of Alanor, sitting in a tangle of limbs on the floor, staring at me.

I met her eyes for a moment and then looked at the empty throne where Death didn't sit.

"Hey, Deathio, we sort of have a situation here," I whispered.

There would never be a reason to yell for Death's attention. Not in the Grey World. It was as though they were stretched out over the entire space of their World, their nerves tuned in to every movement and moment within it. It had been how I saw it, even though I knew there were flaws in my thinking.

Death had many powers and could concentrate on many areas of the Grey World at once. But they were not all seeing. That illusion should have been shattered, but what the brain knew had never seemed to translate entirely to the heart. It always pissed Jen off to no end that I thought so highly of her parent.

She proved to me, time and again, that they could not see all.

"What have you done this time, Lilekai?" Theamin's growl greeted me from the doorway into Death's throne room.

"I called for Deathio, not you, Theamin, so off you pop."

Theamin scowled at me, then at Alanor before turning around and storming back out of the Central Chamber.

Once the echo of Theamin's heavy footsteps could no longer be heard, one of Death's minions shuffled up behind me and relieved me of the Green World's cuffs. They held up a robe against the cold, as though I were merely a visitor. So, technically it was true, but I had never been offered a robe without Death's specific request before. I stared at it and looked up at the minion who offered it.

Whatever they saw on my face scared them enough to drop the lifted robe at my feet and scuttle back to the wall. They retook their position in the shadow of a skeleton, but I continued to feel that scared gaze as it wandered over my skin.

A second minion stood with a robe held up, eyes focused on Alanor but they stood still, out of their shadowed position but not brave enough to approach.

"Detective?" I asked.

Alanor looked over at me, standing up as she did. A glassy confusion coated her eyes, and I suspected it wouldn't matter what I said right now, she wasn't quite with me yet.

"Are you cold?" I asked three times before her furrowed brows relaxed, only then seeming to understand the question.

"Freezing." She nodded but made no move to either take the robe or let the minion place it over her shoulders.

With a shuddering sigh, I stepped over the abandoned robe at my feet and took the other one from the frozen minion. I smiled my gratitude and understood the fear that flashed through their eyes.

My own time as a minion had been filled with snarls, rolled eyes, or worse yet, a complete lack of being seen whatsoever.

A robe bearer was the first rung on the minion ladder. We all began there, when we were the newest and greenest members in Death's service.

I approached Alanor as carefully as that man who approached wild animals on that late night TV show. Stan, Steve, Stewart? Something like that. He made the Aussie accent something worth laughing along with, or at. But his name didn't really matter. He had been walked through many years ago now. Even before my banishment. But still, the mortals watched the old shows and missed the man's enthusiasm for life and the living.

I had never known my mind to cling to such random trivialities before.

I wish I had been surprised. With all that had happened I felt the need to pat myself mentally on the back for holding up as well as I had so far. I clung to this self-appraisal like a bin chicken with a pilfered hot chip. I must have smiled, because Alanor's brows furrowed. I shook my head side to side ever so slightly. I hoped she knew that meant to keep her mouth shut. To just stand there, and I would find a way to get us both out of here.

Alanor did keep her mouth closed and followed my every move, but I suspected it had more to do with the Central Chambers décor than anything being understood between the two of us.

I slid the robe up her arms and onto her shoulders with practised ease. It had been years since my time as robe bearer, but it turned out the skill never disappeared.

With a gasp, like someone breaking through the surface of water after being too long under, she pulled the cloak tight around her body. I envied the warmth she was wrapped in, but I would not show anyone here a hint of weakness.

"Oh god, where are we?" she whispered.

I smiled, it never ceased to amaze me how humans needed so badly to know where they were. They were never happy to simply experience anything without being able to place it into a concrete idea within their minds first.

"My real home." I said the words, but my heart wasn't in it.

She blinked, and then blinked again.

"Okay, listen. I'm sorry about all of this. It takes time to even start processing it all, but we don't have that luxury right now. Just trust me, and I will explain it all later. I didn't mean for either of us to be here, but I'm going to use it as best I can. I need to find Jen and Daria, and you need to stop another murder from happening, yes?"

The laughter that spluttered from her mouth had been expected. The hints of hysteria came as no surprise, either.

"Trust you? I don't even know what the fuck you are." She shook her head, tears caught on her bottom eyelashes, freezing into precious jewels moments after they escaped her eyes. "I thought she was just high, ya know. I thought that the insanity she had always talked about as a kid had the dial turned up to twelve when she went on the drugs."

"Thought who was just high? What drugs?" It was my turn to be confused, but turnabout was fair play. I kept my mouth shut on the matter, realising it wasn't the best time for the discussion.

"Katy," she answered, her voice letting me know in no uncertain terms that she thought I was an idiot for not having figured that out already.

"Katy?" Of course, it was the only thing that connected the two of us.

"Her journals. She wrote about you, about this place. I thought," Larissa turned in a slow circle, and how I wished to experience that first moment of seeing this place all over again, "I thought you had tricked her, and she was high, and she was in love with you."

"Katy was never in love with me. And I never tricked her. I told her the truth. That was all I ever did."

"So why not me?" She must have caught my look of confusion as she clarified. "Why did you never tell me the truth?"

"Because you weren't in a place to believe it."

"I'm bloody well in the place now, aren't I?" She smiled, rueful, but with a slight tremor on her lips.

I returned the smile and for a moment I remembered the things I had kept from Katy, especially that one thing I had never told her the truth about. I mentally shook my head. Inappropriate timing. If I let those thoughts in, they would drown me where I stood.

"Who have you brought to us, Lilekai?" Death, always with the perfect timing and the dramatic entrances.

"Lilekai?" Alanor asked.

I shrugged before turning toward Death.

"I apologise. It was an accident. This mortal got a hold of my phone and didn't know she was sending us on a journey."

"Your phone?" Despite Death's face being half in shadow within their cowl, I saw the eyebrows raise in question.

Shit! I had forgotten I was never supposed to have the phone, especially one with an E.T. phone home button.

"Ah, yes. I-I took it when I last came for recharging," I lied, and the smirk that lifted one side of Death's lips told me they knew. They were not exactly standard issue. Jen had designed the things after my banishment. I'd only had mine for two years now.

Death's smirk turned into a full-blown smile. It sent shivers up my spine. I should have taken the cloak. Pride be damned. It really would be the true death of me one of these days.

"This is the detective?" Death asked as they alighted on their throne.

No matter how many years I worked as a minion and then Necromancer to Death, they still managed to surprise me.

"Have you been investigating the trapped soul?" Death asked casually.

"This is the detective," I confirmed, ignoring the second question.

"You have been stepping where you do not belong, Lilekai." Death tutted, but there was no real reprimand in their tone, and that alone made me suspicious.

"She came to me and found me. I want nothing to do with these murders."

Keep lying to yourself, you might even believe it one day.

Death sat forward just enough for me to know they were interested. I would have been surprised if Alanor saw any movement whatsoever. "There are more?"

"I believe so. I haven't seen the body to confirm yet."

"Is this some kind of really fucking elaborate prank? Because I'm not seeing the fucking humour," Alanor snapped, apparently sick of not being in on the conversation.

She turned in a slow circle, mouth slightly parted.

I remembered when I first saw this room. I hadn't broken down, and I hadn't thrown up. I'd seen many who did at least one of the two. But I had never noticed another do what I had done. I had counted the skeletons and then asked Death if the number of them were important. A question they had not answered to this day.

"What does she have to do with you and Katy?" Death asked, and for the first time I saw the merest glimpse of the cruelty Death could throw out.

Jen swore they were vicious beyond what anyone else would believe.

Death laid down the law of the Grey World. It was their job. But now, I could see how hard they pressed into Alanor's mind as they asked me the questions aloud.

Did they enjoy the torment they inflicted on those who would not follow their command? They had never been cruel, not to me. And they had never brought up Katy's name since the banishment. The name upon Death's lips might as well have been a slap to the face. Perhaps Jen had always been right, and the person I knew didn't truly exist.

I lowered my head. Heat burned through my chest. It had been five years, and I had paid for the consequences of my actions, but still the shame lingered.

"She is Katy's sister."

Death laughed and leaned back in their throne. And the cruelty I had been certain of moments ago disappeared as though it had never been there to begin with. But then, they were laughing at my discomfort, with who Alanor was.

"Ah, it always comes full circle." They gestured me forward with a lazy sweep of their hand. "Why had she cuffed you?"

"She thinks I'm responsible for a murder in my Green World home."

I heard Theamin scoff from somewhere behind me. Of course she'd come back when Death arrived. What I wouldn't do to be able to get that overinflated sense of importance knocked out of her. She might even turn out to be a decent enough human.

Who was I kidding, nothing could burst her ego.

"Multiple murders actually." Alanor spoke up as though being a detective here meant a damn thing. The pull at the corners of my lips told me I found it sexy nonetheless.

"Interesting." Death nodded, taking in the information. "Who are they?"

"I don't know. But from what I've figured—" I began.

"One is the owner of the coffee shop, Lily—Lilekai— frequents, and the other we were on the way to see when we were dragged here. They were killed inside of Lily's home."

"Brian owned the coffee shop?" I spluttered.

"Of course he owned the coffee shop. What did you think?" Alanor looked at me as though she had never realised just how stupid I could be. Me, however, I was far too aware of the potential.

"Daria always called him the manager. I didn't know he owned the bloody place," I snapped back.

"Well now, isn't this entertaining." Death clapped their hands, their smile looking wide and devious.

Entertaining? No.

Nothing about the last few days even hinted at entertaining. Even my laughter, always bubbling up when it shouldn't, hadn't managed to bring a hint of entertainment to my life. But Jen and Daria had.

"Jen is missing, Death. Your child." I wanted to deck Death with a right hook to their jaw. The threat as it bounced around inside my head shocked me. "Did you even realise she wasn't here? She got dragged to the Green World and she can't Shimmer."

While Daria and Jen were missing, I couldn't walk away. I couldn't wash my hands of this bullshit.

I tuned back into the room where I stood and found Alanor, Death, and Theamin all staring at me.

"What?" I glared at them all in turn. Why couldn't they understand none of this was a joke, none of this was ordinary, and even as these things raced through my mind, I knew I was losing grip on myself.

"Lilekai." Death's calm voice washed over me.

"I can't do this, Death. Please, please don't make me do this."

"We do not know who is killing and binding these souls."

Binding, not pinning?

"I task you, Lilekai, to bring the Grim to stand before my ruling. You must also ensure the secrecy of our World."

"I didn't do this, Death." I met their eyes.

After a beat, their look toward me softened, turning into the kind albeit enigmatic look I had always known and trusted.

"Some on the Green World might think you responsible, but the Grey World is not so primitive."

I bristled at Death's assessment, which had all the hallmarks of sanity slipping further out of reach.

I had held that same arrogant and superior opinion. We were better than the primitive mortals. We saw the bigger picture, the Worlds as they truly were, not experienced through the limit of five pitiful senses, science, and logic.

Except, we didn't experience it.

"Has Jen returned? Did she get her Shimmer back?" Hope

blossomed in my chest. Maybe Death hadn't been concerned because Jen had already come home and brought Daria with her.

"No." Death's head dropped forward. "I cannot sense them in the Grey World."

"Look in the Green World for her." I shouldn't demand of Death, I knew better, but did I mention the snapping of my mind? Well, this seemed to be the last sinew.

"I cannot locate her in the Green World." Death did not look at any of us. Their eyes disappeared into the shadow of their cowl.

"Well ,what can you do?" Did I have a final walk wish?

"She has not walked through to the gates, Lilekai." Death narrowed their gaze at me. " faith in me still has not returned."

"I believe you, Death. But that doesn't mean I don't fear where they might be."

"I would have known had my child been escorted through the Grey World to the gates."

"And what if she hadn't been escorted?" I didn't want to follow that thinking down the path it led, but I had never been one to leave stones unturned.

"I know every single soul that steps past my barrier. I would have known. Whether she found the gates on her own or through a Necromancer's power makes no difference to me."

I nodded. I knew that. Of course, I knew that. What the hell was wrong with me?

The heaviness of my body pulled at me with such intense suddenness it was all I could do to stay upright. The adrenaline and the fear had ebbed just enough for my energy to drop and my body swayed.

For a moment, for a dreadful tick in time, I had thought I had lost my best friend. Both of my friends. But if they hadn't walked through, that didn't mean they were safe.

"If not there and not here, then where are they?" I asked, my voice cracking.

"Whoever killed and pinned the soul, is cloaking themselves," Theamin said. "All Grey World minions, ranked and not, have been accounted for. Myself, Kensley, and Sara are the only ones who have the ability to Shimmer from the Grey World."

"Are the Witches investigating?"

"We haven't been able to locate any of the Green World minions. None are answering the calls," Theamin said.

"What the fuck?" I glared at Theamin and then back to Death. And then my mind caught up. I slowly turned my head back to Theamin. "When did you stop everyone from being able to Shimmer?"

Theamin didn't answer, but she would not get out of having to, not if I still had a say in the matter.

"Theamin, did you check the mists outside before locking it down?"

The silence told me and Death everything.

"We were pulled into the Green World, and Jen is now stuck there. She tried to Shimmer back and couldn't. You trapped her there." It took all my strength not to shove my hands at her and push her down to the ground. "You trapped her there with a monster, and she couldn't even Shimmer to save herself."

"Lilekai." Death pulled my attention away from Theamin.

"Is that why you can't find the Green World minions?" The words were cinders in my throat. I had thought about Lita and Isla, I had even planned to go see them, but now not even Death could find them. I thought about my found family, and their house that was a genuine Witch's cottage from the old fairy tales. The forests had thinned around them thanks to humanity and their greed, but enough still boarded their property for the image to remain the same.

The silence rested over us all. I chanced a small glance to my side to see Alanor staring at Death as they relaxed back into their throne.

"We believe that whoever pinned that soul–"Theamin began.

"Souls, Theamin. Have you not been listening?" I snapped.

"They have cloaked not only themselves but all magic in the Green World."

"And how do you know it wasn't your brilliant ineptitude when you locked down the Shimmering between the Worlds?"

"Because locking down Shimmering has never before affected my ability to find everyone."

"So, what you're saying," I snarled. "Is that every single one of you is completely useless to me now? You cannot see us, and you cannot help us. Either of you!"

"Lilekai." Death's magic wrapped around me.

"You're Death," I snapped. "And yet you are powerless to help."

"Enough." The magic that had circled me tightened around my body and my mind. Frustration was already building inside of me.

Theamin had shuffled to Death's right-hand side, and her stare bore holes through my very flesh. Beside Theamin stood her very own minions. They were Death's only in name. In reality, these two Keepers followed Theamin around like sick puppy dogs, and did her bidding like the well-trained little bitches they were.

Kensley hated me for no other reason but that her master did. Sara wasn't as bad, though at that moment, her look could have killed if she were more than just a Keeper.

"Yes, I am Death. But I have my limits, and I have never

misled any of you to believe otherwise. If unlimited power truly existed, then the World would not still be here." Death spoke softly. "You also have your own limits, my Necromancer. And you have once again forgotten your place."

"I have always been and will always be yours. I am your Necromancer for as long as you desire it." The words came easily pouring from my mouth by rote. The passion and the belief I once held for being a Necromancer slipped out of my reach.

"Jen is my child. You are not the only one concerned about where she might be and in what state." Death spoke as though I hadn't bothered to open my mouth.

I dropped my head and mumbled an insincere apology. I didn't feel sorry in the least. Jen and Daria were still missing, and I was no closer to finding them.

I hadn't meant to Shimmer through to the Grey World, damn Alanor and her curiosity. But the moment we had landed in Death's Central Chamber, I had clutched at the belief that Death would be able to ease my concerns.

"What would you have me do, Death?" I asked.

"Jen gave you the power to come here, I can give you the power to go back. You will find the one responsible and bring them to my court to be judged." The look they turned on Alanor was not lost on me, nor was it subtle. "And make sure you protect our Worlds, Lilekai. I trust you to remember that."

My hands shook against my thighs.

"Yes, Death." I bowed low and counted under my breath as slowly as I could. I would not run from this room. My opinions of their words, of their unsaid directions meant little. But if I could stop them from forcing me then I could do this my own way. At least for as long as I could keep Death out of the Green World.

"You have been granted leave to Shimmer despite the lockdown. Return when you have the answers."

I turned and grabbed Alanor's hand. We walked away from Death's Central Chamber. The doors opened by silent unranked minions as we approached, and I thanked them with a nod.

Once they banged closed behind me, I picked up my pace.

"Stop," Alanor said.

I heard her but I couldn't stop, not yet. I didn't run, but I was loath to ease my pace.

"I said stop."

"Soon, I promise."

I hadn't expected my words to stop her demands. And maybe it wasn't my words that did.

I looked at her for just a moment and understood. With wide eyes and slightly open mouth she looked at the skeletons that decorated the halls.

"Are they real?"

"Yes, they're real. Bones are a magic not to be wasted. Without the bones, none of us would be here, and the Green World wouldn't exist."

I pushed on, not stopping until I reached my room at the end of the Necromancers corridor. I closed the door behind us and took a deep breath. These rooms were small and sparse. Luxuries weren't needed for us Necromancers who no longer had the same rights as our Grey World dwelling counterparts. The space was filled with nothing more than a single bed and a chest of drawers with a mirror on top of it.

"You're a Grim Reaper." Alanor spoke as she ripped her wrist out of my hand.

"No, I'm not." I took a step toward her, and she moved back, fear and anger flashing over her face.

CHAPTER

ELEVEN

"Yes, you are," she insisted, her voice strong despite the lingering fear that rolled off of her and filled the room. "You're an honest-to-god, motherfucking Grim Reaper," Alanor repeated with a few extra flourishes of her hands that shouldn't have made me smile.

"No." I took a deep breath, forcing my own rage at being accused as such back down into my belly. "Mortals have so much backwards thinking. I'm not the Grim Reaper, there is no such thing."

"You mentioned the Grim."

"Yes, but they aren't Grim Reapers."

"What are you?

"I'm a Necromancer."

"And that's better?" The words exploded on a sound that might have been a scoff, a laugh, or a sob. "Am I truly supposed to feel better knowing you are a Necromancer and not a Grim Reaper?"

"I don't care what you feel. It's the truth," I said. "And you have managed to put us both in a shit world of trouble."

Alanor sat on the edge of the bed. My bed. Though "sat" might have been too generous a word. She collapsed, as though her legs could no longer support her body.

"Why are we here?" she asked, exhaustion showing in the strain of her voice. Exhaustion but no longer the fear that had shrouded her since we landed in the Grey World.

"We are here because you sent for an immediate full body Shimmer when you fucked around with my phone." I looked down to see both of her hands empty. "Fuck. Where's my phone?"

"I..." She furrowed her brows. "I dropped it."

"Great." I paced back and forth in front of her, rubbing my fingers along my forehead, pinching my thumb and forefinger together without trying to capture skin between the digits.

"Is this real? What are we doing sitting in here? The truth," she demanded, and I had to give the woman credit. She somehow managed to shake off the surreal magnitude of what she faced with an ease that was rare.

"The truth is," I took a deep breath, "I'm supposed to remove your memories of the Grey World before we head back."

"What? Fuck off." Alanor jumped to her feet and moved away from me, her back pressing into the corner of the room, her feet still trying to get further away from me.

I couldn't even bring myself to be insulted.

"That's what Death meant."

"Please." Her chest moved too quickly, belying the calm strength in her voice.

Was this what real fear looked like for her? I couldn't entirely pin it down.

"It doesn't hurt." Words I'd said before. But really, I had no idea if they were true or not.

Her head moved back and forth. And I saw it this time. I saw the fear that filled her grey eyes and set them ablaze.

"Are you scared I will hurt you?" I asked.

She had handled the entire experience better than I had ever seen. Not even Death had seemed to hold any true fear for her.

Nothing had, until I mentioned the mind wipe.

Her eyes skittered around the room, dancing upon the sparse furnishing and lack of personal touches. It was as though she searched for something–anything–to help her. She reminded me of a trapped animal having to decide to wait for the hunter to return and kill it or gnaw off their own foot to avoid the capture.

"It's what you did to Katy isn't it?" She whispered. "It's what killed her."

I collapsed on the bed where she had jumped up from. She continued to stare at me from the corner of my recharge room. An apt name Katy had coined.

"You honestly think I killed her?" The pain in my chest twisted. Somewhere along the line I had convinced myself that if Alanor only knew the truth, she would understand that I hadn't been responsible for Katy's death. "Even after all of this? After seeing this World? You still think I killed her."

"Yes."

"I didn't." I shrugged, a defeated weight pressing on my shoulders. How had I been so naïve to believe something as simple as the truth could have swayed Alanor?

"Well, what the fuck am I supposed to think?" Alanor asked, lifting her hands in the air before letting them fall back and slap against the sides of her thighs.

I let that sit in the air for a few moments. The silence stretched between us, tight and taught as a bowstring ready to loose at the slightest touch.

"What happened?" Alanor asked.

I pulled my eyebrows together in question.

"With Katy?"

"You seriously want to know now, of all times?" A lump formed in my throat, and I swallowed it back as I pushed the memories down.

She nodded. "If you are going to wipe all of this from my mind, can't I know just for a moment what actually happened to her, then? You want me not to blame you anymore, then tell me who I should blame."

"Blame Katy if you have to, but sometimes life just fucking sucks and in the end I don't believe she had any more power over it then we did." I regret this conversation, fearing she might finally believe me. Fearing I had finally placed the right words after each other to create a spell of truth like a fisherman's net over her.

If I didn't have Alanor hating me, how did I rebalance my place in the Green World when my identity rested so much on her vitriol of who I was. But, maybe Alanor deserved the truth more than I deserved absolution or a numb existence for the next twenty-five years.

"I met Katy the first time she tried to kill herself."

"First time?" Alanor muttered. Her eyes blinked rapidly as I nodded in the affirmative.

"It looked to be a successful attempt. Which is one of the many stupidest things I've heard you mortals say about suicide. 'Successful suicide.' But I was there, watching as she sobbed." My voice lodged in my throat. I didn't want to talk about this, I didn't want to go down this path. I had become the Green World Necromancer I was because of all of this. I didn't hate the life I had carved out there, and maybe that was the problem. That was the reason I didn't want to relive this, pick at the wounds just to start hating myself all over again.

"What happened?"

"You called at the same time as someone knocked on her front door. She panicked, thought it was you. She screamed into the phone telling you to leave her alone. Asking why you never believed her, asking why you couldn't trust her, not once."

"I remember that call." Alanor said.

"While she yelled at you, she stopped the bleeding and wrapped her wrists. I'm not even certain she was aware of her own movements. She hung up, but before I could Shimmer away, she spoke to me. She shouldn't have been able to see me or sense me, but she could. Katy was strong in her own understanding of the Worlds. I think that was the real problem. She saw too much. And then, I made it worse."

"What? How did you make it worse?" The desperation in Alanor's voice could have killed me.

"I told her the truth."

"That was it?" Alanor's eyebrows pulled tightly toward each other.

"I thought it would help." I nodded. "And for a few months, it did. She smiled again. She was happy and less withdrawn."

"She was my sister again. She let me back in, and then she introduced me to you," Alanor said, the words holding nothing but an empty flatness, devoid of emotion.

"She was always your sister," I said, and realised what an arsehole thing it was to say at that moment.

Alanor's jaws flexed, and I knew she clenched her teeth. It hadn't been the emotion I had been searching for, but it scared me less than the emotionless tone.

"What happened?" Alanor asked.

The anger rolled off her in waves and I breathed easier. I could deal with anger. It made it easier to remember to hate her.

"I offered her the chance to become one of us. A minion of Death, perhaps even a Necromancer. I thought it had worked, but I suppose looking back, not everyone craves living forever."

"You're immortal?" Alanor stared hard at me.

"Yes and no. Nothing should live forever. It throws the balance of the Worlds off. We don't die of old age, we simply hang around a lot longer than mortals do." She really was good at her job. She managed to weed through the questions of every minion I have ever seen during Minion Class 101.

At the back of my head, near the base of my skull that slow beat began. The one that warned of the headache that would soon follow. But beside the pulse of that beat, an idea had formed.

Alanor saw what others didn't. I had no doubt it was how she had risen so quickly in the ranks. I needed her to see what I couldn't.

"Look." My breath sped up, and white puffs of cold air filled the space between us. "I should wipe your memory now, as Death intended me to. But I need your help to find Jen and Daria."

"I'm not helping you. I need to find the murderer and get the bastard behind bars."

I pulled my bottom lip into my mouth and flicked it out again with a scrape of my teeth. "If I help you find the murderer, will you help me find Jen and Daria?"

"What about my memories?"

"They're yours for now."

"No."

"We don't have time for this." I groaned and ran my fingers through my hair.

"I'll do it. We can help each other. But no, I'm not having my memories 'for now.'"

I stared at her; head tilted to the side trying to work out

what she was getting at. "You want me to take away your memories now?"

"No. I want you to leave my memories intact, not just now but forever."

"I can't do that." I shook my head. I wouldn't make that mistake again. It was too much for a mortal to live with.

"Then I can't help you." She called my bluff, and while I was tempted to push back, the pounding in my skull thumped away with an insistent and building beat.

"Fine." I nodded and focused on the energy that surrounded me. Pulling at the magic, I brought the Shimmer to the forefront of my thoughts. "We find the killer. We find Jen and Daria. And you get to keep your memories."

"Does it actually matter to you who is murdering people?"

My mouth dropped open and with it the Shimmer disappeared before it had a chance to form. "Of course it matters."

"Don't Necromancers only care about bones?"

"No. Of course the bones are important, but it's not all we care about." I slapped my lips together and swallowed down the dryness. "We care that someone from the Grey World is killing mortals." The words tumbled out and exhaustion slumped my shoulders forward. I needed to get us back home, back on our own turf where I could answer all these questions without the cold making my teeth ache, and fear making my heart race.

"So, souls really exist, and someone is not letting them leave their dead bodies? And you can see them?"

"Yes, I can see the souls and yes, Brian's is tied to his body, trapped." I pushed my fingers through my hair trying to stop the frustration lashing out of my mouth. "But can we please play detective once we get back home?"

"What?"

"I need you to shut up so I can get us back."

Alanor opened her mouth, her eyes hard. Before she could say anything, I held up a hand.

"I'm sorry. You are handling all of this better than anyone I have seen, but I need to concentrate to get us out of here. If we don't leave, Death will come investigate my continued presence and they'll wipe your memory themselves if they don't agree we should work together."

Our eyes met and for a moment I remembered the woman I had smiled at, the fizz of attraction that had passed between us. The woman before she became Katy's sister.

"Okay," she acquiesced and for a moment I wish she hadn't.

I hesitated, knowing too well the consequences of following through on this plan. Doing this my way, not wiping Alanor's mind, would likely end one of three ways. Extend my banishment, strip my Necromancy and leave me mortal, or have me sent through to my final walk.

I wondered if Death themselves would do it or leave it to a Necromancer. Would it be someone I knew? I shuddered to think of being left on my own, without Death's magic to guide my path and pull me toward the gate.

I didn't want to die, not again and not in finality.

But the needs of others overtook the risks. I would not stop until Jen and Daria were back home safe. A trade of them for me. It seemed more than fair in the grand scheme of things.

In the far reaches of my mind, in the back corner with the cobwebs and dust, a voice tried to speak about why else I needed to follow this through to the end. I ignored the squeak and nodded. The finality of the movement shifted something within me, and I feared it would be something I would never be able to get back. Growing fear burned my chest. It was time to get moving.

"Let the robe drop, take a deep breath, and grab my hand

as though you can finally break the bones you've been wanting to crack all these years."

She smirked, a small huff of a laugh escaping before she followed my directions to the last letter.

The Shimmer washed over me, and I took note of every hair as it stood on end, the shiver that raced up my spine, and the tug behind my belly button that pulled me from one World into the next. It could be the last time I used it, so I tried to focus on it. But the reality of not being a Necromancer anymore, the reality of not being anymore, I couldn't get my head around. No, I couldn't let myself get my head around. If I did, I would hesitate, or give up. I refused to do either.

"Oh fuck," Alanor cursed the moment we made it to the Green World.

My hand ached as we stood inside the living space of my Green World home.

The heat wasn't as bad as when we had left the Green World. But it washed over us as we stepped into the new day's beginning. The grey sky outside the window made me smile, knowing how close that other World was at this very moment.

"Fuck," Alanor swore again. This time the word came out slurred as though she were drunk.

I caught her before she crumpled to a heap on the floor of my living room.

"Believe it or not, you do actually get used to it." I smiled before muttering more to myself. "After a few decades."

"Oh god." Tears leaked from her eyes, but she pushed herself upright, out of my arms. "It was all real. Everything she saw, everything she wrote. It's all real. And I never believed her." Alanor's voice softened as though inside she crumpled to the ground, her emotions doing what she couldn't allow her body to. "She begged me to, but I didn't. Not even once to humour her."

"She told you what she saw?" I didn't expect her to be able to shock me, but there I stood, shocked into stillness.

Alanor nodded.

My heart splintered again for Katy.

She had only ever wanted to be believed. She wanted to be seen for who she was and believed about the truth that surrounded her, surrounded all of us, daily. She'd had no one believe in her. Not ever.

Knowing and believing would never be the same thing.

"I never really listened that closely. When I packed up her apartment, I found her journals." She laughed, a sound filled with such pain and agony, I wondered when it might all just be too much. She had held on so well through all of this. But it wouldn't last forever. "I didn't even know she kept a journal."

"Did she tell your parents?"

"When we were younger. But she stopped talking to them about anything important years before she died."

Alanor grew heavier in my arms.

"You need to sit."

Alanor looked at me, that line between her eyebrows creasing for a moment before she nodded. She let me guide her to the couch where she collapsed onto the cushion, almost as she had onto my Grey World bed. "I didn't even tell my parents about the journals. I just brushed them off as more of her delusional thinking. So many things were ignored as just another part of her mental health issues."

"You all knew about her mental health issues?"

"Yes."

"And still, you kept blaming me." It shouldn't have hurt. Why did her opinion hurt so damn much?

I searched for other words, light or snarky. Anything to take away the pain that throbbed in my chest. But my mind drew a blank.

"I do blame you." Alanor met my eyes then. No longer glazed over, trying to reconcile a past she had thought she understood.

"You knew she had problems long before she ever met me. Why can't you understand I didn't kill her?" I hated the begging in my voice, the demand to have her see the situation differently.

She shook her head. "I don't know. I guess it's easier to blame you. I've blamed you for so long, I'm not sure how to look at it any other way. You did hurt her, you made it worse. You said so yourself. Why didn't you just wipe her mind?"

"You just freaked out thinking my wiping her mind had killed her," I scoffed. "Now you wish I had wiped it?"

"Shut up. That was then. Answer me now. Why didn't you wipe her mind?"

"Because I didn't know it hurt her. I thought it helped her, and it did seem to for a time. Just not enough for it to matter."

"I still blame you," she spat.

And I understood that, because so did I. That didn't stop the shard in my chest from twisting ever more sharply.

I wish I truly hated Alanor. I wanted to hate her. I wanted not to care. But I did. I cared about the pain she struggled with even now, as her words ripped up her throat and made her voice come out hoarse.

But I had never put much faith in wishes, and they had never cared enough about me to change my mind.

I had wished so many times during the six months of sisters fighting over my existence that I had never met Alanor. Because then maybe I could have extinguished the fire between the two of us that had ignited before we were introduced. The emotions sparked differently then. We could have been able to follow them to a natural conclusion and each gone our separate way. But Katy had introduced us, and her death had complicated all of it.

"I'm sorry." And she might have even been genuine.

"Don't be." I wanted not to say what sat on the tip of my tongue, tasting of bile and blackness. But I wanted it all purged. I wanted her to understand it all. At least until Death found out I hadn't wiped her mind and either ordered me to as they watched or just did it themself.

I sat down on the couch beside Alanor.

"I blame myself too. I fucked up with your sister. It's why I'm here in the Green World and not living in the Grey World like most of the other Necromancers. This," I waved my hands around as though the simple gesture could somehow encompass more than my living room. As though my hands had the power to embrace my shelves of vehicles, and safety panelled technology, "is my punishment."

"How did you fuck up?" Alanor asked, and I heard the edges of her badge as it pressed into the words.

"It doesn't matter. But I did." Nope, I couldn't do it. I wanted to, and yet I sure as hell didn't want to. But in the end, I turned out to be nothing more than a coward.

"And for that they exiled you?" She raised an eyebrow and looked at me. We were on eye level, but somehow that simple gesture made me feel far lower than her.

"Yeah." The word stuck in my throat like day old bread.

"What a prick." Alanor shrugged.

I laughed and shook my head.

"Deathio is the big boss. They need to think about the greater picture. Took me a couple of years to stop being angry with them about it though. Took me a long time to realise I had been in the wrong, and I had given them no other choice." Still, even after this realisation, thirty years of exile smarted more than just a little. "But what I did wasn't just stupid, it was dangerous and reckless and well above my skills. I could have done so much damage. I could have destroyed the balance of our Worlds. But now, I guess it's all coming back to haunt me."

"How?"

"It doesn't matter." Then stop fucking mentioning it, Lily! "Not yet."

"If you want me to help you, then you have to tell me all of it. The specifics. I'm not going to be any good if I'm too focused on finding the truth to questions you won't answer."

I closed my eyes. The woman was good, and perhaps a little more psychic than she realised.

"Whoever killed Brian," I puffed out a breath and closed my eyes. Why did it have to be her? Why had I never felt able to unburden myself on anyone else? And now with her, I couldn't keep any of it in. I had tried to, but the smallest of pushes from her and I was ready to spill all of my secrets. "They trapped his soul in his body."

"Yeah, so I gathered." A small vein pulsed at her temple. I pressed my lips together hard, trying not to smile, remembering Katy calling it the Alanor pissed-off pulse. Everyone in her family had them.

"Can humans, mortals, us, whatever, do that?" Alanor rushed the words. I was impressed with her restraint on holding back something akin to "Get to the fucking point, Lily."

"Not that we've ever heard of," I replied.

"So, that means we have lots of work to do, then." She nodded.

I smiled. She took so much in stride, her ability to simply accept the Grey World had me baffled. No wonder I was drawn to her all those years ago. Had been. No wonder I had been drawn to her.

Something in my face must have caught my thoughts

because she smiled and shrugged. "Oh, I have a million questions, don't worry. And I absolutely reserve the right to freak out at any time, but I only need one question answered for now."

"Okay..." What the hell could be on the top of that list?

"Did you sleep with my sister?"

I wanted to be offended. I wasn't. She had a Green World view of her existence. A view I understood a little more than I ever had before. But still, that hadn't been on my top ten list of possibilities. "Why would that matter?"

She ignored my question and asked another one of her own, her lips puckering together in her frustration. "Did you give her the drugs she used to kill herself? How many different ways and times did she try it?"

"That's far more than one question."

"You didn't answer that one."

I smiled and looked in her eyes. They were mesmerising, but they didn't flash with hate as they met mine. My shoulders relaxed enough for me to breathe.

"No, I didn't sleep with her or supply her with the deadly dose. I have no idea who did."

She narrowed her eyes at me and my ability to handle silence snapped in an instant.

"Damn it, Alanor, I'm a Necromancer, not a mind reader." I closed my eyes and leaned my head on the backrest of the couch.

"And a total geek." She chuckled and the sound brought pricks of tears beneath my closed eyelids.

I nodded, unable to speak. Thankfully she remained silent.

The couch beside me dipped, and I cracked my eye lid just enough to see her sitting back in an approximation of what others might deem as relaxed. Her eyes roamed around the living room of my home. She wasn't looking at the floor, with the muddy boot tracks, the chalk, and other signs of investigators caring not a scrap about my life.

In that minute my stomach flipped. Did I actually worry about what she thought of my life?

It had been a relief not seeing her for five years. It had been easy to push away the feelings and desires. It had been a little too easy to ease my own guilt. But that didn't mean I hadn't thought about her more often than I cared to admit.

I was wrapped up in her World now, and there was no getting out of it. It made my skin too tight and the space between our thighs not nearly wide enough.

"We should get started." She spoke around a yawn. I smiled as she leaned back more into the couch, mimicking my own position. With her head back and her eyes closed, Alanor was less severe and sharp.

I remained silent and soon the exhaustion took over her. A few moments later, her breathing slowed and deepened into the breath of the sleeping. I left her to it and sat cross-legged on the mat in front of the floor-to-ceiling windows. Streaks of light slanted through the rippled glass.

I focused on Jen and Daria. I had to find them. I had to tell them how much they meant to me and that neither of them were ever allowed to disappear from my life again.

I swallowed the lump in my throat and centred my body. Yoga had been one of the only ways I had centred myself since becoming part of the Green World. Alita had introduced me to it, and it made me love her even more.

When Alanor woke, we would go see Alita and Isla. I needed to reach them, I needed to make sure they were okay.

As if on cue, Alanor's phone made so many beeps and blips of notifications that it sounded like a melody all on its own. Not a harmonious melody, but a melody of sorts nonetheless.

"Fuck." She sat bolt upright, all angles and sharp edges once more.

I chuckled, ignoring the heat in my chest as I lost the view of the previously unseen softness, and focused on her verbal reaction instead. It really did seem to be her favourite word. It no longer made me cringe the way it once did. The downside of formative years that occurred before women could acceptably cuss alongside the best of them.

She fumbled in her pocket and pulled out the phone. The discordant melody stopped. Her eyebrows pulled together for a moment, then she looked up and saw me.

"I'm going to sit outside." I smiled and nodded as I stood up, heading out the back door of my home.

"Thank you." The softness of her voice made my arms tingle and oh how I wanted that shit to stop.

I wasn't stupid or blind.

I knew the sensation of flutters I felt in my chest, I knew the impossibility of it all. She still blamed me for Katy's death. I saw it in the hesitation of her words, and the flinch and jerk when our bodies threatened to come in contact with each other.

But it seemed impossible for me to shake the wanting I had for her. The wanting that had all but consumed me at times before Katy's death.

TWELVE

"Do you have a TV?" She cocked her head to one side as she stepped outside of my home and scanned my backyard.

I was proud of it, and my chest swelled with the sensation. I had worried about Alanor's opinion of my house, but out here I knew how beautiful and inviting it was. I didn't worry about anyone's opinion. Out here was the only place I never questioned as part of my home.

I sat on a hammock seat attached to one of the largest branches of the macadamia nut tree that shaded most of my back yard. Near me was a small round mosaic table and three mismatched seats.

The flower beds had already been established when I arrived, but Isla had taught me what each of the plants required. After a few unfortunate deaths, I had been able to keep the colours vibrant and thriving.

"Ah." Well this was going to be fun. "Yes, I do.'"

"Where?"

"In the room next to the living room."

She stared at me, the questions legible on her face.

"Alright, you've handled everything stupidly well so hopefully this one won't be the thing that tips your mind entirely into insanity. But you might want to sit down."

She moved to the chair furthest away, turning it to face me before sitting. I took a deep breath and explained my unique situation to her. She didn't interrupt once. I gave her full props for that one.

"So, you fuck up technology when you are around it?" her eyebrows rose, checking she understood what I had told her.

"More like I fuck up electricity. It's always a risk being around me. Sometimes things last okay for a while. Sometimes it just doesn't work at all."

"So, how do you have a television?"

"I watch it through the glass wall."

"What glass wall?"

"Come up." I begrudgingly got out of my seat and headed back inside. By the time we reached the back door, a giddiness had washed over me. I never got to show this off. The fact I never showed it off because I didn't invite people to my home was entirely beside the point.

I took a seat on the couch and faced the wall. Between the living room and the smaller of the two bedrooms, the wall looked solid enough so long as you didn't step too close.

I picked up the resin coated remote and hit the big shiny button at the bottom. With a surge and groan, the inside wall began to roll up near the top of the ceiling.

"What is that?" Alanor hadn't sat, though she stood in front of the couch as though she had planned to sit at any time.

"It's a flexi garage door. The clear walls are resin."

"How do you hear it?"

"Let's just say I'm glad I don't have any neighbours."

She finally sat and looked at me then. We exchanged a

smile, and I hated the sunshine warmth that spread through my chest when she looked at me that way.

"Why do you need a television?"

"Well, I considered asking if you had a whiteboard but thought that one was less likely."

"Shit." I laughed. "You actually use whiteboards? Like in the cop shows?"

"Yep, just call me Benson." She winked, actually winked, and I forced a groan back down into my chest. Ridiculous didn't even begin to cut it. We weren't friends, we weren't anything, and my actual friends were still missing.

But none of this ridiculous logic stopped the heat as it rushed from my chest to my cheeks. Before it could start the inevitable descent, I forced myself out of my head.

"I prefer to call you Detective Arsehole."

"I'm aware, but minus points for the lack of originality. I've been getting called that long before we ever met."

"So, you really are a bitch to everyone, it's not just me, huh?" I chuckled. "So, what's got you in such a better mood?" I forced my voice to remain light as I smirked at her.

For a moment, a fraction of a second, I thought she might smirk back, she might play along. But then that thing happened behind her eyes, as though she remembered how much she hated me.

"Shut the fuck up. I'm starving."

"I really don't have anything in the house."

"So order something. You're paying."

"I have a better idea." The smile spread over my face, despite the scowl Alanor kept giving me. "And this way we can kill two birds with one stone."

"I hate that saying."

"Get up, we've got a long walk ahead of us." I pushed myself up to stand and offered her my hand.

"Ah fuck no." She shook her head and stayed exactly where she was on my couch.

"Are you going to fight me every step of the way?"

"Probably. Especially if you don't tell me what's going on."

"Fine." I nodded and sat back down beside her. "I need to reach out to some friends. I need to make sure they are okay."

"And this gets me fed how?"

"Alita is the best damn cook you'll ever find."

"Why are you so concerned about her? Is she another Necromancer?"

"Hell no," I laughed and shook my head side to side. "And she'd probably curse you if you called her one. She's a Witch and it's her and her wife's job to investigate misdeaths and the abuse of magic and power in the Green World."

"Witches." Alanor's face alternated between disbelief and fear.

"It's all getting to be a little too much now?"

"It's all getting to be a shitload too much. But I need to do my job, I can't just gallivant around without checking in. Especially if you want me kept on the case."

"They could take you off the case?"

"Of course they could."

"Was that the phone call?" But she had returned more relaxed than I'd seen her in a very long time.

"It was work. But not threatening to pull me off the case."

"Okay," I drew out the word. And she thought I played word games. What the hell did she mean?

"They hadn't noticed I was gone."

"That's why you've been happier, because your work didn't realise you weren't still on the planet? Did you really think they would know?"

"Not that I wasn't on the planet, but that I was AWOL." She

laughed at my obvious confusion. "We disappeared outside of the crime scene, or did you forget that?"

In fact, I had forgotten that exactly. How did she even still have space in her mind for something like that?

"No one saw us vanish. They just assumed I had gone to comfort you and learn what I could about the victim."

"I don't know who he is."

"I know." Alanor nodded.

"So, does that mean I can take you to Lita and Isla's place?"

"Where do they live?"

"The other side of town."

"I'm not walking to the other fucking side of town." Alanor stared at me as though this, out of everything she had heard recently, was the most insane of it all.

"Then I'll give you the address and I'll meet you there."

"No." Alanor got that look again. The one showing actual fear.

"I promise you, I won't disappear. I will help you find the bad guy."

"What if you can't?" Alanor asked. "What if it really is someone from your Grey World? Someone I definitely don't have jurisdiction over?"

I didn't have an answer, and she knew it.

"So, what do you suggest then?"

A smile I didn't like in the least spread across her face.

"Give me half an hour and I'll be back."

"You haven't promised you won't disappear." I had given her a glimpse into my own fear but instead she looked even more frightened.

"Can they just take a mortal and drag them into the Grey World?"

"What?"

"Death. Can they?"

"No." I shook my head trying to understand, but worried any assumptions I made would be just that. "Death doesn't work like that."

"But they could, if they wanted to?"

"No." My answer was stronger this time. "No, they don't have control over the living. And even if they did, they wouldn't have a way of finding you unless you died."

"Are you certain?"

"Yes." I hadn't known I still had any faith left in Death, but there had been no hesitation in my answer.

"Okay." She nodded. "I'll be back in half an hour. You'll need to meet me out the front."

"You want me to trust you but you wouldn't even stand up from the couch when I didn't fill you in on the plan?"

"Basically." She smirked as she stood up and walked to the door. "I've trusted you more than you realised, Lily. Be nice if you could trust me on this one."

I nodded and watched her leave, closing the door without slamming it.

THIRTEEN

I took advantage of being alone to shower and dress and generally wonder what the hell had happened to my life. The worst part of being banished was the alone time. I had nowhere near enough distractions to stop me from contemplating every single thought and action I had ever had or done throughout my entire existence.

But once I had acclimated to this World, I remembered more and more each day who I had been before I became Death's minion. I had never needed to be surrounded by others. That change had occurred solely in the Grey World.

Exactly twenty minutes later I stood out the front of my home.

I had changed into some lightweight pants and over my singlet I'd thrown on a thin checked button shirt that hung open. The wardrobe change might have indicated I had some inkling about Alanor's plans. I did not.

The day had cooled a little, a sure sign that autumn crept in. That had been the extent of my clothing choice.

But now, as the sound of Alanor's motorbike engine roared

toward me, my blood drained to my feet and I wish I had something thicker to pull around my chest.

"What the hell are you doing?" I asked, not stepping any closer as Alanor pulled the helmet from her head and shook the hair from where it pressed against her in unflattering ways. Pity the leather pants and jacket didn't look nearly as unattractive.

"Finding an answer to your solution."

"Every vehicle nowadays uses electricity."

"Ah, but it doesn't run on it."

"What do you mean?" I asked, begrudgingly admitting to myself how beautiful her bike truly was.

"Take Mysty for example." Alanor ran her palm over the silver tank she sat in front of. "The ignition is electric for sure. But once she's running, the engine is combustible, no electricity. It's the same with most cars as well."

"Then..." I tried to process the information. Had I really just taken Lita's word for it that my existence interfered with all electricity? "Why do cars stop working after I've been in them longer than ten minutes?"

"I have no idea." Alanor shrugged and I couldn't help but notice the difference between her and the person Katy often spoke about. The person with a chip on her shoulder about feeling stupid. The person who never admitted when she didn't know something.

"You want me to get on that thing and we are going to ride to the other side of town?"

"Yep." Without getting off the bike, Alanor opened the flap of a side saddle and produced a helmet. It had green lightning strikes on either side.

"Nope, definitely not happening."

"What the fuck, Lily? You're immortal."

"No, I'm not. I can die just like the thousands of souls I've walked through the Grey World with."

We looked at each other. Frozen and processing exactly what I had just said.

"I really want to ask more about your actual job." Alanor's voice held a worrying amount of curiosity and grief.

"Yeah, thought you might," I said as I rubbed the back of my neck.

"You remind me so much of my brother." She smiled.

"Wait, what? You don't have a brother."

"Of course I do." She laughed and shook her head. "He's three years younger than Katy."

I opened my mouth. I couldn't have gotten that wrong, could I? Katy had never mentioned a brother, not once.

"Oh."

"She never talked about him?"

"Not around me, not that I remember."

"That's something I won't be telling the family."

"You can't tell the family any of this, Alanor."

"No wonder you're all fucked up. Keeping secrets is a shit way to survive."

"I think I'm starting to realise that," I muttered as I finally accepted the helmet she held out to me.

"I want to know so much more." Alanor's eyes sparkled with the mere idea of learning more. And yet, she called me the geek.

"I can't tell you much. I'm supposed to have already wiped your memory, remember? I don't have clearance to tell you about the ins and outs of the day job."

She laughed and shook her head.

I narrowed my eyes.

"No wonder I didn't believe Katy. You sound like an ordinary human, maybe with a fucking FBI agent swollen head, but not some mythical otherworldly creature."

"That's because I'm not some mythical otherworldly creature."

"I'm still going to ask those questions." She shrugged. "But right now we should get going before I run out of petrol and Mysty won't start again because you are some weird-arse electrical mutant."

"Mutant?" I asked, watching as she put her helmet back on.

"Believe me, that's one of the nicer names I've had for you over the years." I slipped onto the bike, trying my best not to slide too close to her.

"Good, now hold the fuck on. I like to go fast."

I held on, and very soon forgot about not trying to be too close to her. The bike rumbled beneath me, and I held on tighter.

"You're liking it aren't ya?" We stopped at a light, and Alanor held it and us up by her right leg. Her helmet faced our right as though she were trying to look over her shoulder at me. The words came out a little muffled despite her having pushed the visor of her helmet up, but I heard them clear enough.

"Liking what? Dying again?"

"Again?" Alanor tried to look closer at me, pushing her head further to the right. But the light had turned green and a car behind us honked.

Without snapping her visor back down she lifted her leg from the bitumen, and we were off. We sped forward with a sudden jerk. I reached to grab her, but my fingers brushed the sides of her jacket, unable to grab enough fabric to keep me close. The gap between our two bodies grew, and I saw all the souls who had died on these bloody death machines.

I closed my eyes, preparing to fly off and hit my head

against the road or another oncoming vehicle.

I was yanked forward by a hand wrapped around my left wrist. My hand was then unceremoniously shoved into the pocket of Alanor's jacket. I didn't have time enough to process what had happened before the right hand was given the same treatment.

"Are you trying to prove yourself right?" Alanor screamed as we rode, her voice floating back at me, hitting me with her anger and the wind combined. "Does making me the arsehole all the time mean so much to you?"

"What the fuck?" I snarled, not expecting her to hear me. "Where are we even going?"

It seemed such a stupid move to have jumped on the back of this bike before even knowing where we were headed. I had simply assumed we were going to Lita and Isla's, but she never asked for their address, she never agreed to that being the next step.

The bike turned down a road I hadn't even noticed, the smooth ride turned into a jarring of bumps against my bum. Dust swirled around us, and ahead I could see a small cloud of dust that I assumed was another vehicle willingly travelling this backwater way.

Alanor pulled us off to the side of the road as suddenly as she had turned onto it in the first place. The loose gravel beneath the tire made us fishtail and my heart leapt into my throat. But we didn't fall, nor did we skid.

As soon as Alanor turned off the bike, she kicked the stand out, pulled her helmet from her head, and got off the bike. Without looking at me, she slapped the helmet on the seat and walked away.

I sat on the back of the bike, staring at Alanor's shoulders that moved up and down with too much speed for her to be breathing normally.

I didn't know what had happened. One moment we were almost getting along and the next I was standing on a back road with a Detective who hated me and a vehicle I not only couldn't operate myself but despised.

Why weren't cars good enough? Why did humans have to keep pushing the limits on everything? There was something to be said for contentment.

I scoffed and rolled my eyes at my own hypocrisy.

Carefully, scared one false move would send the entire thing tumbling to the ground and pinning me beneath it, I got off of the motorbike.

"You can do this, Lily." I tried to convince myself with words, head nods, and the shaking out of my hands.

I walked toward Alanor. Thankfully she had now stopped moving forward. I had no idea what I would say, what idiocy would come out of my mouth when I reached her. But I moved closer anyway.

"So, wanna let me know what all of that was about?" Ah, that idiocy. I held back the groan and waited for her to turn around.

She didn't, but at least she spoke.

"Did you really die?"

"Oh." That's what all this was about? "Yes. All of Death's minions die before they can grant us their power."

"So..." Alanor's breath was loud and slow. "Why are you here, and Katy isn't?"

Alanor turned around and I was struck dumb. Her eyes were red rimmed and her face blotched and tear streaked. She wasn't a character on a screen, she was a real human being who cried ugly tears and somehow still managed to be gorgeous.

"What did you do?" Her pain morphed into anger in front of my eyes. "That's why you got punished isn't it? You fucked up and you stole Katy's chance to come back to me, to come back and have a better life."

"Fuck you."

"What did you do?" She lifted her hands and I saw them move as if they were in slow motion. Her palms slammed against my shoulders, pushing me back.

I didn't fight her. I didn't even hate her for it. I deserved it and much more.

Then she did it again and again and again. Each time asking me what I had done. I don't know how many times it took for me to snap, for me to no longer care about holding it back, holding everything back.

"I tried to save her," I finally screamed, my breath coming hot and fast through my nose as I tried in vain to hold back the words. "I tried to make her one of us. I did everything in my power, and I fucked up. Death hadn't wanted her as a minion, but I begged them. I begged them to reconsider. They said they wouldn't consider her a minion until they saw her soul." My own tears came unrelenting over my cheeks. I sniffled and rubbed ruthlessly at my face, but nothing stopped them. "When I found her, I couldn't just let her go. I was selfish and scared. She had become the most important person in my life. She never judged me, and she never demanded more of me than I could give. Even Jen hated how much time I spent with her. And there she was, so peaceful in death and I wanted to hate her. I couldn't let her go."

"What did you do?" The question was so soft, I almost missed it.

"I grabbed her soul and tried to place it back into her body. Just as Death had done to me."

"You pinned her soul." It wasn't a question, and the hardness returned to her voice.

"Yes," I snapped as I got in her face. "Now do you understand?"

"You are trying to clear yourself of these murders, and of your guilt."

"Fuck you!" I screamed in her face. "I don't care what anyone thinks. I am guilty of hurting her. I'm not hiding from what I did, but I know I didn't do it to hurt her."

"You did it." She leaned into my face, her breath warm as it rushed against my skin. "Because you do whatever you want, damn the consequences."

"If I did whatever I wanted we wouldn't be here screaming at each other." My breath was loud in my ears, her own breath just as fast against my skin.

"Then why are you here?" she snarled.

Before I could answer, my hand had reached up and cupped the back of her head. My fingers slipped through strands of her dark hair as I pulled her closer, our lips pressing together hard enough to bruise.

For a second, a second of knowing every mistake I ever made in my life had nothing on this one, she remained frozen against my lips.

Then her lips moved, and she kissed me back. The taste of coffee and strawberries filled me, and her hands grabbed my hips pulling me into her body. I groaned, unable to stop the pleasure from rolling from my core up to my mouth.

"Oh fuck." She pushed me back and I covered my lips with my hand.

She didn't speak as she walked past me, shoving my shoulder with her own.

I tried counting to slow my mind, my heart, my breath. Instead, by the time I reached five I collapsed to my knees, sitting back on my heels while my hands landed heavy and lifeless on either side of me.

FOURTEEN

I didn't want to get up, I didn't want to care. I knew eventually the shock and pain would become numb enough for me to get back to work. I would care again about finding Jen and Daria. But right now. I let the numbness wash over me.

I had fooled myself over the last five years. Convinced myself that the life I had carved out in the Green World gave me the best of both Worlds. I remembered how to live. The rank a minion was granted by Death wasn't just a job. It was an entire way of life. I had lived and breathed nothing but Necromancy for more than fifty years. We were all but immortal, but our lives weren't our own. We didn't live, we served.

Mortals knew they would die. They knew there was an expiry date at the end. And it was true many feared their own deaths. But even then, they embraced their lives. Mortals lived while us immortals forgot how to.

I looked down at the dust and brown weeds that littered the shoulder of the road where Alanor had stopped walking to. Katy would have found this beautiful. Somehow, she would have seen the magic in the dust and desolation. Once upon a time, she would have shown me how to see it as well.

"The bike won't start." Alanor spoke behind me. I hadn't even heard her return. "I've called my brother, he's on his way."

I nodded, not knowing if she looked at me or not, but not being able to speak.

"What's up?"

I laughed, still not wanting to speak. My mouth, however, had other ideas.

"I used to believe in what I did. I believed I helped our Worlds, that my rank and existence were important. I didn't follow rules often, and it always worked for me. I had been smart before I died. I had been brave and curious enough to learn everything anyone would teach me once I died. And then I crossed the line and all of it crumbled. So, I dunno what's up except maybe my whole bloody existence?"

"You done?" I looked up to see Alanor's pursed lips and raised eyebrows.

"What do you think your brother can do to suddenly stop me fucking with the electrics?" I asked, raising my own eyebrows this time. Two could play at that game.

"Snap the fuck out of it, Lily. We have a job to do."

"That's it? Not, why did you kiss me, what the fuck is going on between us? Just snap the fuck out of it?"

"Yep."

"Right, of course. Complete denial is kind of your thing."

"Why would you want to linger in any of this? In the shit that shouldn't be happening between us, or the way Katy's death has turned us into enemies and made us stop living properly for the last five years?, she asked, and damn if I didn't want to kiss that smarmy logical mouth again.

"Because in the end it doesn't matter either way. Things

will happen however they want, and how you look at it isn't going to change it."

"Like fuck it doesn't matter. And no, it won't change the situation, but it can fucking well change you."

"What's the point?" I shrugged, standing up and brushing at the seat of my pants. "I gave up and I killed her."

"Oh, would you shut the fuck up? Not everything is about you. Life just fucking sucks sometimes. You of all people should know that. People who shouldn't live do, and those who deserve immortality are taken away."

"Like me and Katy." I stared at her, my face frozen, unable to express much of anything.

"I didn't mean..." But she didn't finish the thought. She couldn't, because that had been exactly what she had meant.

"If I don't go back with the answers, with the murderer in tow, then I'm done. You'll at least get half of your wish. I'll be taken through my final walk, and you'll never have to see me again."

"Right, so it's a whiney self-loathing pity party of one. Don't you think it's time you finally grew the fuck up, Lily?"

"Screw you."

"One kiss was quite enough, thanks."

"Why do you keep doing your job, if you know how much everything sucks?"

"You think I became a cop because I thought every single thing I did would end with a happy ever after, and there'd be a fucking point to all the paperwork?"

I responded with a steady gaze and raised eyebrows.

Alanor thrust a finger at me, the corners of her mouth trying to betray her seriousness. "Fine, maybe I started out that way, but it didn't take long to realise the world is truly fucked up. But you make a goddamn choice. You either whinge about it and peg yourself out, or you can do something to help. You don't have to save the world, but you can make things better in your corner of it."

I narrowed my eyes at her.

"What?" Alanor asked.

"For someone whose favourite word is 'fuck', you have far more insight in there than you let on. I'm not sure I'm a fan of this version."

"Oh, fuck off."

"There ya go." I smiled and nodded. "Alright, then. It's no Alexander the Great speech, but it'll do.'

"I'm sure that was almost a compliment."

"Almost." I smirked and gave her a wink.

She laughed and we walked our way in silence toward the bike. I didn't notice I had started humming until Alanor looked at me with twisted lips, unsure if she were disgusted or disturbed by my shift in mood.

"For someone who ten minutes ago seemed content to sit there until they turned to stone, you sure seem a hell of a lot better now."

"I do, don't I?" I stopped walking and looked over at her. "Even for me, this change is a little too swift for my liking."

"You don't normally bounce back from your depressing outlook on life?"

"Well," I blinked and we continued walking again but slower this time, "to be honest, I don't normally feel so overwhelmed by my own thoughts."

"Alright, so that's a whole bunch of weird shit I'm not touching."

"I think there is something about your whole denial thing I might be able to get onboard with." I spoke as lightly as I could and was stunned at how easily it floated out from me. "So when do I get to meet this brother of yours?"

"You don't." Alanor ran a hand through her hair, sending

short black spikes shooting off into random directions from her head. It almost looked like tousled bed hair. I coughed and shook my head, grateful that kiss hadn't happened anywhere near a bed.

"Why not?"

"Because my boss sent out a press memo that the police had someone in custody. The less people who know that's you the better."

"I'm not in custody."

"Sure, Lily. You keep telling yourself that."

I stared at her wide-eyed as she placed one hand on her bike and shaded her eyes against the sun with the other one.

"How would anyone know it's me?"

"How did the same person get into your house?"

She had a skill of shutting me up. It was sexy. No, annoying. It was annoyingly sexy? I internally sighed and agreed.

"But why?"

"From what I can tell…" She looked my way, as though making sure I was listening. When our eyes met, she nodded and continued to look toward the main road we had turned off of, hand still at her forehead. "Someone isn't a fan of you. Someone who knows what you did to Katy is trying to frame you for these murders."

"Wait, didn't you just tell me it wasn't all about me?" I smirked, and she looked at me again, bait taken and eyes narrowed.

"I'm not sure I want to risk taking you to the station now."

"Then let me take you to Lita and Isla's."

"How?"

"Death gave me permission to Shimmer. I'm hoping since they can't find me here right now means they can't remove it."

"Hope?"

I shrugged.

"Fine. But I need to work through this. Who knew about what happened to Katy? And why would someone want to frame you?"

One name came to my mind instantly. "Theamin knew, oh boy did she know. And she hates me."

"Theamin, I know that name." Alanor tapped her long index finger on her closed lips as she thought. "She's the hotty who was with Death, yeah?"

"Hotty?" I lifted my lip and snarled at the very idea. "Theamin is an arrogant bitch who hates me because I reached rank of Necromancer faster than she did. She also has her little pets who hate me just as equally because I dared to tell Theamin to buy a vibrator and clear the cobwebs. "

"You seriously said that?" Alanor asked as she smiled.

"I may have also added something along the lines of maybe it would help her clear out the pets trying to crawl their way in there. I learned pretty quickly after that not to go anywhere near them without consuming a decent amount of coffee beforehand."

Alanor pressed her lips together until the little pink colour disappeared.

"Oh, what now?" I asked. "Are you going to be all offended, Detective My Favourite Word is Fuck? I heard about you letting it slip in front of the priest in the middle of the church."

"Katy told you that?" Alanor chuckled as I nodded.

"She did. She thought it was the best thing you had done since graduating."

"Pfft." Alanor rolled her eyes. "She didn't think my graduation was anything worthwhile. I was always too serious and straightlaced for her."

"You're delusional."

"Excuse me?" She looked on the edge of returning to Detective Arsehole, which I knew was inevitable, but I needed to get this out. Who knew if we would ever be able to talk so easily with each other again?

"Did you read all of her journals?"

"No." She shook her head. "There are so many. I couldn't even get through the first one."

"Maybe, when all of this is over, you should try again. She wrote everything important in those things. And I know how important you were to her."

The honk from a white dual cab ute pulling up behind Alanor's bike was rewarded with both of us breathing out a sigh of relief.

"Whatcha done to this beauty now, Lari?" The voice sounded familiar, but I couldn't place it or see the owner hidden from sight by the ute.

"Lari?" I smirked and looked over at her.

She narrowed her eyes, but she couldn't hide the twitch at the corner of her lips.

"You're lucky I actually like my brother, so don't get any ideas about a new nickname. We are going to finish this conversation later."

"Sure." Unless of course Death catches me fucking up their orders again. I smiled grateful I would be relieved of finishing that conversation. Surely, Alanor would be proud, or at least give me a verbal gold star, for finding a silver lining to the ticking clock that hovered over my head.

I decided to keep my own council on the matter anyway.

"Lily, this is–" Alanor waved her hand in front of me, the first real smile lighting up her face, but before she could finish the introduction me and her brother looked at each other and spoke at the same time.

"Etziel?"

"Lilekai?"

FIFTEEN

"Wait, what the fuck?" Alanor's hands gripped her hips. "You two know each other?"

"Well, yeah." I looked at Etziel, to the ute he drove up in, to the scars that covered the back of his hands, back to the ute, and then rested on his eyes once again. "But it's sure been awhile. I guess a lot has happened."

"Well…" The Kid, that's the name we had for him in the Grey World, blushed, looked down at his feet, and rubbed the back of his neck with the flat of his palm. "Yeah. You could say that."

"I…I didn't even know…" I wasn't sure how to finish that sentence. My mind raced. Sure, Alanor knew about me and had even been to the Grey World. But this was a whole other level of insanity for her to deal with.

"I heard about what happened to you. It was a blow to a lot of us. I mean. Accidents happen. But then, I got a new work opportunity, and I ran with it," Etziel mumbled the words, almost too fast for me to catch.

"Argh." I should have known. I closed my eyes and shook

my head. How could I still be so damn stupid? "How long since Death placed memories of you in their lives?"

"Wait." Alanor held up her hands and stepped between us.

I really was stupid to think she wasn't listening. With what she knew, the little we had said told her far more than Etziel could realise.

"You're a Necromancer?" Alanor squared her shoulders and faced him directly.

"What the fuck, Lilekai?" Etziel's eyes blazed.

"It's a long story." I couldn't bring myself to rise to the challenge he looked ready to throw down at my feet.

"Is that why you came to us? As a job for Death?" Apparently, Alanor preferred to skip why she knew what she did and go directly for Etziel's jugular.

"Lil?" Etziel's voice held a tone that dripped more with fear than the anger I had been expecting.

"It's okay, Etziel. She's met Death, and she knows sort of a Grey World 101."

"But, why?" There he was, that kid I knew from the Grey World.

"Because two people are dead, and their souls have been trapped to their flesh." I didn't want to say it. But I had a sinking feeling I'd be saying this several more times before we found the answers.

"Oh shit, just like Katy." Etziel said the name reverently, as though he had known her his entire life.

"You know?" Alanor and I asked at the same time.

"Yeah." Etziel threw his head back, eyes closed, and shook his head. I had seen him do it so many times, my heart warmed at the unexpected colliding of Worlds.

My own eyes closed, searching to feel the hum of power from Death.

"I still can't feel it," Etziel replied, but I kept my eyes closed and focused on my breathing.

"Don't," Alanor snarled, snapping me out of my head. Etziel's hand hovered in the air and Alanor had moved away from his touch.

Her lip curled back and the snarl was so animalistic she might have shifted into a wolf if I didn't know werewolves were an entire fiction made up from mortal imaginings.

"I'm sorry, Lari. It was a job for Death in the beginning, but they let me stay because, well, I asked."

"How long, Kid, and what was the actual job?" My stomach swirled with unease, and my brain wanted to hit itself over the head with a lead pipe just to shut me the hell up.

"I've been here five years. My job was to keep an eye on the family." Etziel's voice rose at the end as though asking if that were enough.

Hells no, that would not do. It wasn't even in the same league as enough.

"More, Etziel. I'm no damn Green Worlder." I said it as though I meant it, but I had no idea if it were true.

"No, but," he flicked his eyes to Alanor, "but my sis is."

I expected Alanor to correct the term, and from Etziel's eyes he anticipated a similar kind of reaction. Alanor remained silent. I didn't know if that was better or worse for Etziel, but I was sure glad I wasn't him right then.

"Tell us everything. I'll find out eventually. You know I will." Alanor stood like a sergeant preparing to inspect the troops.

"Fine. At first, Death wanted to make sure you were all safe."

"Safe?" I asked and noticed from the corner of my eye Alanor's lips open, only to slowly close again once my single word question registered. Who knew we could be on the same page without an argument.

"They just said for me to take all possible threats seriously. To keep you and mum safe."

"Safe from the Green World?" I asked, knowing where this conversation would lead, and hoping I could have misunderstood Death's mission for Etziel.

Etziel hesitated and my own spidey-senses prickled.

Death could be weird and strange and often asked for things that didn't entirely make sense until much later. But the prickles making their way up the back of my spine told me there were far more pieces to this puzzle. And I had barely collected enough to spend the energy trying to connect them yet.

"They said from all corners."

I nodded and Alanor remained quiet, arms crossed over her chest, and lips pressed tightly together. Her jaw muscles protruded as though she clenched her teeth far harder than entirely necessary. I vaguely wondered if it ached or if she was so used to playing the bitch persona the muscles had strengthened far beyond a normal mortal's threshold of pain.

Silence lingered.

"So, what's up with Mysty?" Etziel asked, hope and nervous humour tingeing his tone.

Alanor answered by jerking her chin toward me.

"Ah." Etziel's eyebrows pulled together for a moment, but he didn't ask any follow-ups. He simply nodded and headed over to the bike.

The bike turned over on the second try. He looked between myself and Alanor, eyebrows raised. He clearly didn't want to ask any questions, but he wanted the answers, there were no doubts about that.

Alanor looked at me, eyebrows pulled together before looking back at Etziel.

"Just take her home for me, eh?" Larissa finally released the pressure on her jaw, and I followed suit, not realising I had been mimicking her expression. The relief sent a thrill of sweet pain radiating around my mouth.

"I'm not just leaving you out here on ya own," Etziel snapped. I had never seen him so defensive. No one in the Grey World worried very much about the need to defend each other.

"I'm not on my own. Lily is here, I'll be fine," Alanor snapped right back.

"Lily can't take you anywhere. You'll be stuck walking. And... "

"And what, Etziel?" I asked. I had to know.

"Death told me specifically to never let you around her."

And there they were. The words I hadn't known I dreaded. They washed over me, and I wanted nothing more than to vomit. I had convinced myself I looked too deep into how easily I avoided Alanor. It wasn't a coincidence or a natural missing of each other. Death played a hand in it. How I wished I was more surprised. With all they had to do, the two of us running into each other shouldn't have been anywhere on their radar. Yet it had been.

"We'll be fine." Alanor looked at her brother. She might be angry, but I saw the protectiveness in her eyes as she looked at Etziel. The same look she had given Katy on so many occasions. She would always look out for them, even against themselves. It hinted at being the "older, wiser, listen to me if you don't want to wake up with live spiders in your bed" sister thing I had seen so many times.

The nauseous feeling receded and there I stood, still breathing, and being backed up by my enemy. My my, how the world had flipped.

"You can tell Death that I'm done." I spat the words.

"What? No!" Etziel's face paled, and I bit back a laugh. It would have been more like the scream of a banshee than a mirthful sound.

The dynamics were being bent and twisted everywhere I looked.

"Etziel. I get it. Death was worried I had turned Grim. I haven't, and I don't give a shit what mission they sent you on. This is my last hurrah."

"We can't Shimmer. I've been trying to get back, but I can't." True panic filled his face.

"It's a precaution. Did they know you were here?" I gave Alanor a side-eye but she didn't look as though she were about to tell Etziel about my power granted me to still Shimmer.

"Yes."

"Then they believe you will be able to help better in this World than that one."

Alanor smiled and gave me a small nod. But there, behind the arrogance was a panic in her eyes.

I left them to say their farewells, barely registering Alanor's instructions to Etziel except for the tone that all but screamed "Fuck up my baby and you'll never have any of your own."

Too many things rattled in my head, too many threads I wanted to pull, but it seemed all were snared in a big, knotted ball just out of sight.

I gave Etziel a chin jerk salute as he left, Alanor's bike standing sad and tied down in the tray of the ute. I would never be a biker, but even if I didn't completely understand it, I did appreciate the need for the machines to be ridden.

He nodded in return and disappointment washed through me. The least he could have done was tell me if I hurt his sister I'd be sorry, or ya know, a simple finger pointing at his eyes and then to me. Was a little drama too much to ask for? Especially after discovering Death's instructions.

Apparently so, because after his nod he turned his attention to the road, and if he looked back for even a moment, I missed it.

"You ready?" I asked.

Alanor gave a short nod, but then opened her mouth only to close it again.

"What is it?"

"Can we walk a little first?"

"You aren't worried about time?"

"I know I should be." She rolled her eyes and started walking. "And I know I'm stupid, that things always take such a long time for me to work through, but I need the time before more is thrown my way, and I haven't yet processed all of this."

"Stupid?" I walked at her side, stunned to hear the great Detective Alanor speak of herself like this. "Since when have you ever doubted yourself?"

She laughed and the hard edges cut.

"I doubt myself all the time. But making sure no one sees that is half my job. Even when it's never worked. Took me three times to even get into the academy. No doubt Katy told you all about that."

"No. I only remember her dancing around excited for you when you got in."

"Sure." Sarcasm leaked from the word.

"It can't just be the academy thing." I shook my head. I heard it in her voice, her true belief in her lack of intelligence. "Who made you believe you weren't smart?"

"My sister's ex-lover is a Necromancer, well sure why the fuck not?" She waved her hands in the air, her longer strides speeding up. With my shorter legs, I almost had to jog to keep up. "I can almost be excused for not knowing that one, but I'm a fucking detective and my own brother...I had no fucking clue. I'm the clueless wonder."

"Stop." This time I grabbed her arm, but before I could turn her around to face me, she pulled her arm back out of my fingers.

"Kissing and fucking isn't the answer to everything," she snapped and kept moving.

"You aren't clueless." I ignored the soft scoff and carried on. "You knew from the moment you met me. You didn't have a word for it, or the knowledge to know exactly what I was, but you knew I was something different to your life, and to Katy's."

"Yeah." She scoffed again. "I thought you were her drug dealer, or worse, that she'd moved up in the sleazeball world and you were her pimp."

"Oh really?" I laughed. As soon as the sound came out, my heart pounded louder in my chest. "Is that the reason for the sex quip? You still wondering if I'm pimp material?"

Alanor turned and one side of her lip rose, just enough for her to slow her walking. My lungs appreciated it, or they would once they recovered.

"Well, what else was I supposed to think?"

"That's my point. You weren't supposed to think anything else." I smiled, hoping she could understand how much truth I felt about these words. "I don't blame you one bit for thinking any one of those things. But no, I wasn't either of them. And I've told you over and over I was never Katy's lover."

"Really?" Alanor's eyebrows pulled in toward each other. "Did you ever kiss her the way you kissed me?"

"Really." I sighed. "And I believe you kissed me right back."

"I guess." Alanor shrugged and my heart clenched.

"Why do you think you are stupid?" I didn't need to understand, but I wanted to.

"Because I am."

"But you aren't, ya know."

"Let's get to your Witches and find some bloody traction on this arsehole. I need to catch this motherfucker before they take another life."

"It's not just the lives that are the problem."

"Death said something about the deaths being imbalanced?"

"Yeah." I should have told her more, I should have explained what Grims were, but the shame of what I almost did to Katy stilled my words.

"And let's not forget the ever-looming threat of me being taken off the case." She nodded, her lips a thin line once again.

"Looks like we got another clock ticking us down. Lucky I work best under pressure."

She laughed and the sound surprised me, almost as much as my laugh that echoed hers.

The walk wasn't so bad. I mean, sure it wasn't the best seeing as it was hot as hell, and the silence stretched between us like melted toffee.

"What are they like?" Alanor asked.

"Who?"

"The people we are going to see."

"You mean my friends?" I smiled. "They are more like family, really. They are some of Death's minions, but they weren't banished here. All Witches reside in the Green World. It's where their magic is strongest."

"Are the fairy tales real?"

"Most of them, yeah."

"Bullshit. I'm stupid but not a complete fucking moron."

"If you really think you are stupid, why do you always act so um..." Why couldn't I just let it go? A car drove past, kicking up dust as it did. Dust billowed around us while the sweat from walking made it stick to my face.

She looked over at me, those eyebrows rising. "Like a ferocious ball-busting bitch?"

"Ok, sure, I wasn't going to phrase it exactly that way but hey, let's roll with it for now."

"For someone who has been living in the Green World for the last five years, I'm going to guess you've not exactly been living truly in the world."

"Why would you think that?" I asked.

"Because you have some kind of fucked up idea that the world is equal despite what does or doesn't hang between your legs."

"Oh." I'm certain I blushed. I felt the heat in my cheeks and wished I could Shimmer out of there, just until I got my composure back. Sure, I might have been able to, but I promised Alanor I wouldn't disappear on her, and I intended to keep that promise.

She was not the dumbarse in this situation.

"Well, let me give you a brief refresher. People care. They never liked me when I enrolled in the force, or when I graduated."

"I remember that."

"You do?"

"Katy was so angry at everything you had to overcome to be a cop."

"She really talked about me?"

"Of course she talked about you." I laughed and then saw her face. Softening my voice, I continued. "Yeah, she talked about you a lot. She hated that you two had lost how close you were as kids. But she really was proud of you."

"Did she say that?" The hint of mocking in Alanor's voice stung.

"Many times. Even a few times to you when I was present."

"She was being sarcastic."

"No, she really wasn't."

From the corner of my eye, I saw Alanor open her mouth and close it again.

"I thought I failed her," she scoffed. "I guess I still do."

"Because she lost her battle with depression?" I struggled to catch up, my mind three steps behind her own. I supposed she had a point. I had lived in my own bubble inside the Green World, learning from tv shows and the smallest of interactions mostly seen at the coffee shop.

"Yeah."

"You didn't fail her."

"Why do people do it? Why does Death allow people to suffer to such extremes?"

"They wouldn't, not if they had a choice."

"But, they're Death."

"That's just a name." I remembered saying almost the exact same thing not very long ago. "They don't have power over life and death, only an affinity in feeling death, while also being able to walk through the Grey World without getting lost. Oh, and they're adept with bone magic."

"Who are they?"

"They forgot a long time ago who they were before they became Death."

"How many have there been?"

"No one really knows. Death is asked often. But I've heard them say 22, 3092, and even seen them smile and say they are the one and only that there has ever been. It seems to amuse them, but it's bloody frustrating for those of us who would genuinely love to know."

"How do you know they aren't the first? The original magic wielder who created the Grey World?"

"Because they do not understand things that the original would have to know in order to create the balance."

"How are you certain they tell the truth?"

My turn to act like a caught fish, gasping for air on the deck of a boat.

She smiled.

"And you think you aren't intelligent." I winked at her.

"That's not intelligence."

"Whoever made you believe that needs a swift kick in the butt, in the direction of the Dark World."

Her small chuckle did wonders to me.

"Oh, fuck this." I stopped.

'What's wrong?' She asked.

"I can't walk anymore in this heat, Alanor. Can we at least try to see if I can Shimmer us to their place?"

"Sure." Alanor pursed her lips and her body seemed to shrink in on itself as she tensed.

"Death," I looked at the sky, "I know about Etziel, and I guess I understand what you did and why. But I'm not going to stop until I pull all of it apart. There is more going on than you are telling us."

"They can hear you?" Alanor asked.

"Usually." I nodded. "No idea if they can now, but just in case."

"They can hear you from anywhere?" she asked again.

I nodded again and smiled as I reached toward the familiar power, and it reached back. The force which lit my body felt almost as good as an orgasm. Almost.

Alanor eyed me. "Alright, I'm guessing from that, you can Shimmer. What about me?"

"You're coming with." I reached for her hand.

"Not yet." She moved out of reach as I tried to take her hand. "I need to know why you are the only one who affects electricity."

"Who says I am?"

"The way Etziel looked at you when he realised you were the reason Mysty hadn't worked. He was scared. If others affected electricity, he wouldn't have looked like that."

I reached again for Alanor's hand and this time she didn't step back or pull away. I didn't think about how well our fingers interlocked or how calm the touch made me feel.

"What?" Alanor's eyes narrowed on my face.

"Oh yeah, you are one damn clever detective. You're going to be just fine." I began to initiate a full Shimmer, Alanor's grip on my fingers tightening.

"Wait, what the fu—"

CHAPTER

SIXTEEN

"—C k." The sound came out, accompanied by Alanor falling heavily to her knees on the cement path outside of Lita and Isla's place.

I hissed in sympathy and offered her a hand. She looked at me as though questioning if my hand might turn into a venomous snake poised to strike the moment she reached toward it.

I smiled down at Alanor, impressed she held the contents of her stomach in place this time. It hadn't taken long for her to adjust at all. Still, she didn't take my hand.

"Could have given me a little more warning," she muttered.

"Really couldn't have." I smiled and offered her my other hand as well, both now out toward her.

"Why not?" She took my hands, and I pulled a little too hard, our bodies colliding with each other. Her hands landed on my hips and mine around her biceps. Damn were they muscly.

"Hi," I whispered.

"I can't." Her eyes flicked to my lips and then met my eyes. I would have walked my own soul to have understood exactly what hid behind that look.

"Shit, sorry." I turned away from those eyes and took a few deep breaths.

"No big." She stepped back, looking down at her own body as though checking I hadn't gotten any Necromancer on her.

"Because you would have tried to prepare by doing something stupid like tense up and hold your breath."

"What? I've missed something again."

"You asked why I didn't give you any warning before we Shimmered."

"Oh, okay." She blinked, and I loved seeing the way her face splashed with thought as though it were paint thrown over a canvas. "Why is that stupid?"

"It ends up with muscle spasms." I smiled without humour, remembering my own pain. "It took me almost a year before I stopped holding my breath."

"A year?"

"I'm a bit of a slow learner."

"Mhmm." She finally took in our surroundings. "Where are we?"

"At Isla's." I smiled.

"Thanks, couldn't have figured that one out without your help." Sarcasm dripped from her words.

I laughed and looked up at the faded red sign with three-foot-high white letters spelling out "Isla's Place."

"Isla is a ranked Witch, one of Death's minions. She's also a fortune teller for the Green World."

"And Death is okay with her being so in our face?"

"You know what I like about you, Alanor?"

"I haven't killed you, or arrested you again, yet?"

"Well, yes, that." I smirked and silently laughed. "But I was thinking more along the lines of your tact and gentleness with words."

"Fuck off."

I laughed louder and began my way up the cement path toward the front of Isla's place. The truth was, I had always wondered why she hadn't killed or arrested me, but in two seconds she had jumped directly to the point.

I took the three cement steps to the porch in one leap. I always enjoyed the feeling of that achievement. A mere example of the small things that made those truly living happy.

On either side of the front door a window loomed, and the sensation of being watched was unmistakable. It wasn't an accidental feeling. Lita, Isla's wife, had bewitched the windows to act as literal eyes, scanning visitors and determining their intentions. The curtains, sheer and strung with crystals, twitched.

A mortal could easily mistake the movement for the wind or someone shifting the curtain to see. But Lita and Isla could be anywhere in the house and still be able to see the front porch.

"Can she actually tell the future?"

"In a way." I gave the front door three sharp knocks, then leaned my arse up against the railing off to the side.

Alanor didn't join me, opting instead to stay at the front door, arms down at her side. I would have bet my next decent cup of coffee she was dying to cross them over her chest.

"Care to explain to the moron in the room?"

"When you stop calling yourself a 'moron' then yeah, sure."

"Fuck off."

"I'm pretty sure you should be sucking on a ciggie when you say it like that."

Instead, she flipped me the bird and I laughed. I had never

enjoyed riling someone up as much as I did her. No one's reactions came anywhere near as close to entertaining me.

The door opened, and Lita strolled past Alanor without a sideways look.

"Well, as I live and breathe, hug me already, bitch." Lita pulled me into a hug as she spoke, all in a rush of movement and energy. Her roughness wrapped around me.

I laughed and squeezed her back. She gave the best heart hugs, as Isla liked to describe them. Embracing with her entire body and squeezing until my shoulders lowered from around my ears.

Lita held my shoulders and eased me to an arm's length away. She studied my face and I cringed. I could only imagine what she saw.

"You should be worried. Why haven't ya come sooner?" Lita scolded with her gravelly voice and low pitch. I felt more love in those words than in any of my ex-lovers' declarations of love, before they became exes.

"Life's been a bit of a bitch." I shrugged, hoping and knowing that would not suffice for long, or at all.

"Of course it has, all the ones worth living are." She let me go and turned her entire body toward Alanor. "And I assume you're the cop?"

Alanor's mouth dropped open.

I laughed and nodded.

"Detective Larissa Alanor, meet Lita. Lita, this is the cop."

"Right. Well come on in, both of you," Lita commanded. "Isla is in the back room getting all set up and ready."

"Ready for what?" Alanor asked.

"The reason you're here, of course." Lita smiled, taking the sting from the words.

"And what reason is that?" Alanor snapped.

Ok, not the entire sting apparently.

I looked at them, eyes flicking back and forth between the two of them. There were a few similarities I wasn't sure how I felt about. Lita had always been direct and to the point. She didn't wrap any of her words or actions in cotton wool to protect delicate feelings or people.

As I watched the standoff between them, the "Aha!" moment hit me with such a forceful slap to the forehead I caught myself just in time from groaning in self annoyance.

It would be just another piece of my larger life puzzle that I needed to put a pin in for now. It wasn't pertinent, but the truth of it stung like a bee.

Alanor truly did think she was stupid. Beneath all the bluster and the words. Beneath her even saying those very things to me, I had thought there was still some belief in herself. There had to be, didn't there? She hadn't given up on making it into the academy, she hadn't stopped and been content with being an officer. She worked and clawed her way to the top, no matter the obstacle.

It just hadn't truly sunk in that *she* was her biggest obstacle.

She wasn't a bitch because of gender inequality. Alright, maybe some of that was it, but not just because of gender inequality.

It was to hide what she truly thought of herself.

"To find out who is murdering these people." Lita turned her eyes, half lidded and seeing far too much, to me. "And hurting their souls."

"Of course you know." I closed my eyes and rolled my head around on my neck. I felt and heard every snap, crackle, and pop that echoed from the bones and muscles.

Lita nodded, turned, and walked back inside. She led the way, not once looking back to check if we followed.

Ah, another similarity between the two of them. The confidence that bordered on arrogance. How this existed inside of Alanor alongside her thoughts of being stupid made her more complicated then I realised. I didn't want her to be complicated, I didn't want to be curious about her. I could still taste coffee and strawberries on my lips, and I wanted to badly kiss her again and taste it once more.

Alanor took a few moments before she nodded and followed after Lita. I pulled the door closed behind me and breathed in the scent of love and herbs, and oh, could I dare hope for coffee. We walked through the narrow hallway in silence

My mind wanted to pick up all the pieces of this puzzle that remained turned over, make sense of this whole thing. Was it an adventure, or a bloody nightmare? Either way, I couldn't shake Alanor's idea that I was being framed. It felt right, even in its wrongness. I wanted to believe Death understood it hadn't been me. They must have understood I had been set up even before they sent me back to the Green World.

I wanted to find this bastard who was determined to send me to the Light World.

And then what?

Sometimes I truly hated my own mind. Even as the thoughts continued to spiral and twist around inside my head.

"Maybe it's not about the Light World at all." This time I couldn't catch my mouth in time.

Alanor and Lita stopped at the same time and turned to look back at me.

"What was that?" Lita asked. She stood in a slanted ray of light that streamed through a window in the hallway. On its own, it seemed harmless enough, except the hallway was through the centre of the house and the window was on an internal wall.

"I…" I hesitated, unsure why.

Lita glared at me, and the small snort of amusement from Alanor made my chest heat. I had an audience for a Lita stare down, that would never do. I straightened my spine, hoping some false height would bring some confidence.

"I…just thinking out loud."

"And?" Alanor really didn't have the patience for foreplay. The idea would have made me smile had I not still been thinking so readily about my realisation.

"I've been set up for Death to believe I have interfered with mortals' lives and souls."

"You finally got on board with that then?"

"Yes." I nodded, not letting her snark or her smirk distract my train of thought. "I had been wondering why anyone would want me walked through to the Light World. Sure, it would get me out of their hair. But it doesn't take this much effort to have me walked. I live in the Green World; I can die from mortal wounds. If Death believes I am responsible, they won't have me sent to the Light World."

"Oh shit." An obvious difference between Alanor and Lita, was that Lita rarely swore. Her saying the word now raised the hair on my arms.

"What are they wanting then?" Alanor asked.

"They want me walked to the Dark World. They want to make sure they never have to see me again, that they never have to be confronted when I figure it out. Because they know me well enough that I won't just give up. I won't lay down and accept the judgement for something I didn't do. Not even after I'm walked."

The silence lingered and Alanor opened her mouth.

I cut her off. I had to put this out there before I lost it.

"They aren't from the Dark World, and they can't be a

Grim. They have every intention of being walked to the Light World one day. They really are a motherfucking Grey World minion, and I bet they are a goddamned Necromancer."

"What's the difference between a minion and Necromancer?" Alanor asked.

Before either myself or Lita could reply, Alanor's stomach gave an almighty growl.

"Who knows you that well?" Alanor asked, no doubt hoping the rest of us would ignore her obvious hunger. I forced a small smile. I wish she could see these moments for what they were. She cut directly through the bullshit and asked what was truly at the heart of the matter. "Who knows about Katy?"

We stepped into the largest room in the house. The largest and the most used. It was the heart that made the most regular beat in my chaotic existence.

"That can wait until after food," Lita said as she moved to Isla and wrapped her up in a hug as though they hadn't seen each other in years, instead of the five minutes it took Lita to retrieve us from the front door.

I watched from the threshold of the room. I risked a sideways glance at Alanor, who had pressed herself off to the right of the door. She stood back as though trying to disappear into the cabinets behind her.

Two steps past the threshold I stopped again. I closed my eyes and breathed deeply of smells that made me think of home. Was home a smell then?

The aroma of freshly ground coffee and homemade pastries washed over me, and for a moment we occupied ourselves with greetings.

"Hey, Isla. I need coffee, please." I rubbed my forehead with my fingers, trying to rid the thumping pain that had been growing worse since yesterday morning.

"Perfect timing, my sweet Lily." Swept up in another all-encompassing hug, I waited to be released and then introduced Alanor to Isla.

They sized each other up silently while coffees were poured, and nothing of importance was said until we sat at the rectangular table in the middle of what would look like a nice wholesome country kitchen. Until one looked just a little bit closer.

Alongside cream-coloured tins of coffee and sugar were other containers, both smaller and larger. The labels of those read "Crushed Bones", "Belladonna", and "Snake's Teeth." Hanging beside shiny silver cooking pots were garlic cloves wrapped in thistle weed. And on the bench beside a regularly used MixMaster covered in dents and scrapes, lay a pack of tarot cards. The small cups and saucers could easily be found in a regular country kitchen, but I knew they were used predominantly for Turkish coffee readings.

"What were you asking when you came in, Detective?" Isla asked as she joined the rest of us at the table. She refused to let others help; she thrived on feeding others and never sat until everyone had first been served.

"Please, call me Alanor."

Isla nodded and for a moment Alanor remained silent, sipping her coffee to buy time or to buy courage. I couldn't be sure which, but I found myself mesmerised by her lips, with little care for what had been going on in her mind.

"I asked, 'who in the Grey World knew about Katy?'" Alanor spoke with a confidence in her voice that made me shudder pleasantly.

Whatever must have shown on my face made Isla answer for me. "Unfortunately, too many in the Grey World. And almost all of us here in the Green World."

"What? Why?" Alanor's stare roamed over us all before returning to Isla once more.

"Lilekai being banished was a huge deal. Not many know the exact specifics. But they all know about the cost. The general whisper is that Lilekai had gone against Death. They used the punishment as a warning to the rest of us who might think of playing Death ourselves," Isla said.

"Yep, that's me, the fucking cautionary tale." I leaned back heavily in my chair. The truth of her words still twisted in my chest. "Don't go getting ahead of yourselves, little Necromancers, you fuck with your place in line, and I'll fuck you over."

"She was trying to save her." Alanor's sudden defence of my actions could have knocked me over with a feather, and from the look on her face, she had a similar reaction to her own words.

"I think," Isla answered in her slow deliberate way, as though trying desperately to rearrange the words in her head for the best chance of palatability. "Since the punishment, Death has realised how severe and extreme they were with Lilekai's banishment."

"How on Green World did you come to that conclusion?" I scoffed, snatching up a warm blueberry Danish. Pulling a little too roughly at the edge of the pastry, I tore off a piece and stuffed it into my mouth. It stung a little, too hot against my tongue, but I refused to open my mouth again.

"Lily, do you really think they allow other banished minions to earn back their powers?" Lita asked, rolling her eyes before staring at me as though I were the most naïve person in the history of all the Worlds.

I opened my mouth, but nothing came out. Trying in vain to save face, I swallowed my Danish chunk and ripped off another small piece and shoved that in my mouth as well.

"As my darling wife so tactlessly put it," Isla sighed, but gave Lita a small smile. The way they smiled at each other made my cheeks heat as though I had just interrupted them in the middle of sex. "Since your banishment, Death has allowed you more freedoms than the rest of the banished have been granted."

"You two live here because you want to? Not because of any banishment?" Alanor asked.

The question rankled me. Hadn't I already explained that Witches lived in the Green World because their power works better? But hey, why trust the Necromancer to know what the fuck she was talking about. I closed my eyes and took another deep breath. I needed to calm down. But it seemed an unlikely possibility when everything continued to pile on top of me.

"Witches have existed long before the Grey World came into being. This is our home and without our connection to this land, our powers weaken over time."

I pulled my cup to my mouth to stop a "told you so" from escaping. Instead, all it did was muffle the words a moment before I took another sip of the coffee.

"I'm a detective, Lily. I wouldn't have gotten very far if I believed a single source of information without cross-referencing."

"Well, it's about time you found someone who didn't put up with your tantrums." Lita laughed and lifted her chin toward Alanor. "I think I'm going to like seeing you around. Lily's always needed an equal in a partner, instead of the wisps she's dated in the past."

"We aren't together like that, and what the hell, Lita?" I stared at her.

"What?" Lita shrugged, an expression on her face bared no remorse or guilt over her words. "It's true."

"Isla. Do you know what's been going on?" I asked as the

clock on the wall ticked loud enough to drive me crazy. The threat of time raising its head once again. A countdown had been placed on me, but I had no idea what it counted down to.

"We've heard bits and pieces," Lita's rough voice answered for Isla. "But it'll help if you connect some of the dots for us."

Skipping over the kiss between Alanor and myself, I gave them a quick rundown on all that I knew, and a little about what I theorised.

"You still haven't seen the second body?" Lita asked. "Why not?"

"I..." I blew out my breath and my fringe lifted from my forehead with the pressure. "Honestly, I've had so many things to worry about. I kind of forgot about it."

"Lily, for Gaia's sake. I'm not saying you are wrong, but you need the facts first. You've assumed this second body has its soul pinned."

"Death didn't correct me." I pouted and caught Lita and Alanor sharing a here-comes-another-tantrum look.

"Death can't see the Green World. Or did you forget that?"

"No, I didn't forget that," I snapped, before muttering a little quieter, "I just hadn't put the timeline into place."

"Alright. The first thing we need to do then is to see the body." Alanor tapped her short-nailed index finger against her lip again. I watched each tap as she thought. "Taking a person of interest to see the body isn't as easy as it's made out on the TV shows."

"Really?" Why did I find that so interesting?

"Really. There is so much paperwork and fucking around. It could take days to get you in through official channels."

"And what about unofficial channels?" Lita asked.

"Cops do protect each other. Even ones they don't like. But the risk would be getting caught."

"I could try to Shimmer?"

"No!" Lita and Isla said at the same time. The intensity of their response was hard to ignore.

"Alright." I stretched the word out, flicking my eyes back and forth between the two of them. "Want to fill me in on that very subtle reaction?"

"Every time you Shimmer, they reach out to follow you," Isla said, eyes turned down and shoulders rounded forward.

"You can see them? Why didn't you tell me?"

"We can't see them, only the line that connects you to them."

I pushed my seat back and stood. I paced the room, head shaking and thoughts spinning around in my head.

"How long since you saw the line, Lita? How long have you known this has all been connected to me and you didn't tell me?"

"Sit down, Lily," Lita snapped.

I took two more steps before turning around and slumping back into my chair.

"I saw a faint line when we were on the porch. I didn't know what it meant until we got the full story."

I knew she told the truth. Lita equated lying to the most hideous of sins.

"You have the full story?" A sound, bitter and adolescent, escaped me. "Care to fill me in? Because nothing I have heard or said makes any fucking sense to me."

"Yes, it does, Lily." Isla's soft, gentle voice was accompanied by her hand laying over my own. "You just need to work through the blocks stopping you from thinking clearly."

"Nothing is blocking me." I smiled at her. "I just don't understand any of it."

"Trust me, you aren't stupid enough to really believe that," Alanor said beside me.

"You don't get to lecture me about thinking I'm stupid."

"Fine. Sit there and wallow. I need to get back to work and find this monster. I don't give a shit where they come from. They are killing people and it's my job to stop them."

"Lily has other powers she's forgotten about," Lita said.

"No, I don't." I laughed. "Death granted me temporary Shimmer to get back here, but I can't do half the things I used to when I was a real Necromancer."

"A real Necromancer?" Isla lifted her eyebrows and I sighed.

"How would you know what powers she has when she doesn't?" Alanor asked, and I heard the tone, the confidence of the detective that I always assumed had just been Alanor. But it wasn't. It was a mask she hid behind, a mask she used to feel smart without allowing anything to influence her belief in her intelligence. Humans, the strangest creatures that ever lived.

"That's Lita's speciality. Knowing the powers of others." Isle spoke with pride as her eyes fixed on her wife.

"And what is yours?" Alanor asked.

"Mine is why you came here, is it not?" Isla smiled. And I loved her more than ever before. While Lita might never have meant to make Alanor feel stupid when she arrived, Isla seemed impervious to making anyone feel less as a mortal, immortal, or other.

"Vague non-answer, but that's cool, I guess I'll find out soon enough," Alanor said, and I bit down on a laugh.

Isla smiled and stood up.

"Are we beginning?" Lita asked.

"Time is not on our side." Isla looked at me and Alanor as a single entity. "Am I right?"

"As always, Isla." I nodded as I pushed back my chair and rose, saddened by not being offered a second cup of coffee. The first still hummed in my veins and the headache had dimmed

to a dull throb, but still a second would have not gone unap-
preciated.

"As if." She laughed, light and tinkling like the sound of glass windchimes.

SEVENTEEN

"What can I do?" Alanor looked lost and out of place as Isla and Lita moved around the kitchen, transforming it into a workplace for the fortune teller.

"Sit back and admire their work." I smiled and shrugged. "It sucks, but honestly, they do it all without a word to each other. They are completely in sync."

"You sound envious." Alanor's distaste at the idea radiated in her words.

"Oh, absolutely. What I wouldn't give for that kind of connection with another soul. Where words are beautiful when spoken between us but not necessary for a connection to be made."

"Wow."

I looked away from Isla as she lay the cloth over the kitchen table. The purple darkness, scattered with pinprick lights, rippled as though alive.

"You sound like you suddenly don't hate the idea so much." I smiled, feeling my cheeks heat. I really didn't like feeling like a teenager again. And of all people to have that power over me. I mentally rolled my eyes at life's sadistic humour.

"I've never really thought about it like that, to be honest." Alanor shrugged as though it were no big deal.

"You've never had a connection with someone else?"

"Only if by 'connection' you mean sex." She laughed and shook her head. "There aren't many women who are okay with my career ambitions taking precedence over everything else. Being the partner of a cop doesn't exactly allow for many wonderful connections, other than an orgasm here and there."

"Well, that depressingly makes sense."

"Yep." She nodded as we continued to watch Lita and Isla move around each other like a choreographed dance.

"Alright." Lita stopped the awkward silence from stretching as she clapped her hands and looked at us. Did I like the smirk on her lips? No. Did I also wish I could sit down and talk to her and Isla about all the confusion this woman stirred inside of me? Absolutely. "Come join us at the table, please."

I led the way, and Alanor and I sat on one side of the rectangular table, now longer and devoid of the coffee pot, while Lita and Isla took up positions on the opposite side.

"Tell me again about the events." Lita offered her hand, and I placed my own, palm up, in hers. Isla covered our hands with both of her own.

I gave her a quick rundown, limiting my rants as much as possible with the help of Alanor knocking her thigh into my own.

"It's good you've not spoken to the souls," Isla said softly. "There is no way for their experiences to taint the sight."

"Let's do this," Lita said, all business and impatience. I understood why. I had seen them do a reading before, and what this would take out of Lita, and even more so from Isla, killed me a little.

"I'm sorry, Lita, Isla. I never wanted to make either of you do one of these for me."

"Oh shush, you. We are family." Isla smiled as she looked at me with eyes that seemed impossible of harshness or closed doors.

The lump that lodged in my throat made it easy for me to do just as she had ordered.

The World shifted around us. Above the table, an image grey and misty, appeared as if we saw it through a water covered mottled glass window.

Isla's grip tightened on the top of my hand. I hadn't realised I had tried to pull it away.

In front of us lay the interior of the coffee shop. Brian was chatting to Daria who was keeping herself busy by preparing sandwiches and wrapping them in cling wrap. I smiled as she moved easily and comfortably around the space. It was her space and she enjoyed it.

Brian spoke again, leaning over the counter and asking for his morning coffee. Was he flirting with her? Creepy.

Daria looked up after a while, coffee in hand, and in that moment, her face, no longer full of sunshine, froze. Darkness settled over her soul. The cup she held dropped to the floor, and the coffee splashed over the large cream tiles.

She screamed, and screamed, and screamed.

Our angle shifted and I bit back my own scream.

A black cloaked person stood behind Brian. Their fingers disappeared into the back of Brian's skull. Red blood spilled from the holes and dripped down Brian's neck, onto his previously clean white button-up shirt.

The Necromancer looked up, and grey eyes, lined with crackling fire stared out of the darkness beneath the cowl.

They were familiar. Similar, but not enough to ones I knew. The colour was wrong, but the unique pattern had a twin.

I didn't know who murdered Brian. It wasn't her.

"Enough." I pulled my hand out from between Lita and Isla's. The image disappeared immediately.

"Do you know the eyes?" Alanor asked, her voice taking on a roughness I hadn't heard before.

I shook my head. "They are the eyes of a Necromancer, but I don't recognise them."

"They do look familiar though, Lilekai." Isla's voice, though soft, scolded me for my desire to hide from what I didn't want to know.

"It's not her, Isla. It can't be her." I jumped up from the table again, but I didn't have the strength to pace. Instead, I leaned against the counter far enough away so none of them could touch me without standing up themselves.

"Who?" Alanor asked, an edge of annoyed frustration in the word.

"Jennivieve," Lita answered.

"Jen?" Alanor asked, nodding, her eyes not showing the surprise they should. "She's been on the top of my list for a while."

"What?" I glared at her. "Bullshit. It's. Not. Her."

"Lily," Lita snapped. "I know it seems ridiculous, and it may not be her, but you can't fool yourself on this. Those eyes, they are very familiar to Jennivieve's."

"So what? Familiar isn't the same. It doesn't make it her." I begged, but I saw the resolve in all three sets of eyes. They would follow this train of thought whether I liked it or not.

"It's okay, Lilekai." Isla brushed off Lita's arm and stood up.

"It's not okay. Someone is hurting people and wanting me connected to it. Now they are trying to frame my best friend, why?"

"I don't know, honey." Isla wrapped me up in her arms,

and I collapsed into her warm strength. "But we will figure it out."

"Tomorrow." Lita stood, the legs of her chair scraping against the tiles. "We will figure it out tomorrow. Right now, you all need to rest."

"I can't just rest," Alanor argued. I should have warned her, but she was about to learn the lesson firsthand.

"Yes, you can." Lita pinned her with a look that made even Alanor's stare seem like puppy dog eyes. The two facing off looked to be of a similar age. But of all people, I knew how looks really were only skin deep. The years Lita had on Alanor sparked between them and I had to give Alanor credit, she held her ground longer than most.

"The guest room is made up for you both. Isla needs to rest and recharge. Doing a reading is not a light thing. So, off you go, and no one wakes her or me again until at least sunbreak."

Lita disentangled Isla from my embrace, and guilt washed through me as Isla collapsed into Lita's arms. Lita scooped her up, like a wife being carried over a threshold, and headed down the hallway without a backwards glance.

"I can't just sleep," Alanor said.

"Trust me, fighting Lita is not worth it in the least."

"Yeah, I got that impression."

"Come on. I suspect once we lay down, we will both crash."

But of course, it didn't dawn on me until I opened the guest bedroom that there was only one bed inside. Lita could have summoned a change in situation, but obviously chose not to. I half cursed, half thanked her.

"I'll take the floor," I offered as soon as we stepped into the room.

"Don't be stupid."

"Offering not to barge into your space is being stupid?"

"Yes." Alanor looked at me and damn, I wish I knew what danced behind her eyes. "We kissed, Lily. We were angry, emotions took over. It happens. It doesn't mean anything. We are grown-ups; we can share a bed without being stupid."

"So now kissing me is the stupid thing?" I smirked, trying to stop the sharp pain her words had caused.

"Of course it was, now hurry up and turn out the light so I can strip down to my underwear and get some sleep."

"I thought you weren't tired?"

"I'll give Lita credit, we will all function better after we've had some sleep." She spoke the last of the words on a resigned sigh.

"Ok." I flicked off the light and distracted myself from the sound of her taking off her clothes by ridding myself of my own.

We shuffled and spoke, with overly polite and nice words as we settled into the bed.

I lay on my back, unwilling to move and disturb her, unable to relax into the exhaustion pulling at me.

"Do you really think kissing me was stupid?"

"Yes." Alanor's voice was soft and thick. "But it doesn't mean I regret it."

"So, did you want to kiss me again?" I'm sure my smile could be heard floating around the room.

But the moment of silence stretched, and I deflated. She would ignore the question.

"Yes." A whisper that thrilled me.

"So why is it stupid then?"

"Lily." She groaned a little and damn if that didn't send me over a ledge that made certain parts of me pulse.

"Good night, Larissa."

I searched for her hand in the space between us.

Slowly, giving her ample time to pull away, I interlocked our fingers in the darkness. She squeezed back.

"Good night, Lilekai."

EIGHTEEN

It couldn't have been more than an hour or two before I woke with a shiver to find the space beside me empty. I sat up and smiled at the darkness that greeted me through the gap in the curtains. But the smile faded when I turned back to the empty ruffled side of the bed where Alanor should be.

I held my breath and closed my eyes, searching for the smallest of sounds in the darkness. The muffled sobs weren't hard to locate. My feet whispered across the carpet as I followed the sobs to the small ensuite of our room.

I knocked gently and the sobbing stopped. I turned the handle and opened the door just a crack to make sure my voice could be heard.

"Can I come in?"

"Fine." Alanor's voice came back clipped, but I heard the thickness in the word, a nose blocked from crying and sniffing.

I opened the door and gently closed it behind me, leaning my back against a towel that hung from a hook on the door. Alanor sat on the closed toilet lid, knees pulled in together, a towel tucked under her arms and covering arguably the best parts of her. I appreciated the towel, although curiosity raised her head. I had enough trouble not staring at the tanned shapely legs and bare shoulders and arms.

"Are you okay?"

She tilted her head and gave me her infamous are-you-really-that-stupid-look.

"Alright, alright," I conceded. "Completely stupid question, I mean of course you aren't alright, but can I help?"

"Why are you wanting to help me, Lily?"

"I dunno." I shrugged and took the half step to the bathroom sink so I could lean on it and face Alanor without having to twist my head at an odd angle.

"I fucked up." Alanor's words looked to cost her the last of her strength as she slumped.

"Fucked up what?"

"Everything." A bitter laugh accompanied by actual tears came out with the word. It echoed around the tiles and bounced back to her. Before I could find anything to say, she barrelled on. "I love my job, I'm so fucking proud of how far I've come. I do good things for the World. But I'm so fucking jaded. I can't even believe you would want to help me without an ulterior motive. I question everything."

I watched as she lifted her eyes and stared into mine. I didn't flinch or look away. I don't think I would have been able to if I tried.

"When I first saw you, I felt electricity buzzing beneath my skin. And now I can't help but wonder if I've lost the ability to even feel love, if I ever had it in the first place. Had I been attracted to you, or am I such a cop it was all just that sixth sense when we know something isn't right about someone? You probably don't even remember seeing me before Katy introduced us. I'm such a fucking cop. Did you have any idea of how stupid I was, even then?" More tears ran over her cheeks as her voice sped up and thickened once more, trying to force the words out before another flood of tears stole her ability to speak.

"Oh, sweetheart." I dropped to my knees in front of her and cupped her face in my hands. "I saw you, too. I felt the same moment when our eyes met. You have been the person I've compared everyone else to, and you know what?"

"What?" She kept her eyes lowered, avoiding my stare.

I leaned forward and kissed tears from her right cheek.

"Not one of them," I kissed away tears from her left cheek, "came even close."

I brushed my lips against hers, just soft enough for her to feel it. I moved back but her hand was in my hair, pulling me to her lips. Our lips moved against each other, hungry and desperate. Coffee and strawberries filled my mouth as her tongue teased open my lips and plundered the depths of me.

After a moment, we pulled away from each other, both of us gasping for air.

"How about we get out of the bathroom?" I smiled, and the one she gave back to me had me very eager to get her back into bed.

"Well, this will be fun," Alanor said between kisses as we walked, not letting the other go, while hands explored beneath underwear and towel.

"That's usually the plan." I gasped as her finger slid over the cup of my bra and pinched my nipple through the material, with impressive accuracy.

"I meant–" She pushed me gently away from her, and my knees hit the back of the bed. I fell backward and looked up, mesmerised as she rid herself of the towel. The definition of her body reminded me of something chiselled. An artist's masterpiece for example. "It'll be fun seeing who wins for top."

I laughed and shook my head.

"You not going to fight me for lead?" Alanor breathed.

I raised myself up on to my elbows and shook my head slowly, grazing my eyes up and down her tanned body. Who knew this bronzed goddess hid beneath the uniform.

My libido cockily said, "Me,", raising its head and smirking.

"Good. Now lift your hands." She smirked as she slipped her fingers beneath the band of my underwear and slid them down my legs.

I heard something soft hit the carpet somewhere over toward the window. That would be fun to try and find later. But my mind blitzed out on all other cares as she stepped on to the bed and slowly lowered herself to straddle me.

I remembered her command and lifted my hands above my head, groaning as her wetness settled against my own.

Slowly, she rocked her hips back and forth and I lifted mine up to meet her.

Our breathing filled the otherwise silent room, and damn her instructions, I grabbed her hips with my hands and increased our pace, pressure, and breathing.

She laughed and leaned down, her nipples dangling invitingly in my face.

"What happened to not fighting me for lead?" She laughed as she pushed my hands above my head once more.

"You're on top." I smiled and breathed deeply as she pressed her fingers a little harder against the racing pulse at my wrist.

"Hmm, I guess you have a point." She let my hands go.

I found her hips once more and took one of the nipples hanging in front of me into my mouth and sucked.

"This is crazy," she spluttered out between pants.

"Fucking?" I murmured around her nipple.

"Fucking you," she corrected.

"I can stop."

"Don't you fucking dare!" She ran her fingers through my hair, tugging lightly as she moved her body down, her breast pressing hard to my mouth.

"Then why is it crazy?"

"Because we hate each other."

I moved my hands to her arse and ground us together as hard as I could while sucking hard enough for her nipple to harden beneath my tongue. A guttural moan escaped her.

"Oh god, yes," she breathed as she lifted up a little from me. Before I could dare complain, her fingers found their way through my wetness.

"I don't hate you."

"But you wish you did."

"Yes," I gasped as her fingers circled my entrance.

"Can I be inside you?"

"Please. Yes, please."

She pushed into me and lowered herself back down. Her thumb found my clit as she moved her fingers in and out. The combination of fingers, thumb, and body weight made me scream all the words I had learned from Green World TV shows. They were mixed with a few other sounds that had no language except for pure orgasmic bliss.

Before the rush of my orgasm subsided, I flipped Alanor onto her back, and moved us further up the bed.

Her legs opened for me; her knees bent while her feet pressed down flat against the mattress. I knelt between her thighs, tucking my arms under her knees and gripping her beautiful hips in my hands.

I took in her scent of musk and arousal and ran the flat of my tongue from her entrance to her clit. Her hips rocked beneath my mouth as I circled her clit. Soft and slow, increasing speed and pressure as her hips turned from rocking to bucking.

I worshipped her with my tongue, holding her hips and enjoying every hitch of breath and groan that escaped her.

She writhed beneath me, softer and more sensitive than I would have imagined in my wildest dreams.

And I had imagined plenty.

"May I?" I released her hip and pulled my hand back, circling her entrance as I waited for an answer.

"Yes. Fuck me."

I chuckled and eased first one finger and then a second inside of her.

"Okay?"

She panted, groaning as I moved my fingers in and out.

"Or should I not be inside you?"

"No." She put her hand over mine and pushed me further into her.

I followed directions and after a few thrusts she removed her hand, gripping the sheet beside us.

I moved in and out of her, watching her face as it contorted, her mouth opening and closing, pleasure stealing her power of speech. Reluctantly pulling my eyes away from her face, I lowered my head once more, desperate to taste her need again.

She came with a muffled scream. I lifted my head from her clit to find she had dragged a pillow over her face. She throbbed around my fingers, and I moved them lightly, enough to send another ripple through her body.

I laughed, kissed the insides of her thighs before easing myself out of her, and climbed back up her body to collapse on her shoulder. Her fingers traced patterns on my back, and I closed my eyes.

"I have a question."

"Is it too early to feign sleep?"

She tapped me lightly on my bare back.

"Fine," I chuckled, "what's the question?"

"What is your obsession with all the toy cars? Especially seeing as you can't drive them?"

I had been prepared for so many questions, things about Katy, things about being a Necromancer. But my cars? I swallowed audibly and hoped Alanor didn't hear.

"It's okay, you don't need to answer."

"No." The word came out before I knew if I wanted to or not. "I just. It's probably going to sound strange, and a little sappy maybe."

"Is it about Necromancy?"

"No, it's about before I became a minion of Death."

"Then I think we're safe on the strange front."

"Fair point." I laughed. "Alright. When I was younger, my grandpa loved working on his car. I didn't really know much about it at the time, but he let me help. Not 'help' in the sense of getting oil and grease all over me and learning how to change the tyre. I would pass him tools, and he taught me the correct way to wash it without leaving spots or streaks. He would take me for drives with the roof down and I would laugh at the wind knotting my hair and the rush of flying."

"None of that seems strange."

"I guess I tend to forget what others see as normal or strange. I seem to have developed a rather twisted perspective."

"I'll say." She laughed and a small hum escaped my lips as her fingers lightly drew circles over my back. "But why the models?"

"Because I can't have the real things. I missed out on getting to ride in cars that were made since I became a Necromancer. And trust me, I tried many different cars and many different times. As time marched on, more and more of the workings of vehicles became electrical."

I yawned and snuggled close to her side.

"Oh no" Alanor's hand slipped from my back and squeezed my bottom. "Don't think I'm finished with you yet, Lumbra."

"Lumbra?"

"That's your last name, isn't it?" She asked, eyes still closed and breath still winded.

"Yeah," I laughed, "but since when did you call me that?"

"Since I decided Lily is Katy's, and Lilekai is Death's."

"You want a part of me all to yourself?" I asked, shocked at the power the question held. It reached into my chest and squeezed my lungs. "But we hate each other."

"Doesn't mean I don't get a part of you for myself."

"Oh."

She laughed and looked down at me. I wanted her to tell me she didn't hate me either. But the look of desire pushed that hope aside.

I knew she hated me. I even understood it.

Tonight was a one-night thing. And I wasn't going to waste a minute of it hoping for things I would never have.

NINETEEN

Pressure rested on my chest as warmth lit up my closed eyelids. I blinked them awake, groaning lightly at the sunlight piercing into my eyes. Well that explained the warm eyelids, but what about the pressure on my chest.

I looked down to see spiky black hair. It wasn't another dream.

I smiled and kissed the top of her head, indulging in a moment I might never have again. I still had her taste on my lips, and her smell wrapped around me.

Her fingers twitched against my hip, and I flinched.

How had I missed where those beautiful hands had ended up? They had been all over me, but somehow in this moment, those fingers resting on my bare skin felt far more intimate.

"Oh, fuck." She woke with a start, jumped out of bed, and dragged the sheet with her. She pressed the sheet to her chest covering herself. Meanwhile, I lay completely exposed in my own nakedness.

"Good morning to you as well."

"I...I'm so sorry." She turned around and I wondered who

this woman was. This flustered, precious, and dishevelled human. "I, I, I—"

"Don't normally wake up with them the next morning?" I guessed, taking a stab in the dark.

"Never." Her voice barely made it back to me, but it brought a huge smile to my face. "You can stop smiling now."

"I really can't." I didn't even try.

"Oh, god." She groaned, not nearly as pleasing a sound as last night's groans.

"Look." I got up slowly, hoping not to spook her more than I already had. I brushed my fingers gently over her bare right shoulder.

She squeezed it between her cheek and shoulder, holding my fingers in a strange caress. Was she trying to hug me or hurt me?

I took the chance. I would never get another one like this. I stepped in and gently kissed her left shoulder before whispering. "I'm going to go see if our hosts are up and awake."

"Please don't tell them what we did last night." Her voice filled with regret.

"Okay." I slipped on shorts and tugged a singlet over my head. I didn't look at her as I slid past to the door.

I knew it would mean nothing to her. But her words hurt me more than I wanted them to. She had been right. I did want to hate her. But I never had. It became even more apparent in the harsh light of day that the feeling was not mutual.

I went to the bathroom, before following my nose to the smell of fresh coffee.

"Have I told you two lately how much I love you?" I said, walking into the kitchen.

"I don't remember you begging on your knees." Isla smiled over her coffee cup, a twinkle in her eye.

"I do." Lita winked.

Isla playfully slapped Lita's shoulder.

"Well at least someone's having a good morning," I grumbled, and took my seat at the table.

"Coffee?" Lita tilted her head to the side.

"Please."

"What happened? It seemed like you two finally got over the whole 'we aren't together like that' thing," Lita asked, slipping a mug in front of me.

"Oh shit. Don't mention that to her. One night thing." I didn't meet either of their eyes.

"You two really aren't together?" Isla's voice filled with a soft sadness that filled me with an overwhelming sense of loss.

"Um, no." I swallowed the lump in my throat. "We aren't together."

I'd never had this uncomfortable heat in my chest about not being with someone before. It usually only appeared when I gave in and tried to be what the other person wanted.

"There is something there." Isla nodded and sipped her own cup. It hadn't been a question, and sometimes I hated having these two as family.

"For me there is, there always has been." I admitted the truth easier than I thought possible. "But I'm pretty sure what you sense from her is hate and loathing, not anything else."

"There's something else." Isla nodded again, certain, and I slumped further into my chair.

"Why does that make it worse?" Lita laughed, confusion all over her face.

"You two need to realise the World outside of this home isn't always so clear and simple." I sighed. "If she feels anything else it sucks because what happened with Katy will always stop us following through. But it doesn't matter anyway." I pulled myself back up into my chair. "Once Death realises I took his orders a little too liberally, I'll be walked whether I bring the culprit to justice or not."

"Does Death think you killed the mortals?" Lita asked, always the one to cut through the chase.

"Nah, not at all." I blinked and stopped the words that were going to tumble out of my mouth. "Wait, why the hell doesn't Death think I killed them? I mean, they've had Katy's family watched, thinking I would go back for the rest of them."

Isla and Lita stared at me.

"Oh yeah, okay, I may have forgotten that part huh?"

"Tell us now." Lita was pissed, I could see it in the strong set of her jaw.

I summed up all of it, and even mentioned the poorly timed kiss. After they exchanged know-it-all looks with each other, they nodded.

"So why don't they think it's me?"

"Let's circle back to that one later." Lita shook her head, and I wasn't certain if her exasperation was aimed at me or Death or something else entirely. "Why would Death walk you?"

"She was told to wipe my memory but has since miraculously forgotten," Alanor spoke from the archway into the kitchen.

"Ah." Isla smiled, and I loved and hated her in equal measure right then.

"Have a good sleep, I trust?" Lita asked as she walked to the coffee machine. "Coffee?"

"I'm a cop, the answer is never no."

"That's her way of saying 'yes please, that would be lovely.'" I rolled my eyes at Alanor.

"Oh, sorry." Alanor blushed as she slid into her seat. "Yes, please."

"Stop that, Lily," Isla said. "Alanor, you said nothing wrong. We are family here."

She winked as though making sure Alanor understood what she meant.

The blush that covered Alanor's cheeks was a neon sign we all saw clear as day. Though when she turned to me her eyes were a stormy cloud ready to throw lightning down on me.

"So, what are your next plans?" Lita asked as she slid the fresh cup in front of Alanor and sat again beside her wife, placing an arm over the back of Isla's chair.

Isla immediately leaned into the half embrace.

"I was thinking about that," Alanor responded instantly.

"You were?" I finished my coffee and stood to get another.

"Yes, not all of us snore like they are trying to wake the dead."

I laughed and shoved my cup under the coffee machine. Nothing happened.

"What were you thinking, Alanor?" Isla asked as she stood and shooed me away from the shiny monstrosity that refused to grant me my wish.

At ten paces away, the machine finally began grinding the beans. I turned around, resting my arse against the bench and waited for the fresh cup.

I didn't see the point in sitting down when I had decided I would have my weight in coffee before I left their house again. Plus, I wouldn't want to accidentally brush Alanor's leg and have either of us react and once again announce the detective had lowered herself to my level.

"What exactly do the two of you do?" Alanor held up her hand to me, without even looking. It's like she knew I thought she was being rude to my family. "I know what I saw last night. But I get a feeling there is more here."

"She's cluey, this one." Lita looked at me and jerked her head toward Alanor. "I like her, don't go fucking this up."

I spluttered, unable to articulate a single sound. Lita was swearing as though it were nothing, and what the hell. Had she heard anything I said earlier? Having a family didn't always seem to be such a great idea. Especially moments like this.

"We are Witches." Isla smiled at Alanor as though Lita had not spoken at all. "We became one of Death's minions when the world still believed in magic. Death, a different Death to Lily's, damn near pleaded for us to become Necromancers. We refused but did agree to assist them."

"With a few terms and conditions." Lita picked up the story, and I listened as though I hadn't heard it a hundred times or more. "One being that we retain our magic, no matter what."

"So, what can you do?" Alanor asked.

"Is there a point to this?" I asked. But the way Lita told it, something had changed from every previous telling. "Wait. Assist them? You agreed to be minions, didn't you?"

Lita and Isla exchanged a look that sent shivers running up my spine, as though a thousand spiders had been let loose.

"No, we did not. They bound us later as minions. Because we demanded to be allowed to keep our magic, we were ranked as Witches."

"And you never fucking bothered to tell me this before?"

All three turned and gave their own silent versions of shut the hell up.

I rolled my eyes, huffed out air through my nose, and gulped my coffee. It burnt as I swallowed, hoping it would soon settle my nerves.

"I am good at personification. Which means making inanimate objects human. Like the front windows, they act exactly like eyes," Lita replied.

"Cool." Alanor smiled and a small slithering snake of jealousy worked its way up from the pit of my stomach, scorching a trail over my ribs and lodging itself into the hollow of my neck. "But that's not what I saw last night."

"No." Lita smiled again. "I can also read energies and powers. I transfer what I read to Isla who is a tracer."

"I can find the energy, if I know what I'm looking for. Past, present, and in some rare cases, future energy as well." Isla shrugged as though these things were completely inconsequential.

"Oh, I was hoping you would say something like that." The excitement in Alanor's voice and the energy in her body seemed to vibrate, though she sat perfectly still.

"Who do you want tracked?" Isla asked, ignoring Lita's scowl.

"Jen and Daria," Alanor replied.

"Death already tried to find Jen." I felt a strange desire to contribute to this exchange, almost as though I was at risk of being pushed to the sidelines, where I had been so many times, more often than I realised.

Lita scoffed and from beneath the table she kicked my chair out a little further from where I had left it.

"It's time for you to sit and finally listen, Lilekai." She nodded to the chair, pointedly telling me to sit down and shut up.

"No." The word came out before I could stop it. I wasn't sure I wanted to stop it.

"No?" Lita lifted her eyebrows slowly, and I felt my resolve melt like butter under heat.

"Not when you use the mum tone and look at me like that." I forced the lightness in my words, but anger sparked. I was hotheaded, I knew that. I was impulsive and reckless but being treated like a child and kept from the truth hurt.

"Come sit down, Lily." Isla laughed a little as she spoke softly, an attempt to calm my bristling nerves.

I topped up my cup. I had a very strong suspicion that three cups were not going to be nearly enough for this conversation.

"What do you know about Death and their powers?" Isla asked once I finally took my seat back at the table.

"They're Death. They can find souls no matter where they are. They told me once that all souls have a unique trace, like fingerprints. And they can find anyone at any time."

"Ah." Isla held up a finger. "Then how do they not know where Jen is? How do they struggle to stop the Grims when they are in the Green World?"

"Because they are Grims." It sounded weak, even to my own ears. "And Theamin explained that whoever is killing these people is cloaking the Green World.'

"The Grim are still souls. And someone capable of stopping Death from finding souls? Death is not so easily stopped, or so they'd have us believe."

"Okay." My spidey-senses were tingling in all manner of hyperactivity. "Then Death should be able to find Jen and Daria. Why would they lie to me?"

"Because long ago, the previous Death was more open

about what they could and couldn't do. They were forced into the Dark World, and things were very bad for a very long time."

"The Dark Ages?" Alanor asked, and I wanted to slap my palm so hard against my head.

"The one and the same." Lita nodded, a beaming smile on her face. She had never looked at me with such admiration.

"What can Death actually do, then?" My heart seemed to be slipping out from behind my ribs and right down to the very soles of my shoes.

"Death can do many things, but they cannot find all souls at any given time. If a soul does not wish to be found, it is easy enough to hide themselves from the great Necromancer."

"But–" Alanor's smile was beautiful. I admired her strength. My Worlds were disintegrating around me and I felt stuck in place. Her entire life had just changed, and she carried on, excited at prospects she had worked out on her own. "You can find the souls with your magic, can't you?"

"I can locate a soul if I have the right information." Isla looked pointedly at me and waved her hand a little in the air. "Or I've met them and shook their hands."

"That's why you insist on shaking everyone's hand when they come here?" My jaw dropped.

"And it's considered polite in most circles," Isla said, nose slightly lifted.

Lita chuckled beside her wife.

"Y'all have been holding out on me." The words came out as petulant as a teenager learning their parents had a life before they existed.

"Not at all." Isla reached out and patted me on the back of my hand.

If anyone else had tried it, I would have scowled and pulled away, despising their patronisation. But Isla meant the things she said and did. That didn't stop me from being hurt.

"Why didn't you tell me about Death's limitations?"

"Honestly," Lita answered, "you weren't ready to hear that they weren't a true god."

The information hit hard, a punch to the chest. But it didn't unsettle me as it should. Things had been off, ever since my banishment.

But that shit could wait.

"Okay." I nodded. "So, you can find Jen?"

The silence that answered me stifled the air in the room and pressed down like too much gravity against my shoulders.

"I can, but I think you need to focus on the investigation for now."

"I need to find Jen."

"It will take time, Lily," Lita snapped. "And while we are finding her, you need to be fulfilling your promise to help Alanor with the case."

And just like that, I felt abandoned and kicked out. They had known her for a minute and already, they took her side over my own.

"Fine, so what now?" I asked.

"You need to see the other body. We need to know for sure if they have been trapped as well," Alanor said. I wanted to be impressed, but a red haze of anger had fallen in front of me.

"Jen could be responsible for all of this. You do understand that right, Lily?" Isla asked.

"No." I shook my head. "I don't care how similar their eyes are. This isn't Jen."

Alanor's hand slipped beneath the table and rested on my knee. I jumped a little, the touch unexpected, but no one at the table reacted and I thanked them all for the small mercy. But Alanor still hated me, no matter the touch. I repeated that several times, trying in vain to stop my head and my heart running away with me. The touch meant nothing, I couldn't let myself believe she actually cared.

"You need to prepare yourself for that possibility," Lita snapped.

"No," I shook my head again, biting back the desire to tell them to go fuck themselves, all of them. "You're talking about Jen. She's the only one from the Grey World who stood by me. She helped me find Katy's burial and–"

"She hated Katy, you even said so."

"She hated how much I enjoyed spending time with Katy. She was jealous, but she's not the kind to hurt anyone. Besides, she was the one who convinced Death to let me take the cottage so I could visit Katy."

"The cottage isn't yours?" Alanor frowned.

"Nothing is ever ours," Isla said, a rare edge to her voice. "Once you become one of Death's minions, nothing ever belongs to you again. You can take leave of the Grey World, but even then, you are little more than an indentured slave."

"Is that the real reason Witches live solely in the Green World?"

"There are rooms in the Grey World for Witches, but it doesn't take long for any of us to leave and become part of the Green World."

"Do you hate them?" The words were a shock to me as they tumbled from my mouth.

"No." Isla patted my hand again then removed her fingers. "We do not hate your Death. They never lied to us. They've never lied to any of those they have recruited. Do you remember what they told you?"

"As a Necromancer you belong to me, all that you have and all that you are will forever belong to me, this day forward," I repeated the words without a second thought.

"And you agreed to this?" Alanor looked disgusted.

"My options were that or the final walk of death."

"Oh." That deflated Alanor's anger instantly.

"We were never told this. We were told we would be like gods; we would know the secrets of life and death and be able to control those that remained with their mortality."

"What?" I stared at Lita. "Are you serious?"

"It was called the Dark Ages for a reason. That's only one of the many reasons that Death ended up being walked to the Dark World."

"Why is none of this known? Why don't all minions get told this history?"

"Because," Lita shrugged, "it can all be used against them. Death now is a far kinder soul and they never did enjoy the role they played in their predecessors final banishment. But they also know how precarious their throne is. They will protect it every way they can until they find another Necromancer they believe will serve our Worlds, and not their own purposes."

It made sense. Too much horrid sense that made me hate my stupidity and youth. I had been so willing to believe, to question only those things I wanted to.

"You will help me find Jen?" I asked. "When you have everything you need?"

"What do you need?" Alanor asked.

"Only time and energy. She has everything else she needs." I smiled knowingly, rolling my eyes at Lita's big grin.

"Absolutely," Isla said with a smile and a nod.

"Wanna clue the moron in?" Alanor snapped out the question.

"You aren't a moron," Lita said. "These two have their own language. They always have. All Isla needs to find a soul she has previously met, is another one searching for them. She will not do it for anyone who wishes ill intent on the first soul."

"But you can't do it now?" Alanor asked.

"Not yet. Lita and I must summon more power. But during that time, Lily, you should go learn what you can about the bodies and how the souls have been stitched."

"Alanor, you're up. What's the plan?" I asked.

"You're not going to like it."

"Well now, that's not really a shock, is it?"

All three at the table laughed and I smiled. Pain still throbbed around the outside of my heart, but inside I knew I would never stop loving any of them.

"And this is why I get paid the big bucks, you fuckers," Alanor called out to the room of cops as she pulled me by my arm. I breathed through my mouth, forcing away the memories of other fingers gripping my upper arm.

Seriously, what was it about authority and this grip? Did they have a training day or something?

My wrists were cuffed behind my back, my heart jackhammered away in my chest. She had asked me to trust her, but this...this made my breath come in short sharp gasps as she walked me through the office and into a small room.

From the doorway, the room seemed plain enough; a desk, a bookshelf, a filing cabinet with a second drawer that didn't quite close flush, and the piece de resistance, an uncomfortable looking "guest" chair.

She nudged me, not too kindly through the door of the room. I looked back over my shoulder to see a whole host of faces looking back at me. A range of expressions stared back, from smug to terrified. I assumed the latter might actually be on my behalf. It did little to calm my racing heart.

"Sit."

It irked just how easily my body complied to the order,

taking the seat she pointed to, the uncomfortable one that proved looks weren't always deceiving.

Once I sat, she closed the door with a decisive and altogether too loud bang, then snapped the blinds on the window closed.

She turned to me, her face hard and cold. The face I had known far longer than the one who smiled at me when she believed no one else was looking.

We stared at each other, and my stomach tightened, remembering the same standoff only a few days ago when the first body had been found.

"Well, that went well." Her face broke and her cockiness reigned supreme. "I never knew you were such a good actor, but I shouldn't be surprised. You basically do nothing but act."

In such a short number of words, I had relaxed only to tense back up again. Is that what she thought of me? An actor, nothing more than a liar?

"I don't act."

"It's okay. I understand it to a degree now." Her eyes narrowed, boring into my face and I flinched, wondering what she saw. "What's wrong?"

"You think all I do is act some part? Like I'm just a persona for the Green World?"

She didn't answer, her face processing thoughts she didn't allow me to be privy to.

I pulled against the cuffs, wanting to wave my hands and arms. "The cuffs?"

"Right, sorry." She stood and I lifted my hands higher for her to reach them easier. But she didn't stop at where I sat.

"Time to act scared." She said as she put her hand on the door handle.

"Who's acting?" I scoffed.

She opened the door in the middle of her laugh. It hit the

wall as she pulled it open before returning to where I sat. She grabbed my arm and pulled me to my feet.

I was genuinely considering death for the next arsehole who grabbed my arm like that.

"You want to know what this is all about?" Alanor snapped. "Why don't I show you?"

The hush in the station settled unnaturally. We walked past people frozen as statues and I saw their faces. The range of emotions slapped me in the face. No wonder she hadn't let me in on her plan. I would have nixed this bullshit the moment she suggested it.

I was wound up like a jack-in-the-box, ready to spring. Those things were terrifying, and I knew if I had to, I could truly scare Alanor just as well. But I had never enjoyed doing that. I had used that part of my powers only a handful of times in all those years.

I gasped as I realised what it all meant. They had been right. I had never had to earn these powers back. I had simply not tried to use them having believed every word Death had said. Why had Death returned them without a word or any acknowledgement. Why did they care so much about having banished me? They had banished others before, so why was mine so out of line?

Alanor swore at people who got in her way, and she rumbled words at me to create fear. And while a good part of me hoped she was the one acting, enough uncertainty remained for me there that the fear I showed needed no pretending.

Alanor pushed open the door. The cold air whooshed out and washed over me, but I knew where we were without needing to be told. Death, that of mortals and not the person who had recruited me as a minion, hummed inside, past the threshold of the room.

Alanor pulled me through behind her, but as soon as the door closed she moved around me. Behind me, she unlocked the cuffs.

"I'm sorry. But I needed a real reaction from you. Plus, I kind of enjoyed you in handcuffs." Her cheeks pinked in uneven splatters of colour.

"Are you always such an arsehole at work?" I rubbed my wrists, giving her a chance to get back in control of her body's reaction.

"Honestly? Nah." She looked sheepish with her grin. "They all know it's just a show for the bad guys."

"So, you don't call them 'fuckers?'"

"Oh, no.'" She barked out a laugh. "I absolutely do that. And the fuckers really do hate me."

I laughed but it stopped short and sharp, as I looked around taking in everything in the room.

"Oh, shit." I fell to my knees. Even the impact of my kneecaps hitting hard tiled flooring couldn't pull my attention away from what I stared at.

And what stared back at me.

"It's the same?" Alanor's voice was soft behind me. Soft, but not gentle.

All I could do was nod. There were no words for what I saw. Two bodies lay on tables beside each other. They were covered except for their faces, but the white sheets did nothing to hide what I saw.

Their souls sobbed and rocked back and forth.

"Oh, Death," I murmured. Something tickled my cheeks, and I lifted my fingers without blinking. My fingertips came away wet. Only then did I realise I sat on the floor of the morgue and sobbed as two souls shifted between sobbing and the screams of the damned.

"I'm so sorry. I don't know who did this, but I will find them. I will help you get out of there."

"You can't help us." The souls, transparent and grey as a campfire's smoke, turned as one and glared at me.

Dead souls didn't talk, didn't interact with the Green World, not unless granted permission by their transfer Necromancer.

I had not invoked any such permissions.

I gulped air and moved to stand. The world tilted, and I no longer saw the souls, or the dead bodies that tethered them.

Darkness embraced me and I sighed with relief.

"Where are they?" I asked. My eyes flew open, and my hands curled, ready to channel whatever power remained in me. "Ouch."

The morgue had disappeared, replaced by a much nicer room. I lay on a black couch. It was made with something less sticky than leather, and it pressed against my skin with a softness that reminded me of a warm hug.

"Hey." Alanor knelt beside me on the couch, brushing fingertips over my forehead, and through my hair.

"Well, not exactly the way I thought I'd ever see you on your knees again, but I'll take it."

She laughed and shook her head, but her eyes remained focused on me, and what I saw in them turned my stomach into a springboard diver in the Olympics.

"What happened?"

"You scared the shit out of me," said, "I thought you had fucking died and I'd have to explain to my boss that I showed a potential suspect two dead bodies and that had killed her."

"Right, can't have you losing your job." I tried for light humour. I failed.

"What happened?"

"It's the same." I nodded, confirming for myself the truth of what I had seen. "The second soul had the same dark shape around it, the fear and pain surrounding them."

"Is that what happened to Katy?"

"No." I shook my head. "Katy was scared. She couldn't hear me and I couldn't hear her. But these ones can."

"Why does that matter?"

'I'm not entirely certain. But I don't think this is just about me anymore.'

"What is it about?"

"It's about Grims."

"What?" She blinked at me. "You said you aren't a Grim."

"I'm not," I snapped and then took a deep breath. "I'm not a Grim. A Grim is a Necromancer who has turned against humanity. They use their powers not to guide the dead, but to enslave souls. They unbalance the Worlds and threaten the Grey World's existence."

"So Grims can cause the whole World to what? Explode?"

"If there are enough of them, and they collapse the Grey World, then the final gates will collide with us. Every soul that has ever been will be able to return to our World."

"But what can that do?"

"Souls are the strongest part of us. A soul can manifest anything and everything."

"What does that mean, Lumbra?"

"It means, the souls of all those who have been walked to the Dark World get another chance to wreak havoc on the World. A havoc that only Death stopped. In your World, in your terms, it means murderers will be free to do whatever they want without end, and they won't be stopped by something as simple as Death, because Death will no longer happen, not in any way it does now. There will be no power strong enough to force them back through to the Dark World and to shut those doors again."

"How do you know that?"

"Because it happened once."

"Why can't the doors be closed again then, like they were last time?"

"The cost will be too great." I shook my head. "So yes, fine. It can be done. But the cost is too great."

"What is the cost?"

"You have seen the Grey World. You have seen the bones that decorate it."

"Yes." Alanor's face darkened and I knew her thoughts were heading down the right track.

"Those bones were all once magic users. They sacrificed themselves to create the gap between Worlds again. To shut the doors on Death."

"That's horrible."

"Oh," I huffed out a shuddering sound. "It doesn't end there. The mists of the Grey World."

"No." Alanor shook her head, horror widening and filling her eyes. "No."

"The mists are the souls of all those who died, who sacrificed themselves. The souls of those bones that remain in the Chamber of Death. The skeletons that line the halls, the bones beneath the floor. Every single one of them. They *are* the Grey World."

Alanor rushed to the bin beside her desk and threw up. I left her to her processing and forced my breath to ease down enough to sit back up.

"What are you doing?" Alanor was beside me in seconds as I stood up from the couch.

"What I need to do."

"Stop." Alanor reached for my arm.

I yanked it out of reach. "Do not grab me again like I am some kind of bad guy here."

"I wasn't going to."

"I'm not the bad guy here. I never meant to hurt Katy. I didn't understand. I was broken and grieving, and I fucked up. But I'm not going to let you or anyone else stop me from all of those sacrifices being in vain. I will not let the Grey World disappear."

"What do you need?" Alanor's face had paled, but the strength in her words remained absolute.

With a little more preparation, I managed to stay conscious the second time I stepped into the police morgue. The two souls looked up when I crossed the threshold. Alanor hovered beside me, keeping pace step for step. I assumed she remained so close in preparation for another black out.

The souls remained tethered, I didn't expect anything else, but still the sight unsettled me. Their shadowy forms lingered above the sheets, the bottom of their bodies disappearing beneath.

"Hi." Well, I couldn't blame them for their tilted head responses to that idiotic introduction. "Can you understand me?" I inched closer.

Alanor did the same. Nope, definitely not disconcerting at all.

I stole a look at her, and while she managed to keep a neutral expression on her features, in her eyes I could see the questions building. I looked forward to the questions, even if it were in the hopes of getting another taste of coffee and straw-berries.

"Do...do you know who did this to you?"

"Who killed us?" Brian answered. His soul shivered, as though it was in a freezer.

I closed my eyes. He *was* in a freezer. This was all levels of fucked up.

"Yes, do you remember anything?"

"I remember a dark cloak. Death came for me," Brian answered.

"And me also." The other soul's voice was softer, sadder. "They never spoke. They swept in and the pain exploded in my head. It's still there, throbbing. But then she picked me up by my head and I screamed, and she laughed, muttering something about the stars."

"She?" I latched on to the word. That would rule Theamin in, and she already sat right at the top of my list.

The dead man nodded. "I...I think so. I don't know. The laugh, so high pitched."

Brian shook his head. "No, it was a man. He was too strong to be female."

I bristled at the binary sexism, but they couldn't know that strength as a Necromancer came from somewhere entirely different.

"What's happening?" Alanor asked.

"Sounds like they were killed by a Grim," I replied.

"The Necromancers that go bad. How the fuck do Necro-mancers go bad?" Alanor's eyes were so wide they were almost comical.

"Because humans are fucked up no matter which World they live in."

I no longer wanted to put the pieces of the puzzle together just to understand. I wanted to make sure this Grim was revealed and stopped. They had a goal that seemed apparent enough. But the goal didn't make sense, not really.

Were they trying to frame me and get me sent to the Dark World? Had I simply been an easy scapegoat?

My curiosity shifted into an angry rage.

"If this Grim wants me out of the way, they've got another think coming." I turned back to the souls, to Brian and...the other one. "What are your names?"

"Brian."

"Geoff."

"Alright. I'm so sorry for what has happened. But I'll find them, and I'll help you move on."

"But our bodies are right here." Brian's insubstantial-looking hand waved to the dead flesh attached to him, though thankfully hidden beneath the sheet. "Just put us back."

"I can't." The words lodged in my throat.

"Can't or won't?"

"I can't. I don't have that power. I can only find a way to help you move on. Separate the soul from the body."

Geoff's soul sobbed and I wanted to comfort him, but my comforting skills came from being a walker. I couldn't give them the same words as I gave Rose and the million others I had walked through the Grey World with.

"I'm sick of being behind this fucker." Alanor broke the tension in the room.

"Alright, Detective," I snarled, turning away from the men and slamming my hands onto my hips. "How do you plan to proceed?"

She glared back at me, and I no longer cared. She could go right back to hating me. Sure, the hiatus was a nice break, and damn did I ever want to touch her and taste her again. I wanted to kiss her into oblivion.

But I was over caring about anyone's opinion of me, even hers.

"First, you need to channel your pissed off attitude toward the Grim, not toward me." She tried to project calm, but I saw that pissed off pulse at her temple.

"And then?"

"We get Lita and Isla to do their thing and we find this motherfucker."

I nodded, a sharp single head down movement.

"I'm coming back for you both. I promise." I turned to them both before I followed Alanor to the door of the morgue.

"But the stars, they hurt so much. Please can't you make the stars stop?" Geoff's soft voice followed me to the door. The soft whoosh as the door opened almost drowned out his next words. "Orion's belt hurts."

My blood ran as cold as the freezer.

Before I could say anything, before I could step back inside and check that Geoff didn't just say what I thought he'd said, the room went black and the door swished closed again, separating me and the trapped souls.

TWENTY-TWO

I moved in a haze, smiling and brushing away Alanor's concerns without meeting her eyes. I needed time to think. I needed space away from all the voices and outside noises pressing in against me. I didn't want to think about the stars, I couldn't. There was no way I had heard Geoff correctly. There couldn't be. I didn't have the time. And I couldn't, I wouldn't disappear on them, not even to work things through. I should have gone back to the morgue; I should have demanded Alanor show me how they died. But fear filled my chest and instead, I Shimmered us to Isla's place.

"I don't know what happened in there," Alanor whispered to Isla and Lita as though I couldn't hear them. "But something at the end spooked her."

"My sweet Lily?" Isla approached me as though I were an easily startled animal. Her hands were half raised and her shoulders tilted the slightest bit forward, as though I could spook at any time. To be fair, she wasn't too far off the mark.

"What happened at the morgue?" Lita cut through the tension and the bullshit.

"They're the same," I spoke, in a voice not even I recognised.

"That doesn't mean we're right about it being a Grim." Lita's answer pulled me out of my haze, enough for me to glare at her.

"What else could it be? They are trapped to their bodies, they can speak without permission, they can hear me, and they can feel the cold."

"What?" The colour drained from Isla's face.

"What does that mean?" Alanor glanced around at all of us.

We still stood in the hallway, in the beam of light shining through the window that shouldn't be able to see outside, let alone bring the outside in.

"It means," I swallowed, "that whether or not the monster who killed them is a Grim, their intentions are to make Grims."

"Make Grims?"

"I didn't know until Katy, that Grims weren't just Necromancers turned dark. There are other ways to become a Grim. And not all of them are with the consent of the soul."

"Trapping a soul turns them into a Grim?" The tremor in Alanor's voice made me snap back from whatever numbness had overwhelmed me.

"Only if they are left too long tethered to the body," Isla answered.

"How long is too long?" Alanor asked.

"Let's move into the kitchen." Lita spoke with such command we all moved further into the house without argument or delay.

Isla made coffee, while Alanor excused herself to the bathroom. Lita sat across from me at the table, as Isla started to softly hum and leaned forward.

"What else?"

"What?" I had a shit poker face, but that didn't mean I didn't at least try.

"What aren't you telling us Lily?"

"There's something Geoff said." There was no point arguing with Lita on the best of days, let alone when her eyes narrowed at me like that. "Something that I don't know what it means yet. Or if it means anything."

"What did he say?"

"Please." I looked at Alanor as she came back into the room and walked directly to Isla.

They murmured soft words I couldn't make out.

"Just trust me. Once I know if it matters, I will tell you."

"You better not be thinking of stupid shit, Lily." Lita's voice returned to its normal volume and Alanor responded with a guffaw.

"Lily, doing stupid shit? Never." Alanor smirked as she sat in the chair next to me.

The words were good, and even her delivery hit pretty close to the mark, but the tension that lay over all of us remained thick, dampening the space between us.

"Time to begin," Lita announced, once everyone's coffee cups were empty.

Isla placed her hands palms up on the table.

"I need silence from all of you." Without need for any other instruction we held hands and soon, we breathed in the slow same rhythm Isla set.

It didn't take long. It didn't take nearly long enough to prepare me for what I saw.

At first, the image was innocuous enough. I recognised the room. It was Jen's. The same washed-out colours that tainted all of the Grey World permeated the room.

One of Jen's rebellions against Death came in the form of bright yellow sunflowers painted over every wall. She had to reapply the paint regularly to overcome the draining of the Grey World.

Death once told me they loved visiting her room, because they missed the colours of the Green World. But they played the annoyed parent, knowing if they didn't Jen would stop reapplying the paint.

The relationship between daughter and parent had always been a strange one. But this admittance of theirs to missing the Green World had shocked me. They rarely stepped through the Barrier, and Shimmering didn't work for them. But it hadn't occurred to me until then that they actually missed it.

We scanned the room, Isla's images pressed into our minds. I squeezed the hands I held on to, and both hands squeezed back.

Jen sat at the foot of her bed, knees curled up to her chest and fingers locked into her hair. She looked up, as though sensing our presence, and I gasped. Her eye was black and dried blood covered the gap between her nose and top lip.

Laying on the bed, head on the pillow, body too still for my liking, was Daria.

"What the fuck?" I heard Alanor's words as an echo, once in the Green World and again in the Grey World.

Jen jumped to her feet, eyes wild and crazy searching the room for the source of the words.

"Shh." It was a low sound, barely audible in either World, but I knew it to be Lita's command.

I felt Alanor's fingers pull against my own, trying to disengage. I held tighter, wishing I could reassure her, alleviate her of what I could only imagine she might be thinking, of herself and of the situation.

"Who's there?" Jen pulled me back to her.

At Jen's words, Daria groaned and moved slightly on the bed. I let out a relieved breath and swallowed over the lump in my throat. Something had happened, and Daria had been hurt. I knew where the others would go, but I couldn't.

It wasn't Jen. She was not the bad guy.

"You can't touch me you arseholes. Do you know who I am? I am Death's daughter. I will remain long after you. I am heir to their kingdom and you cannot touch me!" Jen screamed into the void of her room.

The image disappeared, and the Green World around us took back over my senses.

The small tick of the clock above the bench with the jars of herbs all labelled in Lita's cursive writing slowed my racing heart. Other sounds filtered in slowly. The faint calls of children came in from outside. The sound of the water bubbling in the coffee machine.

"Drink up, you'll warm up soon enough." Lita placed a second cup of coffee in front of me and only then did I realise I was shivering.

"Thanks." My fingers tingled around the warm cup. Warmth flooded back to them after the chill of the Grey World.

"What the fuck was that?" Alanor, half her coffee already drunk, asked the room.

"Jen is in the Grey World, with Daria," I answered.

"Lily," Isla began.

"No." I sipped, shaking my head."She's not the bad guy."

"The wounds on her are consistent with someone defending themselves," Alanor said.

"Consistent with her being in a fight, any fight. You're only wanting it to fit because you want all of this to end, no matter the consequences, just so you can get another tick on your career jacket."

"You don't know shit about me, so don't act like you do. If you won't help me question her, I'll find some other way to get my answers."

Something itched at the back of my head. I rubbed small circles at my temples as I struggled to find the missing pieces. I could see the shape and form taking place in my mind, but there was also something else that hinted around the edge. If only I could see it more clearly and connect the dots that my mind insisted were there.

"How were they actually killed?" Why had I not asked such a simple question before now?

"What?" Alanor snarled at me.

"How were they killed? Brian and Geoff?"

"Three small calibre wounds in the back of their skulls. We still don't know what the weapon was," Alanor said. "Though the image you showed me last night showed Je...the green-eyed Necromancer jamming their fingers into Brian's skull."

I turned to Isla and waited for her nodding confirmation.

"That's not a way one would normally kill a human." I shook my head.

"What's your point?" Alanor asked.

Silence settled over us. The connections I was making didn't make any sense. None whatsoever. Even minions could go crazy, and I couldn't risk them thinking that before I determined how everything connected.

"I know you don't want it to be Jen, neither do we, but—" Lita began.

"No, it's not that. I know it's not Jen, but the other pieces don't fit yet. It doesn't make sense." This was not the way to prove to them I hadn't gone crazy. I stood and started to pace the kitchen.

"Do you want to see them, the wounds? Do you want to see the bodies again?" Alanor asked.

I blinked and met Alanor's eyes. After a few seconds I shook my head. "No, that's not going to give me the answers I need."

"What's the question, Lily?" Isla asked, while Lita narrowed her eyes at me.

"How all of it fits together."

"Very vague." Alanor rolled her eyes.

"What do you want, to grab a white board and list all the pieces to a puzzle that makes no sense?"

All three sets of eyes looked at me, and small smiles broke on their faces.

"That's a brilliant idea, Lily."

"It wasn't an idea, it was a snarky comment."

"Either way." Alanor smiled and shrugged.

Lita and Isla chuckled and for a moment I wondered if I were the only sane one in the room.

Katy and I laughed as we ate Chinese omelettes over a small table in the restaurant across the road from the tattoo parlour.

"I can't believe you've never got a tattoo before." Katy laughed between mouthfuls of her dinner, washing it down with lemonade.

It had taken me three months of intense time and energy to convince her that not all meals needed to be consumed with alcohol. I had no issue with alcohol in a broad sense, but I knew more about Katy then even she knew. She used any substance she could to make the things she saw, the Grey World and the monsters that went bump in the night, fade from her mind and for short moments, her eyes.

"I never really thought about it before now, to be honest." I shrugged.

"You aren't going to back down on me, are you?"

"Hell no." I smiled and shook my head.

I didn't admit how much I looked forward to the experience. I had been around for so many years, new experiences were few and far between.

It had taken less time than I thought possible to find an old-style tattooist who used a hammer and nail to tattoo instead of an electric gun. But nothing would stop me from going through with it. Seeing Katy's excitement had been icing on the cake.

The tattoo itself was simple enough. Three stars in a not quite straight line. Placement had been my biggest concern. In the end, the back of the neck had been the most logical place, hidden when needed and shown off when desired.

"Lilekai!" The name may as well have been accompanied by a slap to the face. Everything stung, so maybe a slap really had been involved.

"I think I know who did this, and it's not Jen," I blurted.

"Okay?" Alanor looked at me. We were on eye level. She crouched in front of me and only then did I realise her hands cradled my face. So, not a slap?

"I just don't know how it's possible. Or why her eyes look so much like Jen's."

"Whose eyes, Lily?" Isla asked.

I looked around at the small living room at Lita and Isla's that I rarely ever saw. When had we moved in here?

"Why are we in here?"

"You decided to go all catatonic on us. We moved you in here." Lita was the only one standing. Her shoulders rested lightly on Isla's shoulders, one of Isla's hands covering one of Lita's.

"How long?" My mouth was dry and parched.

"A few hours," Alanor answered.

"How many?"

"Five," Lita snapped. "Five hours of you being entirely unresponsive and scaring the shit out of all of us."

"I'm sorry." I spoke the words, knowing I apologised for far more than they realised. I never apologised before, I always asked forgiveness afterwards. But I didn't need forgiveness. There would be no coming back from this. I didn't have all the pieces, but I knew where to go to get them.

"What is the thing you aren't sure is connected or not?" Lita asked.

"If it's not connected it will just create pain when it's not needed," I pleaded. I didn't want to bring it up. Not again. Too many feelings warred inside of me.

"We can help you work out if it's important." Alanor sat back on her heels and the lack of contact had been all I had been waiting for.

"It's Katy."

The room fell silent. Eyes widened with emotions I didn't look close enough to examine. I couldn't.

"I need air. I'm sorry. I promise I'll be back."

Unless I get walked.

Before they could respond, before Alanor could reach forward again, the Shimmer washed through me and the last thing I saw was three sets of eyes staring at me. None of them look pleased.

TWENTY-THREE

The cold chill of the Grey World washed over me for the third time in just as many days. This shit was not what I signed up for when I accepted my banishment. How I ever put up with these constant whiplash changes was now beyond me. Hot and cold, Green and Grey, Light and Dark.

I shook my head, turned in a circle, and took in my surroundings. This Shimmer had not gone according to plan. I supposed it made sense. I had rushed and made too many Shimmers in quick succession. First to home, in case Lita or Isla bothered to track me, then to the cemetery, before heading to the Grey World.

But more importantly than the timing was the adrenaline rushing through my body. It might have been fear, but it had been so long since fear had taken any true root within me it was hard to tell.

I had aimed to Shimmer directly into Jen's room.

I had instead landed just outside of my own Grey World room. The bare one I used only when I came to recharge.

I walked back toward Death's Central Chamber so I could make my way down to the Resurrectionists' corridor and then on to Jen's room. My teeth chattered and my breath came out in frosted swirls, reminding me of dragon's breath as all the kids called it when I was young.

I slipped unharried into the Resurrectionists' corridor. It didn't seem possible Death would be unaware of my presence, but why they hadn't sent someone to fetch me uncurled vines of worry in my chest. I could focus on that later. First I needed to find Jen and Daria.

Jen's room was a dark oak door, three from the right.

"One, two." I reached out my hand to take the handle of the third door, but my fingers enclosed around an unfamiliar shape. Looking down, I blinked uncomprehendingly at the skull doorknob that greeted me from a bright purple door.

This was the fourth.

"For fuck's sake." I rubbed my forehead and paced back to the start of the corridor. I counted again and at three found myself looking at the skull once more.

"What the fuck? A room can't just vanish."

Stiff and sore from the cold and fear, I kicked at the base of the purple door. At least if I pissed someone off, I could at least ask what the fuck was going on. The quiet of the corridors scared me to my very bones.

"Where the hell are the minions? I need a fucking robe." I wanted to giggle. I had spent too much time around Alanor, that was for sure. The curses rolled off my tongue as though the language were natural to me. But nothing actually felt funny, especially when you were freezing your tits off.

A robe landed warm and heavy on my shoulders. I turned to thank the minion responsible and stared instead at Death's face.

"Death," I managed to say before they collapsed into my arms. "Well, shit."

They should have weighed more.

"I mean, sure you're nothing but skin and bone, but still," I huffed between grunts while I half carried, half dragged Death down the corridor. "This should be a lot harder. I mean, I haven't worked out in years and all the pastries and cakes I have with the coffee. This should definitely be harder."

I finally stopped rambling, my nerves shot, and my anxiety and fear had both taken to the sky with rocket speed. I stood in front of the door to my own room faced with another conundrum.

Death occupied both of my hands, arms, and thighs because of the struggle involved in wrestling them there. I had no way to open the door without dropping them.

"Sorry, mate, but needs must." I had been in the Green World longer than I had realised. But despite the exertion I smiled, even as I lowered Death to the ground. There was temptation to simply drop them, but after all the years, despite the recent knowledge I'd gained of their fallibility, Death still created me, and I remained one of their minions.

I opened the door and froze. No more than a foot inside my door stood a second door. The dark oak door that belonged three doors on the right of the Resurrectionists corridor.

I opened the door and Jen's room looked almost exactly like it had in the vision Lita and Isla had shown us.

Daria still lay on the bed, but Jen was nowhere to be seen. I picked Death back up and dragged them over both thresholds and laid them top and tail with Daria on Jen's bed. That will be fun to explain later. If I had a later.

The sunflowers that covered the walls were almost devoid of colour, the barest hints of yellow petals and dark green leaves the only signs they had ever once been coloured.

"Where are you, Jen?" I chewed on my bottom lip. It'd been five hours. How long had they been here, and how long ago did she leave?

"Please don't wake up. I've no way to explain any of this just yet. But please don't be fucking *dead* dead," I muttered as I pushed Death's cowl back from their face.

"They aren't dead, but they won't wake up, not yet at least. Not after what they've been through."

I whirled around to find Theamin standing at the threshold of my room, not having stepped inside even to Jen's door.

"Seriously, you?" I groaned, rolling my eyes. "And here I was thinking you were too damn obvious."

"You'd like that, wouldn't you?" She scoffed and stepped over my threshold and then Jen's. "It would be all so easy for you wouldn't it? A nice, neat mystery all wrapped up, if you could pin me as the bad guy?"

"Yep. I'd be good to roll with it. But we both know you aren't. And you know I'm not your bad guy either."

"Since when did you start speaking like you knew what was going on outside your own small sphere?" Theamin stepped up to Death's side, my body tensed, coiled and ready to spring into action should she move an inch closer to me. But she brushed long fingers, nails painted bright red, along Death's cheek.

"You mean my own little bubble?" I chuckled, but begrudgingly gave Theamin credit for at least trying to connect with the Green World.

"Whatever," she snapped, waving her hand around as she stood back up.

"If you had any proof of my involvement, you would have been shoving it in Death's face that very same second. Just like I would if I had any proof you were to blame for any of this.'

"And what makes you think I'm somehow above blaming you for everything, whether I have the proof or not?" I knew she bluffed, but I didn't have any more time to fight ego against ego.

"You wouldn't. I'm sure you have some crazy noble reasons you still hold on to as important. But I know you wouldn't do that, because then you would be less in Death's eyes."

"I think you're mistaking me for your own reasons at not throwing me under the bus, Lilekai." Her words made my jaw drop. Could they have just paid me a compliment? Surely not. If so, it would be the first compliment they had thrown my way since the day I died. "You wouldn't risk losing your station. Even though you haven't slipped a single fraction in Death's view. Not even after your colossal fuck up."

"Somehow this rant, and you hating on me all these years, means I shouldn't think you're the big bad wolf?"

"I'm going to let you in on a little secret, Lilekai." She smirked and I imagined the sharpened teeth of a shark lurking behind her lips.

"Oh, this sounds fun. Should I grab some popcorn, or do I wait for intermission?" I knew I should stop. But antagonising her gave me joy and lately there had been little enough of that. And my future didn't look to be much longer.

She growled and I gave myself a mental pat on the back.

"Shut up and listen," she snapped.

"Oh, it's going to be good, I can tell."

She narrowed her eyes but didn't bother with another "shut up," which I thought showed a lot of personal growth and development on her behalf. Telling me to shut up took up at least a good hour of her day while I was in training.

"I'm not your bad wolf." Theamin spoke slowly as though I hadn't just said the exact same thing less than a minute ago.

"Oh, but calling you Rose is going to be my new favourite thing."

She narrowed her eyes at me, though I noticed the flicker of confused curiosity. Another point for the arrogant upstart. I was on a roll.

"Oh, you bloody Grey World dwellers need to start indulging a little in the awesomeness Green Worlders are doing. Next time you are there, check out their Dr Who. It is," I mimed a chef's kiss. "And I reckon even you would like the oft-discordant beauty of some of their sapphic hottie musicians."

"Are you done?" The question resonated and I remembered Alanor asking the same thing. But now I had left her behind and Death had been attacked, and knocked out, and nothing made enough sense and I wanted to scream or rip the skin from my flesh. Maybe both, at the same time. I think one would likely precede the other. What I knew, I didn't want to know, and that made even less sense than everything else combined.

"Not at all." The honesty of the words fell from my lips and I couldn't seem to stop them. "I'm freaking the fuck out and instead of focusing on what I need to be focusing on, I find I'm enjoying myself by pissing you off. Why? Because, let's be honest, if we're all about to disappear in a smash of Dark and Light, I want to at least have enjoyed my last few minutes. Because if I focus on the crazy shit I'm pretty sure is happening, I'm going to die only after I've lost my fucking mind."

"Oh, do shut up." This time Theamin didn't snap or growl. Her words might as well have been accompanied by an exasperated sigh and a rolling of her eyes.

I smiled and nodded. "Nice."

"Death isn't dead. But Death *has* been attacked."

"Thanks for that recap, but sure I'll bite. Who attacked them, oh great and wise Necromancer?"

"The same arsehole you've been supposed to be tracking down."

"Oh, of course, how silly of me. No wonder you came swaggering on in. You can now lay all the blame of this at my feet. Clever. I was wondering how you'd manage it." I paced back and forth. "No *thanks for all your hard work, Lily,* or *we understand it was hard for you to have to confront your mortal enemy, Lily,* not even a *hey, I've realised I'm a major douche and I'm going to back the fuck off now, Lily.*"

"Nope, none of that shit."

"Well, thank fuck for that then."

"That's the spirit." Theamin chuckled.

That's when the lump in my throat formed. That's when I knew Hell *had* frozen over, and we really were all doomed.

"So, what do you know, and what the hell is going on here?" I didn't have another smartarse comment. I hoped the smartarsery would return before things all went big bang in the wrong direction.

"Jen." Theamin pursed her lips as though saying her name was distasteful.

"You've seen Jen?" A wash of relief raced through my body, and I breathed a sigh of relief.

"Oh yeah, I've seen her." Her tone was almost as angry as when she spoke of me. Go Jen. "Jen did that to Death."

"What? Not you as well." I wanted to argue, but as much as Theamin made me want to high five her with a chair to her throat, I'd never known her to lie.

"She came up behind Death and shoved her fingers into their skull." Theamin shuddered and I wished I had kissed Alanor again. I envisioned a world where we kissed every morning as we headed off to our jobs, nights in the backyard of the cottage with gin and tonics in hand with our bare feet propped up on the extra chairs. Chairs only used when Jen, Daria, Lita and Isla came to visit.

"How do you know it was Jen?" My voice wavered despite pouring all the strength I could into remaining calm.

"I saw her." Theamin's smirk brought back the itch to find a chair.

"Okay." I took a deep breath. *Enhance your calm, Lily.* "What exactly did you see?"

"Her eyes, she had turned Dark, the lines of the Grim now run through them."

"They weren't her eyes." I shouldn't have felt the relief, I shouldn't have felt the weight lift from both inside and outside of myself, but I did. I wasn't the only one being set up and framed in this shit show.

"And how would you know that?"

I opened my mouth and shut it again. But she knew. I could tell by the look in her eyes that I had worked something important out.

"Eyes shift when influenced by the Dark," she reminded me in that fun, wonderful, patronising tone I enjoyed, oh so much.

"Yeah, I know that dipshit." I smiled as sweetly as I could. There was a whole new level of freedom I could express when I knew Death might be out of action for a while. Even more, knowing the Worlds were all doomed anyway.

"Then what's your point, Lilekai?" The iciness of her words caused an entirely different shudder up my spine.

"I saw Jen, after the first murder. And her eyes weren't shifted." I wanted to fist pump the air, but first I had to find Jen, and the real culprit.

"It could have happened after the first kill. After you saw her."

"Why are you so determined for it to be her? It's not like she's some kind of threat to you."

"And here's what I've been looking forward to telling you." Theamin smiled like the proverbial wolf in sheep's clothing.

I didn't like the tone of her voice or the smile that made her face look wrong. All Picasso angles. It gave me the wiggins.

"So, tell me already, you creeper."

"Death chooses who receives the power next. They transfer the power before they step through the last gate."

TWENTY-FOUR

"What?" I sat on the edge of the bed. Jen's bed. Where the fuck was she? Death's still form was an uncomfortable pressure against the small of my back. A comfort quickly chased by disquiet raced through me at the touch.

"Death chooses who will be their successor."

"But, Death told Jen years ago that they had no control or power over their successors."

"They lied." Why was she so pleased about this? Was it about stumping me, or were they happy Death was a big liar liar pants on fire?

"Ok, so why are you telling me this now?" Fury raced beneath my skin, warming my body to near uncomfortableness.

"Jen found out the day before your first trapped soul."

"What?"

"She. Found. Out." Theamin's words were slow and deliberate as though I didn't understand them individually.

"How?" I snarled in return.

"She overheard Death telling me who they believed would be best for the role."

"Why would they even be considering that now? They aren't ready to walk through." I looked over at Death, at the form that had once seemed so flawless to me before. "Are they?"

"No. But that has never stopped Death discussing options and always being prepared. They respect the intelligence and sound advice I can offer them. I'm not just a pretty face and big muscles to them."

"Well, that's a disturbing and horrible thought." I shuddered, begging my mind to reel itself back out of the gutter. "I need to bleach my memories when we're done here."

"Theamin," Death interrupted whatever Theamin might have said.

Theamin raced to Death's side. But all I saw was the space where Daria no longer lay.

"Where's Daria?"

"Gone. Shimmered away."

I stepped back, not wanting to see Theamin paw over Death. I didn't want to see Death either, to be honest.

"I'm done with this shit." I moved to the door. My hand was on the knob before Death called out to me.

"Where are you going, Lilekai?" Death asked.

"To find Jen and Daria."

"Come." Death's rattle pierced my room.

I wanted to ignore the command, I wanted to be older and stronger. But their words wrapped around me like rope. I turned only slightly, appeased by Theamin doing the same.

"Lily." Death's voice came out softer, but they hadn't released their command over me.

Breath caught in my throat. Death had never called me my Green World name before.

"Death?" I hated the quiver in my voice.

"I am not dying, child. There is no need for fear. But I cannot finish this. It was never mine to begin with, though I interfered when I should have known better. You must end it."

"Why me?"

"Because it has to be." Thin skeletal fingers reached for my own and I offered my hand freely. "You need to find her, and you need to stop her. She's been looking for you."

The lump in my throat made a reply impossible.

"She who?"

Please don't say Jen. Anyone but Jen.

"You know who. I can see it in your mind. You already know, Lilekai, you just wish you didn't."

I wanted to believe that my defending Jen was because I knew her so well. And part of it was, but it was a lot easier to hold that belief when I had never told her about my tattoo.

"I'm right about the tattoo, aren't I, Death?" I couldn't say her name, not again.

"What tattoo?" Theamin asked and I started, having forgotten for just a moment that she was there.

I looked at Theamin and back to Death.

"Please show Theamin." My will was once again taken from me, despite the manners Death used.

I lifted the back of my hair and turned my back to Theamin despite the goose pimples that popped up over my skin.

"And the significance?" Theamin asked.

I spun quickly on my heel to face her again.

"It is identical to the wounds on the victims, is it not, Lilekai?" Death asked, but it wasn't a question, really. Just a confirmation.

I nodded. I didn't need to have seen them to know it was true.

"You can track her through this." Death pressed something

circular and flat into the palm of my hand. It vibrated as I wrapped my fingers around it.

"I can take care of this, Death." Theamin stepped forward, as though trying to put herself between me and our leader.

"This is not your fight, Theamin. We aren't done, we aren't ready to hand over the reins, old friend, but the young ones need to find their own place."

"Their place?" I snapped, pulling back from Death and pushing past Theamin. "People are dead. You lied to all of us. You told Jen you had no choice over your successor. You lied to her. But lies come out, Death. And she found out and she's pissed off and right now I don't even blame her. And because of that everyone thinks the monster doing all of this is her."

"Lily, I know it's not Jen."

"That's not the point though, is it?" I waved my hands around the moment Death relinquished their thrall over me. "You lied to her. You dragged her here and told her she can never be anything more, no matter how hard she tries because you don't get to choose. And then..." I paced in front of the still open doors. "And then, she finds out you are full of shit. The one person she should have been able to trust over any others. But you kept her at arm's distance her entire life. So yeah, she has every fucking right to be pissed off. But it's not Jen. And she doesn't deserve to have people hunting her as though it were."

"Lily, it's not that simpl–"Death began.

"Nope, I've had enough. I'll find Jen and Daria. And then I'll be back. Because you, Death." I lifted my arm straight at them, finger pointing to their face. "Owe us all some pretty fucking big answers."

Theamin reached out toward me, but I was already Shimmering, using the flat circle in my hand to guide my way.

The rush of a Shimmer from Grey World to Grey World

landed me in a tangle of limbs and dizziness on another room's floor. A Green World Necromancer's room. Small and bare except for the single bed, the three-drawer bedside table, and the stand-alone mirror angled in the corner.

Identical to the one that Jen's room, far larger than these cells, now rested in. No wonder Dr Who had popped into my mind. The swirl of bone and black cinders were as comforting as ever, which was to say, not at all. I didn't want to look up, I didn't want to see what state Jen was in.

I hated Death. I hated myself for ever saying yes to being a minion. I hated myself for being caught up in the Necromancer's existence.

There were too many thoughts and emotions bubbled up inside of me and the overarching thought seemed simple enough.

The Worlds could still survive, even if we didn't. But before we got to that, Daria needed to get out of the mess safely.

No Necromancer should ever be allowed to live in the Green World. We should not be allowed to remember what living is truly about. All we did was cause the living pain.

And I should know, I was the worst culprit.

"Lily?" Jen sobbed and I looked up instinctively, despite my previous anger and determination to let all of us minions rot in the Grey World, sacrificing ourselves to stop the living from dying in a fiery death of Worlds colliding.

"Jen." My voice shook, but there wasn't much I could do about that now.

"Did you find them? Have you stopped them?'" She sat at the end of her bed, Daria's bare feet within her reach.

"What are you talking about sweetheart?" I shuffled toward the bed, toward Daria's head. The one killing and trapping souls might not be Jen. But something had happened to my best friend. Something bad, that kept her eyes from focusing and her limbs jerking intermittently.

"I had to bring her here. It wasn't safe for her. She smells like you."

Tears sprang to my eyes. "Jen, I don't understand. What happened?"'

"We ordered pizza." She sniffled and looked at Daria. "The doorbell rang and Daria answered while I grabbed plates from the kitchen. She screamed. By the time I reached the door, they stood there, a man dead at her feet and Daria crumbled over by your fake wall thing."

She sniffled, tears running freely down her cheeks.

"I ran to Daria but then the pain. So much pain. It won't go away."

"Where's the pain, Jen?" I asked, fingers trembling.

Jen just stared at me, wild eyes holding wild fear.

"Jen, is the pain at the back of your head?"

"Oh, no." Jen leaned toward me and pulled me halfway to her. We hugged awkwardly, my arms wrapping around her on habit and instinct. "Have they hurt you?"

"Jen, did you see them before they hurt you?"

"The fake cloak with my eyes."

"You saw the eyes?"

"No, yes. I don't remember." She pulled back out of the awkward embrace and threaded both hands through her hair, pulling at the strands.

"Jen, why would it matter that Daria smells like me?"

"They are looking for you." The clarity of her words sent a shiver up my spine. "You're easier to get to than Death, and you're next in line."

"What?" I laughed until her eyes met mine. "Jen. Do you know who the fake cloak is? Did you do something to send them after me?"

"What?" Jen jumped up and stepped back until her back pressed against the opposite wall. "You think I did this? I have nothing to do with this, Lilekai."

"Jen." I forced my hands to uncurl from fists I hadn't remembered curling.

"No, Lily!" Jen spat my name and I cringed backward. A laugh that sounded more like a sob escaped her. "You don't even want it, do you? The most coveted position in our entire realm, and the Green World as well, and you wouldn't even want it."

"Of course I don't want it! I'm not Death, and I don't ever want to be." My heart raced in my chest. "Jen, is the pain still there?"

Her eyes had sharpened as anger and frustration filled her.

"Oh, no." Her eyes wouldn't meet mine, but not because they flitted around as before. They wouldn't meet mine because they were focused entirely on something they saw over my shoulder.

Before I could turn my head, the pain seared through me. The tattoo had been nothing compared to this.

I screamed. The sound never ending, the pain building to beyond anything I had ever experienced before in my life.

"They lied." Katy's voice, warped and filled with such agony, was the last thing I heard before the blackness took over.

TWENTY-FIVE

"Don't move," Jen whispered in the darkness.

"Where are we?" The words came out raw and red.

"I don't know."

"What do you...ouch!" She had said not to move, but I had gone and moved.

"Shhh." Jen's gentle fingers brushed across my forehead. "I know it hurts. But it's okay. You'll be safe now."

"Jen, what did you do to me?"

"Lily, it wasn't me." Jen's voice was back to the strong and assured voice I had always known.

"Please, what happened?"

"They found us," Jen whispered.

"Not they, Jen. She."

"You know her?"

I nodded.

"Who is it?"

"Katy."

"The suicide?"

"I saw Death take her soul. They told me it was done. They

had taken Katy on her final walk and seen her step through the Light door. Why would they lie to me?"

"They lie about everything."

"Where are we?"

"Another room. But I'm running out." Jen sighed and after some sounds of shuffling, her hand found mine in the darkness. "It's how we've been getting away."

"Lily?" In the darkness, close by but somehow miles of space away, Daria's voice called out to me.

"Daria. Oh, thank Death. Are you okay?"

"My head is really sore, and I can't see a thing."

"It's dark. It's okay," Jen answered, far too peppy for this situation as far as I could tell at least.

"Who is that?" Daria's voice quivered in the murky light.

"It's Jen. We met at Lily's."

The only reply was heaving sobs.

"Daria? Daria, what's wrong?" Alarm bells made me sit up, what was I laying on?

"You're one of them, aren't you? I thought you were here to rescue me."

"I am."

Hiccupping sobs were the only reply I got.

"I'll get us out of here, Daria. I promise."

"You can't go out there, Lily, not while the bad one of me is still running around looking for you. They keep tracking Daria because she smells like you."

"Jen." I took a deep breath. "I don't think it's Daria they are tracking. If anyone smells like me, it's you."

"Oh." Jen's verbosity seemed to have abandoned her.

I opened my mouth to say something but hands were suddenly on me, and a full Shimmer pulled me away.

I burst out of the Shimmer, sprawled on the floor of Death's Central Chamber.

Compared to the darkness of the previous room, the light stung my eyes as though I had been Shimmered outside in the midday sun of Green World. It felt as though it burnt my eyes, despite how quickly I slammed my eyelids closed.

Thuds hitting the floor and sounds of oomphs and curses echoed around me, one after the other.

"Stay away from her, you bitch!" Alanor's voice called from behind my too bright eyelids. I smiled. Her words sounded familiar, a movie or TV show. Either way, I forgot about the searing pain in my eyes and at the back of my head.

Okay, not entirely forgot about it, but I pushed it far enough away for me to think wildly inappropriate and tantalising things about the detective. Wait, why the hell was she back in the Grey World?

"Get your hands off me. It wasn't me," Jen yelled, before a thud vibrated the ground beneath me and she let out an oomph and then an expletive for extra measure.

"You got her?" Alanor asked.

"Has who got whom?" I asked, my eyesight still fighting to focus over the scattering of too many overexposed spots of light.

Something, no, someone touched my arm and I flinched. But the fingers didn't grab or grip. Instead, they gently stroked it, and I leaned into the familiar touch of Detective Alanor.

I relaxed into the rhythmic brush of fingers making slow circles on my arm.

"Hey, Lily!" Behind Alanor's closeness, I recognised the second voice as well.

"Etziel?" I smiled but I didn't want to open my eyes again to confirm his presence.

"Couldn't let you two have all the fun." The Kid was here, and he'd brought his sister with him. It had been a long time since I got to smile with The Kid.

"Let me go. If she finds us there won't be any fun at all." Jen's words were accompanied with scuffles.

"Shut up, Jen," Etziel replied.

"Etziel," I snapped, forcing my eyes to blink a few more times, and allowing the World around me to come a little more into focus.

I locked my eyes on Alanor, as though my body instinctively knew where to find her. We smiled at each other, and I wondered if we would get a chance to kiss one more time before the Worlds collided.

I knew instantly the moment my smile slipped. I could read it clear as ink on paper, written all over Alanor's face.

I had been right, I knew I had but seeing her standing there, cowl thrown back, hit me like a clenched fist to the guts.

"Hi, Katy."

TWENTY-SIX

"Katy?" Alanor asked, voice flat, head tilted to the side.

"I've been looking for you." Her voice ripped my chest open. It was filled with pain and tears.

"Katy." Alanor spun around, and Katy smiled even as those eyes, darkened with signs of the Grim, flickered and flashed. "What's going on?"

I saw it in slow motion, but my body wouldn't move fast enough.

As Alanor twisted her body to look at me, Katy moved forward, hands up and out in front of her.

"Alanor!" I screamed as Katy ran through her.

Alanor's body shuddered for a moment when the two sisters took up the same space in the Grey World. She screamed as Katy burst through the other side.

I stood my ground, chest moving rapidly with my breath. But really, what the fuck could I do against an incorporeal spirit who could influence themselves on the Grey and the Green World?

"Freeze!" Death's voice filled the Chamber, and we all did as commanded. Even Katy.

"Death?" The question came out slowly, like it was stuck in molasses, and for a moment I wondered if their command also tried to still my tongue.

"It's okay, Lilekai. I have her now." Death's voice filled the quiet stillness.

"How? How is she here?" A lump caught in my throat, unspilled tears filled my eyes.

But Katy's ghost, the essence that I had been preparing to find, let out a wailing sob and dropped to its haunches.

"It didn't work, it didn't make anything better. Please, I don't want to be here anymore. Just let me go, just let me go." She repeated the words over and over and my stomach roiled.

I turned to Death.

"You have been keeping her here? Keeping her prisoner?" I barely contained the scream from roaring up my throat.

"I..." Death shook their head slowly. "It is a very long story, Lilekai."

"I don't give a shit. Condense it for me."

"Mind yourself, Lilekai." Theamin stood behind Death, her pet minions flanking her. I hadn't even noticed any of them until Theamin hissed her order at me. Damn, the Chamber was getting all kinds of activity today.

"I could not send her through," Death answered as though Theamin had not spoken.

"You lied, again." The lump in my throat dissolved under the heat of my anger. But no surprise filled my words.

"No." They tilted their head and I saw them searching for something. Was it words or were they trying to find the minions that remained absent. "I did walk her through. I watched her go into the Light. But she has not stayed put. She keeps returning."

"Keeps?" Alanor roared, and I suspected if I had the courage to turn my head and look at her, I might find her head transformed into that of a lion.

"I thought the last time had worked. And I didn't realise it was her. She had never hurt anyone before," Death said.

"Until now." Etziel, sweet boy Etziel, sounded as pissed off as I felt.

"I didn't know it was her, not until you returned and told me about the second soul." Death spoke as though our anger, the raging heat that roiled off us—me, Alanor, Etziel, and even Jen—was inconsequential. "I went searching in the Grey World hoping to find some answers to all of this."

"And then what? You just let us go, no warning and no idea what we were facing. You set her loose on me."

"What are we facing?" Alanor asked.

I really liked the squishy grey matter of this mortal.

"Katy, it's time to move on now." Jen spoke softly. She moved to the shifting soul that flickered as though reception were a bit spotty in the Grey World. Like she channelled some of my own magical deficiencies.

"Jen, step back." Fear prickled up the back of my skin.

"It's the bad me. But she's not bad. She's trying to help."

"Help?" Alanor asked, and I heard the small catch in her voice.

"She wants to be seen. She wants to understand."

"She's killing people, Jen," I said.

"I know." Jen lifted her hair at the back of her skull. I stared at the three holes, precisely where I expected them to be.

"Death?" Theamin asked.

Death turned around and dropped their shawl, revealing the same three holes.

"What the fuck is she looking for?" I heard my own voice but still wondered where the hell the question had come from.

The straining grunts coming from Katy were growing louder as she fought against the magic Death trapped her in.

We didn't have time for feelings or diplomacy.

"What happened when you tried to walk her through, Death?" I asked.

"I walked her through fine," they said with a sniff as they pulled their cowl back up over their bald head.

"I know, but you felt it, right? Something was different." I stabbed at the dark, but by the look on Death's face, I stabbed correctly.

"Yes." Death scowled.

"What?"' I rolled my hand over in a circle. "We don't have time for this shit."

"She resisted. She pushed against it, she called for you."

"And you never told me?" I huffed out a breath but shook my head. "We don't have time. Okay, so she's been looking for me."

"That's a leap," Alanor said.

"No, Alanor. It's really not."

"How do you know, Lily?" Alanor asked.

I lifted my hair for her to see.

"What the fuck?"

"I know. I'm sorry. I should have told you what I suspected but I didn't know what we would find. I didn't want to hurt you more."

'What did the souls say?'

"Geoff said 'Orion's belt hurts.' And I didn't want to be right, but I knew it had to be Katy, somehow."

Alanor looked at me, too closely for my liking because she saw what none of the others were looking for. "What the hell are you planning to do?"

"I'm going to give her what she wants," I answered. My

voice was steady, and my body was still. The calm was a relief washing over me.

"No!" I'm not sure how many people exclaimed their disgust, maybe everyone, but it didn't matter. I was not going to run away anymore.

Death might have banished me, but I never fought it and I never once wanted to stay, not even with Jen at my side.

I had one more question before I did this, because I didn't expect I would survive whatever Katy needed to be able to move on.

"Death, why do her eyes look like Jen's?"

Death hesitated but I didn't take my eyes off of them. Instead of looking at me, Death kept their eyes on Jen.

"I tried to turn her into a Necromancer once her soul touched the Light World door, before she stepped through." Death's voice was a whisper we all heard.

"You said—"

"I know." They nodded, grief and regret rolling off of them in waves. I wanted to feel bad for them, to take that pain away, but my anger still lingered. "But you never meant to hurt her, I understood that. And she was such a sweet soul, I would have offered her the chance to be a minion. But you didn't trust me."

"No, I didn't." I accepted that guilt many years ago, but I would not relive it now, or ever again. "And her soul is still sweet."

"Jen." Death might have heard me but their eyes remained on Jen.

Jen's eyes flashed and flickered. Similar to Katy's but not identical. "I don't want to hear it. Nothing you have done will excuse the lies."

"Lily," Jen turned to me. "She's going to kill you if you give her what she wants."

"We can figure something else out." Alanor's voice dangerously bordered on begging. I didn't want her begging. It would be hard enough to do what I had to as it was.

"She's been searching long enough." I smiled and shrugged. "Let her go, Death."

Nothing happened. No one moved, and it seemed even Katy's struggles lessened.

"Please, Death."

A nod, barely perceptible, and then a scream escaped from Katy.

I turned and tried to smile the best I could at her, but sadness pulled down the corners of my mouth.

"I'm sorry, Katy. I didn't know how much pain I would cause you. But it's okay now. I'm here."

Heart pounding in my chest, blood roaring through my ears, I took a slow step, pivoting on the balls of my feet and showing Katy what I had turned Katy into—the star tattoos that were still visible despite the small spiky growth over the top. So often, the tattoo hid beneath the longer strands of my hair, but I never forgot it was there. Never.

Noise exploded around me. Screams and feet slamming on the bone dust floor. But the pressure of the presence as it drew closer filled my entire concentration. Nothing else mattered.

At first the touch was gentle and kind, Katy's fingers gently stroked against the tattoos. The three stars marking the three Worlds I lived in.

I had argued with her that I only needed two, but she had been adamant that I lived in three Worlds: Grey, Green, and electromagnetic. I had liked that. She had been the first person who saw my technological repelling as something beautiful, something wonderful.

"I'm sorry, Katy."

"I know." Her voice was stuff of nightmares, guttural and fierce as it scraped up her throat.

I stiffened as the pressure against the back of my skull increased. My mouth opened, the sound rising as the pressure became pain, and pain became agony. It built, stacking up inside of me, until it blinded all else.

It twisted inside, wrapped around me, and turned me into nothing. I no longer existed. There was only pain and despair and agony.

Before darkness took me again, I understood, and I wept. Katy had never deserved any of the agonies she showed me. I had once believed I deserved punishments far worse than I had been granted, but someone else deserved to never feel a moment of peace again.

The darkness was all consuming. Flickers of pinprick lights danced around me. No, it danced around her. I saw through her eyes and felt the thud of panic replacing what was once a heartbeat.

Do you want your freedom? A voice, disembodied in the darkness, vicious and deep in a whisper we could not recognise. There was no escaping it, it wrapped around our body with sharp incisions on our flesh like the thorns on a rose vine.

"Please." Our lips moved and Katy's pleading voice filled the darkness.

Then you know what you must do.

"Please." A sob, choked back until the power raced through our body, sending nerves and muscles into fiery spasms.

Do you want your freedom?

"Yes. Yes." Katy's words sobbed and screamed again as the vine of thorns tightened around her flesh.

Good.

TWENTY-SEVEN

The time between reliving the horror and sweet oblivion was not nearly long enough. Sounds and screams infiltrated my ears. The pain had lessened at the base of my skull, but it lingered enough for me to be aware of it.

"Let her go, Katy!" Alanor screamed, her voice bouncing off the bones and walls alike.

Other voices shouted. Words blended together and I understood none of them. There were too many people. Why were they all here?

I moved my head. A thick sucking noise came from behind me, followed by something falling with a thud. Slowly, I moved the rest of my body, one shuffle at a time. People fought around me. I watched, cocking my head.

Alanor had her baton out, standing between me and a solid line of Death, Theamin, and the minions, Sara and Kensley.

But no, she wasn't just protecting me.

Looking down, I expected to see my own body, like I had all those years ago when I had died. But the body at my feet, the one that had thudded to the floor at the movement of my head, had curled into a foetal position, eyes wide and staring up at her sister's back.

"Katy?" Even my voice felt slow and thick. My body wavered, or the room moved, I wasn't sure which.

"I didn't know. I was lonely. I didn't realise," she whispered.

"You saw my memories just as I saw yours?"

She nodded.

"You were always so smart."

"I hurt them. I'm sorry, Lily."

"I know. I know," I hushed and nodded. I wanted the thickened air around me to disappear, but it lingered. I moved to crouch beside her, intentions of wrapping her in my arms cut short.

"Don't you touch her. You and your kind have done enough already." Alanor raised her baton higher, the muscles in her shoulders rippling, and ready to strike out at the first provocation. For a moment I believed she spoke to me, but then movement caught my eye and Death stepped back.

"Alanor." I had spoken softly, unsure of the ringing in my ears.

"Lily." My name sounded so soft on her lips. I wanted the tears and relief in her eyes to be about me, about my being awake and okay. But she had said "Death's kind," and I knew where I belonged.

"Alanor, please."

"I saw it too, Lily, we all did." Alanor turned away from me and back to the line of Necromancers.

"Where are Jen and Daria?" Like ears popping on a flight, the bubble of sluggish sensations dropped. Breath raced in and out of my mouth, cold air drying out already too dry lips, as I got back to my feet.

"Lil." Jen's voice was honey to my ears.

"I'm here." And Daria's was the icing on the cake.

I turned to see Jen and Daria sitting together, limbs wrapped around each other. For cold or comfort, I didn't care. They were both breathing and that was all that mattered.

I wanted nothing more than to sit with them, hold their hands and reassure myself they really were okay. But the stand-off remained and the energy in the Chamber buzzed inside every part of me, from my toes to my still tender head.

"What did you do to Katy, Death?" I turned and stepped around Katy, adding my body to the defence Alanor had created.

"I told you; she wouldn't stay put." Death stopped, mouth opened and energy swirling around them. "I told Theamin she would not stay still."

"What. Did. You. Do?" I spat the words.

"I..." Death had confusion knitting their brows. It was all levels of wrong. I had never seen them confused before. "I did nothing else. I believed she had finally found peace and stayed in the Light World."

With a whoosh followed by heavy footsteps, Etziel, Isla, and Lita joined me and Alanor.

"Theamin?" Death asked.

"I had nothing to do with this, Death." Theamin shook her head, body vibrating with emotions I didn't want to get any closer to. Was she offended at Death's accusation? I would have been. I had been.

"You are the only one I told," Death repeated.

Theamin opened her mouth and slowly closed it again. For a moment she closed her eyes. Her words were quiet and dangerous. "What did you do?"

No one moved or spoke.

Who the hell was she talking to?

A beat and then another.

"What. Did. You. Do?" Theamin's roar raged with a fire that burned the chill of the Grey World from my very soul.

"I did what I had to do," Kensley spat from beside Theamin.

Well, fuck me. I hadn't seen that one coming.

"I did what you wouldn't dare do against your beloved Death. But she drained you both, every time she came to visit. Every time she made you care for her and carry her back. She drained you, and we all suffered."

"No one suffered," Death growled back.

"We did," Kensley spat. "We all suffered from your softness and your weakness."

"You suffered." I spoke softly, eyes pinned to the darkness that flickered in Kensley's eyes. All heads turned toward me. "Who did they choose, Theamin?" I shifted my gaze and pinned Theamin with my stare.

She blinked, and I almost wanted to fist pump the air, having figured out the thread before her. "Choose for what?" she asked.

"Who did Death choose as their successor?" I asked. I already had the answer, but now I had the question as well.

"You," Kensley spat, a thick finger jabbing at the air between us.

"What have you done?" Death asked. Their power vibrated around us, twanging like a plucked overstrung guitar string.

"You act like I'm the bad guy here." Kensley threw his hands up in the air and started pacing the small space between the two sides. With each stride the gap was closing, but Kensley seemed entirely unaware. Etziel, Lita, and Isla were inching their way closer, as were Death and Theamin. Sara slid behind them, as an alley to Kensley or in fear?

"I could have just killed her, hurt her, but I didn't, I kept her and them both safe. She had her own room, everything she wanted. A luxury room within a room. A skill I learned from your own dear daughter, Death." Kensley kept going without any more prompting from any of us. I kept my eyes on his, watching as the gap continued to close. "How could you possibly still be Death when you didn't even know you had succeeded in turning her into a Necromancer? But she wasn't right. Not entirely a Necromancer and not entirely dead. You were too close, too weak to see what you had created."

I looked back to where Katy still rocked against the bone floor.

"She couldn't stay in the Light World because she was no longer a mere soul." Kensley really enjoyed the sound of his voice. "You were both so confused and scared."

I didn't care what Kensley had to say, not really. Katy was more important. I crouched down and helped her to her feet.

"I kept her safe," Kensley all but screamed.

"Until you didn't." I turned toward him; my arm wrapped around Katy's shoulder. "You let her out, you tried to frame me. You put her on my scent, literally. After you traumatised a soul who didn't understand what was happening to them, you let her loose to create Grims. And why? All to get me out of the way?"

"You aren't worthy to be Death," Kensley spat between clenched teeth.

"And you think you are?" Etziel snarled. Who knew The Kid had it in him? Being around Alanor had obviously been good for him.

"Of course not." Kensley looked affronted by the very notion. "I didn't do any of this for me. I did it for the Death we all deserve."

"Kensley, you idiot," Theamin growled, low and dangerous in her throat. I had never heard the venom behind it, but I knew she reserved the term "idiot" for when she truly thought the lowest of a person. I had heard her call me it many times now.

Kensley blinked and stared, mouth slightly open at Theamin.

"I did this for you. You deserve to be the next Death. Not that idiot. I'm not the idiot." His voice rose in pitch as he spoke.

Katy leaned heavily against me, her breathing laboured.

"Is she okay?" Alanor asked softly, taking some of Katy's weight on her other side. Lita, Isla, and Etzial filled the gap we made, protecting us.

"I don't think so." I spoke just as softly, trying to meet Alanor's eyes, but she avoided my gaze.

"Theamin is the only one who can return Death to its proper place of power," Kensley continued on, monologuing like a genuine villain.

"You locked a new Necromancer up, alone and without any help or understanding, and then let her loose, knowing she was damaged. Even more so from incarceration. To frame what you think is my competition for the top job?" Theamin hissed, stepping into Kensley's face and I smiled.

"Kensley," Death said the boy's name with a spark that pinned him to the bone floor. He stood and looked between his frozen feet and back up at Death. "You are relieved of your position as minion." Death stepped between the two Necromancers facing off with each other.

Kensley laughed, loud and heavy. He threw his head back.

I didn't catch the movement of his hand until it squeezed around Death's throat.

"Your time is over, Death," Kensley snarled.

"You forget your place," Death coughed out.

Kensley's dark eyes had grown deeper and flicked faster, the jagged lines of darkness crossing over the colour.

"He's a Grim!" Theamin shouted, stepping forward and

trying to pry one of Kensley's hands from around Death's throat.

"Let them go!" I roared.

"You can't stop me, Lilekai. None of you can." He smiled with a knife's sharp-edged gleam to his lips. "When Death dies, the power will transfer to Theamin, and I will be forgiven."

"You think we can't stop you?" Etziel growled and moved forward.

With a flick of his free hand, Kensley sent Etziel flying.

Etziel crashed against one of the skeletons and fell in a pile of bone and limbs all tumbled together.

"Etzi." Alanor dropped Katy's weight entirely on me once more as she raced over to check on her brother.

"You will not be one of my minions!" Theamin spat.

"You are Grim, and the fire will burn through you!" Lita and Isla clasped hands as their words carried a magic older than the Grey World.

"Witches," Kensley spat, dropping Death. Theamin stopped Death from falling to the floor.

"Yes, we are." Lita and Isla spoke as one, and vindication and pride raced through me, for they were so much stronger than they ever let on.

"But you aren't the only ones who have learnt the old ways." Kensley spat on the ground. The glob of his spit that landed, hissed black and oozed into the air.

"I can't see." I blinked furiously, but the other Necromancers all echoed the same.

"Who will stop me now, Witches?"

"I will," Katy muttered as she pulled away from me.

I tried to reach out to stop her, but without my sight she avoided my grasping fingers.

"You will not be forgiven for your crimes!" she screamed,

and soon Kensley's roars of pain filled the air, the black cloying blindness slipped.

First, all I could see were the vague outlines of those around me. Kensley and Katy were the only two figures not leaning against a wall or a piece of furniture. The two of them looked like nothing more than people lining up, exhausted with slumped shoulders as they waited their turn at the checkout.

As more of my vision returned, I could see. And how I wished for blindness.

Katy's fingers were lodged within Kensley's skull. Not just the three fingers like all the others, but all five fingers of both hands. Her face, a twisted mask of all the darkness that had brewed within her as she lay deserted and abandoned, trapped in a room by a monster parading as a good guy.

Kensley screamed, hands flailing wildly around beside him.

"Feel what I felt, you bastard. Know what it's like to be locked away for years, taunted with false promises of freedom and oblivion."

I watched, frozen.

I wanted to revel in his demise. But the darkness swarmed around like a tornado searching for ground to truly take flight.

"We need to stop her." Lita and Isla spoke as one.

"How?" Even as I asked, I shook my head back and forth in the negative. All scenarios I could think of ended with Katy's death. "I can't kill her, not again."

"Death is a gift, Lilekai." Death stepped forward. The black swirling energy pushed against them, and with each step, skin peeled from their bones, growing only to be peeled away once more.

"No!" I called out. I searched Katy's face for the girl who sobbed, for the woman who goaded me about my lack of ink on skin. But I saw only the monster Kensley had created. "He deserves it."

"But she doesn't." Alanor's words were soft, as she took her own steps forward, clothes pressed back against her skin as though walking against a hurricane's wind, the force of power and the taste of magic surrounding us.

Alanor reached Katy first and tears sprang to my eyes.

"I'm sorry." I heard Alanor say, before she lifted her gun and pressed it to her sister's temple.

The sound exploded around us.

I fell to the ground, and then the world stood still.

I didn't want to open my eyes. Sounds invaded and again, I existed. I squeezed my eyes shut tighter but the tears, betraying salt water, slipped from between the lashes and slid down the sides of my face. I sobbed, big gulping gasps of air.

"Come on, sweetheart." Isla's voice, alone and individual once more. "Let's go home."

I didn't fight her or the arms that wrapped around me and helped me to my feet.

I let them take me home, though I wasn't certain just where that would be.

TWENTY-EIGHT

Sun pushed against my closed eyelids and for a moment, I wondered why the hell I hadn't closed the blinds before I went to bed. Sleep wasn't entirely necessary for Necromancers, though I ached for more oblivion, but why?

Like a freight train coming out of nowhere, the memory of the abandoned Grey World invaded my mind. I was out of bed, eyes wide, head swivelling around like a praying mantis. I couldn't quite do the entire 360-degree exorcist twist, but it was close.

"What's wrong?"

I turned slowly. I was in the spare room at Lita and Isla's. Had the room in the Grey World all been a sick and twisted nightmare?

Alanor scratched sleep from her eyes with slow fingers, not bothering to stifle a yawn.

"Alanor, what happened?"

"Lita and Isla brought us back here." She looked at me, without quite meeting my gaze. Her eyes were red-rimmed while dark grape-coloured bruises stood out beneath.

"Oh." I took a deep breath, as deep as I could, trying desperately to slow my heart rate. Relief washed over me. I hadn't dreamed it. Pain and hurt followed closely behind.

"Everything's wrong, isn't it?" The pain in her voice made everything in me ache.

"What?" Oh yeah, I was firing on all mental cylinders.

"I was supposed to be the good guy, and you were supposed to be the villain. But now I'm the one who killed my own sister."

Ouch.

"You didn't kill her." I buried my own pain behind the need to comfort her.

"Of course I fucking did." All traces of the sleepy woman I had woken up beside vanished in the snarl and growl of her words. "And now I'm a monster, just like you."

I met Alanor's eyes and the whirlwind within couldn't stop me hearing her words on a repeated playlist in my head.

"That's right, I'm one of them," I spat and quickly scanned the room for anything of mine.

"I didn't mean, oh fuck." Alanor ran her hands through her hand, and I didn't find it sexy at all, nope not one single bit.

"Fuck you." The words fell as my heart broke, and I slipped out of the door before Alanor could try to stop me. I didn't hear any effort on her behalf.

Lita and Isla might have been in the kitchen, I didn't head that way to find out. I slipped out of the front door and walked home.

I might have been able to Shimmer, but I didn't want to find out. I didn't want to know what happened after; I didn't want to relive the horrors. But each step I took reminded me of the darkness that had wrapped around us all, ever since I tried to go beyond my powers.

The walk took longer than I remembered. The back of my

neck burned as the sun rose behind me, my stomach growled, and I should have at least found a way to smuggle out a cup of coffee before I left.

The only place I wanted to be was home. The cars I could touch without breaking them, the kettle that boiled as long as I used the gas stove top, the sounds of the backyard so many others didn't hear, or took for granted when they did.

"Fuck." I looked up in front of the coffee shop.

It was open. Through the window, I saw Daria serving customers. I watched as she smiled and laughed, and I envied her for her existence. Would she be able to forget about it? Had Death even given her a chance to live with it before they wiped her mind? I doubted it.

I didn't stop, despite the pull of the ground coffee aroma teasing my nostrils.

Halfway between home and the coffee shop, the breeze taunted me with the sounds of someone calling my name. The sounds of someone wanting my attention, needing my attention.

I sighed as I heard "Lily" called out again.

I kept walking.

"Goddamnit! Stop, Lilekai!"

I froze in my tracks.

Footsteps raced up behind me, drawing closer as I still looked ahead, toward the cottage with my false sanctuary and sense of isolation. Maybe my entire sense of identity. I had no bloody clue.

"You forgot your coffee," Daria gasped out between heavy breaths.

"You know who I am?" I asked, frowning.

"Yep. You're kinda hard to forget!"

I turned around and stared at her. "Why didn't Death wipe your mind?"

"I asked them not to." Daria shrugged.

"They gave you a choice?" I was certain my eyebrows disappeared into the mop of disarray that was my hair.

Daria bobbed her head side to side, indicating a yes but no kind of answer.

I narrowed my eyes and she laughed.

"Jen told Death that if they threatened to wipe my mind, she would start resurrecting whoever she felt like, paperwork signed and approved or not."

"What?" The smile pulled at muscles I had feared would never be used again.

When Daria held out the coffee cup to me, I accepted with a nod and a laugh.

The first pull warmed my chest. I rolled my shoulders and took another sip. I could have floated with the pleasure of the addiction.

"Oh shit." I looked at Daria. "You raced out of work. Are you going to get fired? I can't give you a lift home."

Daria laughed and threaded her arm through my free arm. "I'll walk you home."

We walked while I sipped the jumbo coffee, and Daria told me what happened once Lita and Isla took Alanor and myself home.

"Death entombed Kensley in some resiny kind of forcefield thing, and then cleaned up..." Daria's voice stopped in her throat like a needle pulled quickly from a playing record. I gave her a sad but reassuring smile. "Cleaned up Katy's body. It happened so quickly, and I didn't really understand most of it, but Jen explained what I didn't understand later."

"So you and Jen are becoming good friends huh?" I smiled and took another sip, saddened by how light the cup had already gotten.

"She's amazing." Daria's cheeks pinked and I wanted to

whoop aloud, but the caffeine energy still didn't have enough oomph to brush all the weight from my shoulders.

"She is."

"Death approached us once they returned. Jen stood up and wow, she let them have it. She asked all these questions about eyes and who she was. I didn't understand all of it, but she told me that if I saw you first, she would come and explain as soon as she could."

"She really is okay? Since the attack?"

"Physically, yes."

The implication hung heavy in the air and no amount of coffee could make up for my lack of faith in my best friend, or the fact that shit was never going to be the same again.

"You wanna come in for a bit?" We stood on the patio of my home and the idea of Daria leaving curdled like week old milk in my coffee.

"You knew I was living at the coffee shop, didn't you?"

"I figured it out." I shrugged and gave the best apologetic look I could.

"When you found me?"

I nodded.

Daria walked over to the railing and leaned on it with her forearms.

"My folks kicked me out when I came out. Nothing unique or interesting in the tale, just the same old horrid rhetoric of homophobic arseholes."

"Did Brian know?"

"Oh hell no, he would have charged me rent and electricity." Daria laughed.

"So, what happens now?"

"Turns out his kids want nothing to do with him, or his café. I mean, they want the money, but they don't want to do anything for it. So, I've been officially upgraded to manager."

"No way." I smiled.

"Yeah." Daria smiled back, and then pressed her lips together so firmly that they went white.

"So, what's up?"

"I know it sounds crazy. Jen thinks I'm more traumatised than I'm letting on. But I don't think Katy was bad. She didn't know she was hurting those people. She was just looking for you because you always helped her, you always found a way to make things better."

It wasn't as though this idea hadn't crossed my mind, and the coffee was certainly helping to clear the cobwebs, but I needed time. Time alone and aware enough to process everything that had happened in the space of a week. That alone blew my mind.

"Thanks, Daria." I wanted to say goodbye, but I still didn't want her to go. "Do you have somewhere to stay?"

"Yeah. I'm okay."

"Good." I leaned next to her, both enjoying and hating the comfortable silence between us as a light breeze made the overgrown grass down the side of my house, my home, wave and dance for us.

"Everyone just needs a bit of time." Daria nudged my shoulder before standing up. "Jen stocked your cupboards, but that's no excuse to avoid everyone forever."

I hung my head, a small, sad smile brushing my lips.

"Bye, Daria."

"I'll see you around, Lily." She had such confidence, and the sunshine within her managed to still shine despite all she had been through.

TWENTY-NINE

The longer I stayed in my self-imposed isolation, the more questions formed. Questions that refused to float away.

I couldn't answer them, not without stepping back into that World. My friends, my found family in the Witches, had kept their true selves hidden from me. Death, who had lied so many times I had no idea if anything they had ever told me was true. Alanor, who still thought of me as a monster. Jen, who had her own deeply fucked up shit to deal with.

Nothing I did at home seemed fulfilling or satisfying. I even took down every single one of my model cars, cleaned them and the shelves and replaced them all. I even rearranged them. But they didn't bring joy like they once had. My affliction tormented me.

We had found the bad guy, and I no longer cared. Death had imprisoned Kensley, but the victory seemed hollow.

I blew out a heavy breath after rearranging the cars for the third time. These untethered thoughts and moments reminded me far too much of my first six months of isolation. I wasn't that person anymore, but here I was allowing myself to fall into the self-pitying spiral again.

I knew where I had to begin. Before I could, I had to go to the one place I dreaded more than any other.

I tapped into the power, and it buzzed to life as though it had been waiting all day for me to finally reach out to it.

Shimmering had never been so easy while simultaneously being so hard.

"Lilekai." Death's voice was soft and welcoming the moment I Shimmered into their Central Chamber. A minion hadn't even had time to place a cloak over my shoulders.

"Death."

"I have taken care of Kensley, I—"

I held up my hand to stop them. They tilted their head and nodded.

"Then what brings you here so quickly?" They asked with a gleam in their eye that twisted the knife in my guts.

"I was hoping to get another experimental phone from Jen. But not as a secret. I won't be putting up with any of the secrets anymore, not even from myself."

"Ah." Death clicked their fingers; the sound like those hollow sticks people clacked together for music embellishments. The phone appeared in their hands, and they handed it over immediately.

A minion approached, but I shook my head at the offer of the cloak.

"Thanks, but no need."

"So you don't wish to have the answers, either?"

"I have all the answers I need."

"Jen will not speak to me either."

"Do you blame her?"

"No, but I wish she would let me give her the answers she has always wanted."

"If she wants them, she will. But it's about time she got something on her time and terms, don't you think?"

Death nodded and I pulled at the magic.

"And what about you, Lilekai?"

"I am your minion; I assume we will need to talk about that from time to time."

"And the answers?"

"I don't know, Death." I let the power wash over me. The familiar sting in the invisible pins and needles I long ago got used to, hurt for the first time in far too many years.

I Shimmered, closing my eyes until the tingles on my skin stopped.

"What do you want?"

I blinked, mouth fallen open, as I stared at Alanor. She looked hot with her blazing eyes and fists jammed onto her hips. I hadn't imagined she would still be there, not after so many days.

"Where are Isla and Lita?"

"Busy." Alanor's chest rose and fell a little too fast. "Now, what do you want?"

"Are you okay?"

"What, now you suddenly care?"

"Of course I care."

"You left, Lilekai."

"Of course I left. You wouldn't meet my eyes. And even now you see me as a monster."

"I was ashamed." The words fell from Alanor's lips in a boom.

Silence rested over us, and for a moment, we simply stared at each other.

"Ashamed?" I whispered the word, scared to break the eye contact we had finally found.

But Alanor sighed, closed her eyes, and stepped out onto

the patio. She closed the door behind her and moved to the railing, forearms resting on the white painted wood. She was a mirror image of what Daria had been on my own patio.

I waited a beat, and then followed her. I brushed her arm; I needed it and I wasn't going to let myself feel bad about it. The warm relief flooded through me at the touch.

"For someone as old as you, you really need some lessons in Human Nature and Psychology 101."

"Oh, I'm well aware." I let out a self-deprecating scoff.

"You jumped out of bed as though being next to me was a nightmare come true." She looked at me and I cocked my head, forcing my teeth closed so I didn't interrupt her. "You raced out of here as though there wasn't enough distance you could get from me."

"I'm sorry." I forced my eyes away from her and lowered my head, letting it half hang over the dead garden beside the railing.

"So why did you come back? To tell me to leave you alone?"

"What?" My neck cracked, a knot letting loose at the sudden movement as I looked up to her.

"It's okay. I get if you can't be around me. Right now, I'm not sure I want to be around me anymore."

"No. That's not why I left."

"Don't lie to me, please?"

"I'm not lying. I'm shit at talking about all this stuff. But I'm not lying."

She didn't look convinced, though she didn't pull away from where our arms touched.

"You know more about me, than anyone else alive, or in the Grey World has ever known. I want to know the things about you no one else knows." I tried to catch Alanor's eyes. "Please look at me?"

"I killed my own sister, Lily. How could I look anyone in the eyes, especially you. I hated you for years, blamed you for doing what I have just done."

"Sure, in those words it sounds bad, but words are only a part of it. You saved us all. Katy needed to finally get the peace she deserved. And you granted her that wish."

"I killed her."

"She killed herself. You gave her the freedom I denied her."

The silence stretched until I swallowed down my pride and repeated words she had brushed away so easily.

"I want to know everything about you, Alanor. Not just the hero cop stuff, not just the profile anyone can discover stuff. I want to know all the things you are scared to say, all the dreams you push aside thinking they are stupid. I want it all, and I want it with you."

"I." Alanor's profile twitched as her face scrunched and relaxed, only to scrunch again. "I don't know, Lily. Things are too complicated and honestly, I just want to move on. I've held on to Katy's death for too long, and now I have more guilt to add to it."

"Oh." I nodded, trying not to show how her words shattered things inside my chest. And then my own words to Death, my determination not to keep secrets flashed warning-sign red in my mind. "I won't pretend this doesn't hurt. But I won't beg, or add to your guilt."

"Are you two ever going to come inside?" Lita's voice was loud and hard.

"I wasn't invited in." I turned to see Lita standing just outside the now open door. I hadn't even heard it open.

"Shut up, since when did you ever need to be invited?" Lita turned and walked inside.

"Are you coming?" I asked at the door, realising Alanor hadn't moved to follow me.

"In a moment." She didn't look up, and I swallowed back words that would have me beg.

Inside, I followed Lita to the back room. At the table, covered in the spelled cloth of space, sat Isla and Jen. Lita sat beside Isla. With them both facing Jen, I knew exactly what Alanor had stopped me from interrupting.

"Hey." I smiled, or at least gave my best forced approximation. "What's going on?"

"I'm a Necromancer." Jen blinked.

"What?" I slid into the seat beside her and placed my hand over her own.

"My eyes, they are just like Katy's."

"Yeah?" I drew out the one-word question.

"I'm not Death's child in the mortal way, like they allowed everyone to assume." Jen let that hang in the air for a beat. "I was a child they found. I was three days old, and I was dead. But they found me before my soul slipped through. They stopped my soul crossing over, and they turned me into a Necromancer."

"Death said you couldn't be a Necromancer."

"They were scared of me." Jen's voice was low. "I could do things others couldn't. I was always my own person. I could hide from them, they couldn't enthral me, and Resurrection always came far too easy for me."

"Scared of you?" I blinked and a world of avoidance for their daughter began to make sense. "That's why they thought they could help Katy?"

Isla nodded.

"But Katy was older, she didn't change the same way?" Lita supplied more, without me having to ask.

"And Death's fear interrupted the process from truly succeeding." Isla provided, unasked.

Okay, so the Witches lied about how much power they had, but they were still family, and still the people I trusted.

"Death really is just a name, isn't it?" I asked the room.

"It always has been. At least your Death, this Death, tried not to let anyone think they were an omnipotent god," Lita said.

"At least sometimes," Jen said, but the right side of her lip rose a little and I smiled.

Maybe, just maybe we could all survive beyond this nightmare.

"I'm dying for a coffee," Alanor interrupted, and Jen and I laughed, relieved at the lightness.

"I'm on it." Lita jumped up, kissed Isla on the top of the head and headed over to start another pot.

"So, Isla helped you learn this? You haven't spoken to Death?"

Jen pursed her lips and shook her head.

"Well, if you want to, I'll come with you."

"Thanks." Jen leaned her head on my shoulder and closed her eyes. I kissed the top of her head.

By the time I ventured back outside to find Alanor again, the patio was empty.

I suppose not everyone could let the nightmare fall away.

"Alright, alright," I called out as I raced from the garden, through my house, and flung open the door.

Daria and Jen had been due to show up for board game night, so it never dawned on me to check who stood on my patio.

I lost my breath. I didn't hold it, unable to let it go. It was completely lost, disappeared into thin air at the sight of Alanor at my front door.

"I used to write poetry," she blurted.

I couldn't hold back the surprised laugh as I asked, "What?"

"And I once climbed a macadamia nut tree and carved a heart with my initials and those of the first girl I had a crush on. A few people know that, but what they don't know is that I live in that same house where the tree is, and when things get too much, I climb that tree and trace the letters and try to remember how it felt when that was the only secret I held in my heart."

"That's entirely adorable, but I have no idea what's going on."

"I'm sorry."

"Okay."

"I ran away because it was all too much."

"I know. I mean it's not every day you find out the World is filled with monsters."

"You aren't a monster. Not really."

"Thanks."

"But, that's not what was too much."

"No?" I pulled my head back, as though trying a different distance between us would let me focus better on what her words meant.

"No." She shook her head and reached out for my hands. Her fingers trembled and I met her halfway. She squeezed my fingers as she spoke. "This was all too much. I'm Detective Arsehole. I don't have a beating heart, or a softness people can touch. But you saw beyond the walls and the bluster. Right from the start. And I'm pretty sure I hated you for that as much as I hated you for the influence I thought you had over Katy."

I let the words settle around us for a moment. They floated over my skin with a sincerity that made me shudder.

I opened my mouth and closed it again. I took a deep breath and tried again. "We really are dickheads sometimes, aren't we?" I smirked at her.

She laughed and pulled me close, wrapping her arms around me.

"*You* certainly are," she said as she kissed my forehead.

I laughed and reached up to pull her lips down to my own.

"I'm sorry I left. Emotions aren't exactly my strong point," she said when we came up for air.

"Yeah, and I'm so tuned-in." I rolled my eyes before holding her close and pressing my ear to her chest.

The rumble of her chuckle filled me with hope and light, and a desire to spend every moment I possibly could with this woman. I smiled as the rhythm of her heart raced a little faster than it would have normally.

"Do I smell coffee?" I murmured into Alanor's chest.

"I had to have some bargaining chip if you didn't let me into your house."

I watched as she picked up a carry tray from my coffee shop. Two of their largest take-away cups in a spaced four cup holder, with a bag of grounds in the middle.

"Well, by all means, we can't have the gesture go to waste." I pressed my back against the hallway wall and waved my hand for Alanor to come on in. She brushed her arm lightly across my chest as she walked past. My nipples pebbled instantly at the touch.

"Oh, Jen and Daria told me to tell you, board game night is off this week." Alanor threw the words over her shoulder a few more steps into my home. "Any idea how we might keep ourselves entertained for the night?"

"Oh, I have a sudden craving for coffee and strawberries," I called after her.

"Perfect," she said as I closed the door behind me.

About the Author

Neen Cohen is an Aussie. She writes sapphic speculative fiction and while she tries to take things seriously, she thrives being the hyperactive bookworm who rarely stops smiling or laughing.

If she had to decide between never reading or never writing again, she simply wouldn't. Rules were never her strong point.

When not writing, or working at the day job, Neen loves nothing more than dancing, Nerf wars with her boys, playing the latest PS obsession, dancing without rhythm, and crafting wild and crazy things.

In her ideal world, she would spend her days wandering graveyards for inspiration before finding the perfect tree (usually within said graveyard) to lean against and write.

To keep track of all things Neen Cohen and her books head on over to www.neencohen.com where you can sign up to her newsletter, and find all the social links and bookish love.

facebook.com/neen.cohen.82

instagram.com/neenauthor

patreon.com/NeenCohen

tiktok.com/@sapphicspecficauthor

amazon.com/stores/Neen-Cohen/author/B07VSYZF7K

DEEP SOUNDING CHAOS

A target to capture. A murder to avenge. A life to honor.

Zendalia is a soldier at heart, but when her father is brutally murdered, she must seek vengeance for his death. She dives deep into the ocean to find her father's murderer and bring them to justice. Her plan goes haywire when she ends up kidnapped by the very mermaid she's set out to capture, her life suddenly in the hands of a stone-cold killer.

Kaelin isn't strong-willed or confident or even particularly smart. Banished from her tribe, she wants nothing more than to reclaim her life and do what is right. Instead, she finds herself with a captive she didn't want. To protect both of them from the real monster lurking in the depths of the ocean, Kaelin breaks her silence and the rules of her exile.

Overcoming animosity, Zendalia and Kaelin make a startling choice. Work with the enemy to save the ocean. But will they find more than they bargained for? Will they find love in the deep soundings?

Prepare yourself for a romantasy of mermaids. If you want sapphic mermaids, action, and a snarky octopus, this fantasy romance book is just for you.

Read it today